THE MAN FROM POMEGRANATE STREET

THE ROMAN MYSTERIES
by Caroline Lawrence

Also available:

— A Roman Mystery —

THE MAN FROM POMEGRANATE STREET

Caroline Lawrence

Orion
Children's Books

First published in Great Britain in 2009
by Orion Children's Books
a division of the Orion Publishing Group Ltd
Orion House
5 Upper St Martin's Lane
London WC2H 9EA
An Hachette UK company

1 3 5 7 9 10 8 6 4 2

ISBN 978 1 84255 193 6

Typeset by Input Data Services Ltd, Bridgwater, Somerset

Printed in Great Britain by Clays Ltd, St Ives plc

www.orionbooks.co.uk

To Antonia Arnoldus-Huyzendveld
who showed me beautiful Lake Albano
and to Lisa Tucci and Susan Micocci
who showed me the Sabine Hills

THE MEDITERRANEAN IN AD 81

Tyana

Ephesus
Halicarnassus
Athens
Corinth
Rhodes

Alexandria

MEDITERRANEAN

Reate

see map
of the area
around Rome
in AD81

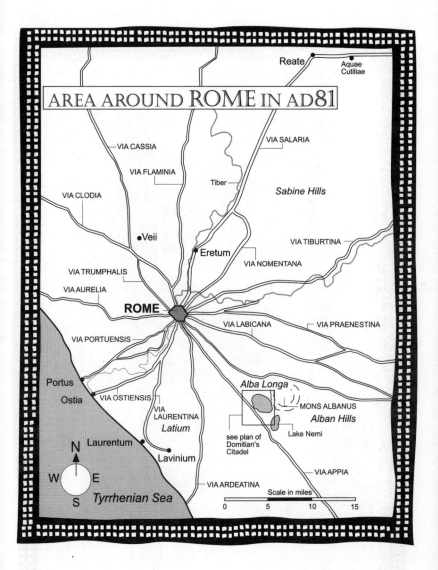

AREA AROUND ROME IN AD81

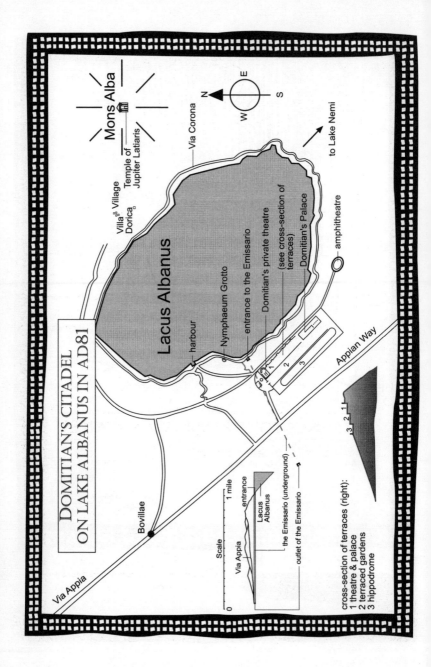

DOMITIAN'S CITADEL
ON LAKE ALBANUS IN AD81

Via Appia

Bovillae

Mons Alba

Temple of
Jupiter Latiaris

Villa° Village
Dorica □

Via Corona

Lacus Albanus

harbour

Nymphaeum Grotto

entrance to the Emissario

Domitian's private theatre

(see cross-section of
terraces)

Domitian's Palace

to Lake Nemi

amphitheatre

Appian Way

1
2
3

N
W — E
S

Scale

0   1 mile

Via Appia

entrance

Lacus Albanus

the Emissario (underground)

outlet of the Emissario

cross-section of terraces (right):
1 theatre & palace
2 terraced gardens
3 hippodrome

3 2 1

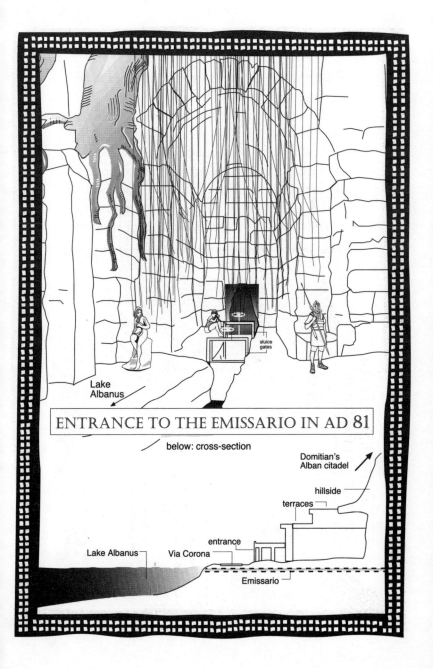

Lake
Albanus

ENTRANCE TO THE EMISSARIO IN AD 81

below: cross-section

Domitian's
Alban citadel

hillside

terraces

entrance

Via Corona

Lake Albanus

Emissario

sluice
gates

This story takes place in ancient Roman times, so a few of the words may look strange.

If you don't know them, 'Aristo's Scroll' at the back of the book will tell you what they mean and how to pronounce them.

This book is the final story in a seventeen-book series. If you haven't read any of the others, you might like to start at the beginning, with *The Thieves of Ostia*, to avoid plot spoilers!

SCROLL I

*F*ifteen-year-old Flavia Gemina trembled as her stepmother advanced steadily towards her, a spear pointed at her head.

'Are you sure it's supposed to be so sharp?' whimpered Flavia.

'This is the same one they used on me three years ago,' said her stepmother with a smile. 'And so far the gods have blessed my marriage to your father.'

'But couldn't you just use a very dull spearhead?' pleaded Flavia. 'Instead of the whole thing on its shaft?'

'No. We have to part your hair seven times with the point of a sharp spear. That's the way it's done.'

A lovely blond girl stepped forward. Pulchra was almost a year older than Flavia. 'When I got married last spring,' said Pulchra, 'three women held the spear. Nubia, come help me.'

Flavia's dark-skinned friend Nubia came forward. She and Pulchra grasped the shaft behind the spearhead while Flavia's young stepmother shifted her grip slightly. Then the three of them carefully used the point of the spear to part Flavia's light brown hair, first in the middle, then three times on either side. Flavia tried hard not to tremble and it only pricked once.

'There,' said Pulchra. 'That wasn't so bad, was it?'

'I suppose not,' said Flavia, but she kept her head perfectly still in case she lost the partings. 'Are you going to plait in the blue ribbons and pearls you brought me, Pulchra?'

'Me? Do the job of an ornatrix? Certainly not! Leda will do

your hair. Now sit in this chair by the balcony. We can use the last of the daylight.'

Flavia glanced at Pulchra's slave-girl Leda and smiled. Although she and Pulchra had been writing to each other regularly for the past few years, Flavia had forgotten how imperious her friend could be.

'However,' said Pulchra, 'I will do your make-up, because that requires the skill of a true artist.' As Leda and Nubia moved behind Flavia to do her hair, Pulchra went to get the make-up tray.

'Don't listen to her,' laughed Flavia's stepmother over her shoulder. She had draped the gauzy, saffron-yellow wedding veil over the balcony so that she could sprinkle it with rose water. 'You've become a lovely young woman.'

Pulchra sat on a small stool in front of Flavia and rested the tray on her lap. 'All I meant,' she said, 'was that tonight is the most important night of her life. We don't want the bridegroom having second thoughts.'

'He won't have second thoughts,' said Flavia's stepmother. 'He's besotted with Flavia.'

'Humph,' said Pulchra, and to Flavia: 'Are you nervous?'

'Of course not.'

'You're not nervous that in a very short time your bridegroom is going to burst in here and snatch you from our arms and carry you off to his bed while boys in the procession sing lewd songs and pelt you with nuts?'

'No,' said Flavia. 'I'm euphoric. It's my dream come true.'

'I do wish you'd tell me more about this man you're marrying.' Pulchra unscrewed a little tin pot and sniffed the contents with satisfaction. 'You're so secretive about him in your letters.'

'You'll meet him soon.'

'So you keep telling me.' She dipped her finger in the face

cream and started to apply it to Flavia's forehead. 'Speaking of mysteries, I have a little mystery I'd like you to solve.'

'I'm sorry, Pulchra, but I gave up being a detectrix three years ago.'

'Really?' Pulchra sighed. 'That's too bad.' She smoothed some of the lemon-scented face cream onto Flavia's cheek. 'Are you sure you're not nervous?'

'Yes.'

'Then why are you still trembling?'

'I'm a little nervous.'

Pulchra laughed. 'Well, why don't you take your mind off things for a while? Tell me about one of your adventures?'

'All right,' said Flavia with a sigh. 'I'll tell you about our last case. The one that made me give up being a detectrix. The one that showed me how dangerous it can be to search for the Truth.'

It was a hot afternoon in Ostia, the Ides of September in the third year of the Emperor Titus. Three merchant ships were standing out to sea, waiting for the afternoon breeze to rise and carry them into port. The local sailors called this wind Venus' Breath, because it was cool and fragrant. It finally rose at about the second hour after noon and filled the ships' sails. Two of the ships headed towards Portus, Ostia's big new port, but one turned towards a smaller harbour.

Beneath the shady reed awning of the customs booth of the Marina Harbour, a young official was dozing. He had tipped his wicker chair onto its two back legs and was resting his sandaled feet on the wooden table. The cicadas chirred soporifically in the umbrella pines and the heat was like a drug, but Rufus was only skimming beneath the surface of sleep. Now the distant crack of canvas and the feel of the cool breeze on his face brought him instantly awake. He squinted at the approaching ship and its sail. His eyesight was good and he could easily make out the image of a leaping dolphin there, painted in black on the pale linen sail. Rufus let his chair fall forward with a thump. It was the *Delphina*. The ship they had all been waiting for.

This was his chance for recognition and maybe promotion. He had to alert Glabrio, his superior.

Rufus stood up and stepped out from the striped shade of the awning and into the brilliant sunshine. Ostia had three harbours: the new harbour up at Portus, the river mouth harbour and this small marina harbour, mainly used in the sailing season by fishermen and local craft. This was the slow time of day. Most men had gone home for a siesta, or to the baths. There were only five or six old fishermen on the docks, mending their nets and chatting. Further down the beach three boys stood knee deep in the water, skipping stones.

'Pueri!' shouted Rufus, clapping his hands. 'Boys! Come here!'

The boys looked at each other, dropped their stones and ran to him. When they stood before him, panting and wet, he said, 'Do any of you know who Manius Acilius Glabrio is?'

The two older boys frowned at each other but the youngest nodded enthusiastically. 'I do,' he said. 'He has black hair and a big belly.'

'Well done,' said Rufus. 'What's your name?'

'Threptus,' said the boy. He was about seven years old and naked apart from a sun-bleached loincloth. His tawny hair was damp and his brown skin still beaded with drops of water.

Rufus fished in his coin purse. 'Threptus,' he said. 'I want you and your friends to run to the Marina Baths

4

and find Glabrio. Tell him to come here at once. He's probably dozing in the solarium about now.' He flipped each boy a tiny quadran. 'There's another coin for each of you if he's here within half an hour. Tell him,' he called after the running boys, 'Tell him the *Delphina* is coming into port. The ship of Marcus Flavius Geminus.' Rufus cupped his hands around his mouth and shouted: 'Tell him that enemies of the emperor Titus may be on board!'

Threptus the beggar boy felt terrible.

He and his friends had brought big-bellied, hairy-backed Glabrio to the Marina Harbour in time for their reward. Now they stood on the shore pretending to skip stones as before. The harbour looked deserted, but Threptus knew there were two magistrates and a dozen soldiers hiding behind the arch of the Marina Gate. They were waiting to arrest the emperor's enemies, who were certain to be aboard the *Delphina*.

Threptus couldn't read, but like everyone else in the port of Ostia, he knew about the decree that had gone up in the forum six weeks earlier.

The notice informed the public that the Emperor Titus was offering a huge reward for the capture of four of his enemies. These four enemies were children: two boys and two girls. Their names were Flavia Gemina, Jonathan ben Mordecai, Nubia and Lupus. All four were residents of Ostia. And all four were known to Threptus, especially the last-named: ten-year-old Lupus.

Threptus and his friends often told each other stories about Lupus, who had once been a beggar boy like them. They told how Lupus could swing from branch to branch like a monkey. They told how Lupus once fought off a pack of rabid dogs, single-handed. It was well known that

Lupus had faced a lion in Rome's great arena and driven a quadriga of the Greens to victory in the Circus Maximus. Lupus had climbed to the very top of the Colossus of Rhodes – it was a mile high – and there he had battled three armed warriors, tossing each one to his death. Lupus had wrestled a giant octopus guarding sunken treasure. He had killed an evil slave-dealer, too, and won for his reward the slave-ship *Vespa*. The ex-beggar-boy had renamed the ship *Delphina*, and he himself had painted that leaping dolphin on her sail.

And now he, Threptus, had betrayed his hero for two tiny coins. He felt sick as he watched the *Delphina* ease up beside the wooden dock.

Should he warn Lupus? Or was it already too late?

He and his friends watched the lanky red-haired customs official and his big-bellied superior move forward. The two men strolled casually, but Threptus guessed their hearts were pounding as hard as his. They would receive a huge reward and an imperial pat-on-the-back if the four young criminals were on board.

After a few moments of activity, the gangplank thudded down and a figure appeared: a short man in a toga. He had thinning hair and pale brown eyes. Threptus recognised him; he was one of Ostia's junior magistrates.

The man paused at the top of the gangplank, where everyone could see him. A black dog appeared on one side of him and a golden dog on the other. Threptus could see their panting pink tongues.

'Salvete!' cried the magistrate in a loud voice.

'Marcus Artorius Bato!' cried Glabrio.

Threptus could hear the surprise in the official's voice.

'Are there any children on board that ship?' called Glabrio.

'There are indeed!' cried Bato, spreading both arms triumphantly. 'I have ten freeborn children who were cruelly snatched from their parents' arms some time ago. Today,' he proclaimed. 'I am restoring these poor lost lambs to their families!' Bato was using his orator's skills and Threptus could hear him perfectly.

'Is there a Captain Geminus on board?' cried Glabrio.

'Up here!' cried a voice from the rigging. Threptus saw Marcus Flavius Geminus, a good-looking man in his mid-thirties. His face was also familiar around the docks of Ostia.

'Is your daughter Flavia with you?' bellowed Glabrio. 'And her friends?'

'No,' said Captain Geminus, and hung his head in grief.

'The captain's daughter and her friends,' cried Bato, 'are dead.' He paused for a moment, looking suitably grave, and then proclaimed: 'They died bravely, saving the lives of these wretched children.'

The two dogs wagged their tails and panted happily as the first of the kidnapped children appeared at the top of the gangplank and began to descend.

Down on the docks, the old fishermen rose to their feet and ran towards the *Delphina*.

'Have you any proof that your daughter and her friends are dead?' called Glabrio, but he was drowned out by the cheers of townspeople. Men and women were pouring out from the Marina Gate to embrace the children they thought they might never see again. The two magistrates were rushing forward to congratulate Bato and some of the soldiers had shown themselves – against orders – and were cheering, too.

Threptus swallowed hard. The missing children of Ostia were home. But Lupus and his friends were dead. They had given their lives to help the children. He would never see his hero again. Tears filled Threptus's eyes and he turned away from the joyful scene on the docks. He did not want the older boys to taunt him for his soft heart.

Through the heat haze, a movement further down the beach caught his eye. Just beyond the synagogue a fishing boat was coming ashore.

Threptus blinked away the tears and frowned. It was old Robur's boat. He was based a few miles south, in Laurentum, and he hardly ever brought his boat up this far.

A figure jumped down into the shallow water. Threptus stifled a gasp. A young man with curly hair was helping three children out of the boat.

Threptus glanced at his friends, but they had run off towards the *Delphina* to take part in the celebrations.

Threptus turned back. The curly-haired youth and the three children were wading ashore. In a few moments they would disappear behind the synagogue. Threptus shaded his eyes and squinted through the shimmering waves of heat. From this distance he could only see their silhouettes. The children all wore wide-brimmed sun hats and boys' tunics, but two of them *could* have been girls. And the smallest one – he was sure of it – the smallest one might have been Lupus.

SCROLL II

Lupus stood carefully on the lofty branch of an umbrella pine in Ostia's necropolis. He had seen a movement among the myrtle bushes to the north and he wanted to make sure it was not soldiers or a magistrate. He balanced on tiptoes, almost fell, but grasped a higher branch and steadied himself. Now he could see a flicker of brown between the branches of the trees. Someone was definitely coming from the direction of the Laurentum Gate.

Lupus had no tongue and could not speak, but he could imitate the call of an owl perfectly. He crouched down, steadied himself against the rough bark of the trunk, and did so now.

Below him there was no movement among the tombs of the necropolis.

Lupus grunted with satisfaction, then carefully stood up and peered through the branches again. Now he could see who it was: Marcus Flavius Geminus, sea-captain. He wore a brown workman's tunic and carried three hoes over his shoulder. Three dogs followed behind. Lupus cupped his hands and gave a different call, the throaty call of the ringed-dove, twice. It was the all-clear.

Lupus looked down again, and this time he saw three figures emerging from the Geminus family tomb: his tutor Aristo, and his friends Flavia and Nubia. Their upturned faces seemed very small as they gazed up at him. He nodded, pointed to the north and gave them a thumbs-up. Then he swung himself down – branch to branch – agile as a monkey.

When Lupus reached the lowest branch, he hung from it for a moment and looked down. It was a fair-sized drop – at least a dozen feet – but a thick layer of pine needles cushioned the earth. He couldn't resist trying a backflip dismount, but he was out of practice and ended up lying on his back, gazing up at the blue sky. The girls rushed forward and each extended a hand to help him up. Both were disguised as slave-boys in short, coarse brown tunics and broad-brimmed straw sunhats. However, they had each begun to develop in the past month and were not entirely convincing. Lupus grinned.

Flavia saw his look and gave Nubia a rueful smile. 'I don't think we'll be able to disguise ourselves as boys much longer.'

'I know,' said Nubia. She glanced at Aristo and whispered in Flavia's ear.

Lupus's ears were sharp as a rabbit's and he heard her say: 'Especially as we are both becoming women on the voyage here.'

Lupus blushed and turned to the north in time to see three dogs emerge from the bushes, followed by Captain Geminus.

Scuto, the golden dog, greeted Flavia first, and black Nipur ran to Nubia. The third dog, Tigris – also black – had not been on the voyage with them. Tigris sniffed them all hopefully, and Lupus realised he was looking for his master Jonathan. Finally, Tigris came back to Lupus and looked up at him with large brown eyes and whined.

'Poor Tigris,' said Nubia, and Tigris went to her. Nubia

crouched down and gazed into Tigris's eyes. 'Jonathan is not with us. Is he with you? Have you seen him?'

'Well, Nubia?' said Aristo. 'What does Tigris have to say?'

Lupus and the girls laughed, but Captain Geminus did not even smile. He glanced over his shoulder and then handed Lupus and the two girls a hoe each.

'Pater?' said Flavia. 'Is something wrong?'

'You know very well what's wrong. You're wanted by the emperor and there are people looking for you everywhere. They're even watching me.'

'But we didn't do it!' said Flavia.

'I know,' said Captain Geminus grimly, 'that's why I've agreed to let you go and explain yourselves.' He turned to Aristo. 'I've arranged a cart to take you and the children to Rome. Atticus is standing in for a sick driver who was supposed to deliver some glassware to the Quirinal Hill. He'll pick you up on the Via Ostiensis in about an hour.'

Lupus rested his hoe on his right shoulder, the way he had seen slaves do.

'Good,' said Captain Geminus. 'That's good.' And to the girls: 'Carry your hoes the way Lupus is doing and remember to walk like boys. Anybody on the road will think you're slaves with their foreman going from one field to the next. Join the road about a mile out of Ostia, at the place where the aqueduct begins to move away from it. Whatever you do, avoid the town gates, as we discussed. Go through the necropolis. Do you understand?'

'Yes,' said Aristo.

Lupus pointed at himself and gave Captain Geminus a thumbs-up. He had lived in the necropolis for two years and he knew a good route through the tombs to the Via Ostiensis.

'All right,' said Captain Geminus. He ran his hand through his hair and Lupus thought he seemed more distracted than he had on board the ship, when they had first come up with the plan. 'When Atticus comes by in his cart,' continued Flavia's father, 'pretend to flag a lift. He'll take you the rest of the way. You should arrive at dusk, when carts are allowed into Rome. Under cover of dark, Atticus will drop you off at the foot of the Clivus Scauri. Go to Senator Cornix's house and make sure it isn't being watched. If it's safe, spend the night there, then go straight to the emperor the following morning. You've been to the Palatine Hill before, haven't you?'

'Yes,' said Aristo with a glance at the others. 'We've been there.'

Lupus grinned when he remembered how they had once dressed up as a troupe of travelling musicians.

Captain Geminus nodded. 'When you reach the imperial palace, tell the guards you need to see Titus on a matter of life or death.'

'We'll tell them that Titus's brother wants to kill him and seize the throne,' said Flavia.

'Great Neptune's beard, Flavia! How many times must I tell you? Don't *you* say a word. Let Aristo do the talking. If you get a private audience with Titus, *then* you can tell him what you've learned about his brother.'

'Yes, pater,' sighed Flavia, and added: 'Can't you go with us?'

He shook his head. 'I daren't go with you, Flavia. They're watching me constantly. That red-haired official is lurking on Green Fountain Street and I think I was being followed when I was in the forum. If they catch you before you see Titus, then Domitian could execute you. You must see Titus in person. I believe he is an honourable man. He will vindicate you.'

Lupus frowned and Nubia asked: 'What is vindicate?'

'It means he will clear you of blame,' said Aristo.

'And revoke the decree against us,' added Flavia.

Captain Geminus looked at them all. 'If necessary,' he said, 'clasp the emperor's ankles and beg for mercy. At the games last year, Titus pardoned two men who openly conspired against him.'

Lupus nodded. He himself had exposed the conspiracy against Titus. That should count for something.

'That incident proves that Titus can be merciful,' Captain Geminus was saying. 'So even if he suspects you of conspiring, he will at least hear you out.'

Captain Geminus handed Aristo the burlap shoulder bag. 'There's a change of clothes for the girls in there, for when you go to see Titus, and a wig for Flavia. She can't very well address the emperor with short hair.'

'Where did you get the wig, pater?'

'From Cartilia's sister Diana. I saw her in the forum just now and asked where I could buy a wig and she said I could borrow one of her mother's.' Captain Geminus looked at Aristo. 'And you've got the money I gave you? Five hundred sesterces in gold?'

Aristo nodded and patted the coin purse at his belt. 'It's far too much,' he said.

'You never know,' said Captain Geminus. 'You might need something to bribe the guards.'

Lupus patted his belt pouch to remind Flavia's father that they had money for emergencies, too. But Captain Geminus did not notice. He put his hand on Aristo's shoulder. 'I'm trusting you with the life of my only child and her best friends,' he said, 'Don't let me down.'

Lupus looked at his tutor. Although Aristo was twenty-three, at this moment he looked very young.

'Yes, sir,' said Aristo.

Captain Geminus turned to Flavia and embraced her. 'May the gods protect you, my Little Owl, and may they grant you favour in the eyes of the emperor.' Then he put one hand on Nubia's hat and the other on Lupus's. 'May the gods protect you, too,' he prayed.

Flavia waved goodbye to her father and the three dogs, then turned to follow Lupus through the necropolis. She had her hoe over her shoulder and her straw hat on her head. It was late afternoon now. The air was still warm and the sun made the needles of the pine trees glow like emeralds. After hiding in the tomb for two hours, being outside was like being reborn.

As she moved through the pine-scented necropolis, the memories washed over her, like waves on a beach.

She remembered the first time she had seen Lupus, climbing an umbrella pine here: swinging from its branches, then falling and glaring up at them with feral eyes. How much he had changed in two years.

She remembered how Nubia had calmed the wild dogs with her haunting song. She remembered how Aristo had often hunted here in the pine groves, and how he had once killed a giant bird called an ostrich. That reminded her of Diana, the nineteen-year-old huntress who had cut her hair and renounced men after being spurned by Aristo. Diana's sister Cartilia came to mind: a beautiful young Roman matron whom her father had loved. Flavia flushed with shame as she remembered her mistake. She had convinced herself that Cartilia was an evil sorceress after her father's wealth. In reality, Cartilia had been warm and wise and loving. When she died of fever, Flavia felt she had lost a second mother.

'I'm so stupid sometimes,' she muttered to herself.

'What?' whispered Nubia behind her. 'What are you saying?'

'Nothing,' said Flavia. She glanced over her shoulder. Nubia's golden-brown eyes were filled with concern. Flavia felt a rush of affection for her ex-slave-girl. She wanted to squeeze her hand, but they had a role to play and fieldworkers didn't hold hands. 'Just memories,' she said, and Nubia nodded.

The sky was blue and the woods were cool and green. The cicadas creaked softly in their branches and the umbrella pines filled the air with their spicy resinous smell. Flavia inhaled deeply and closed her eyes for a moment. She loved Ostia, even the graveyard. Especially the graveyard, where she felt close to all those she had lost. Her friends believed that after you died you went to a beautiful place which Aristo called Paradeisos in Greek. Flavia knew the word meant a royal park. She wanted to believe in a beautiful life after death, and on such an afternoon it almost seemed possible. Then she caught sight of the epitaph on a small tomb, painted in faded Greek:

Eat, drink, be merry and make love; all below here is darkness.

She thought of her mother, and of Cartilia, and blinked back tears.

They reached the main road to Rome a few moments later. With a hesitant look to the left and right, Lupus beckoned them out onto the dirt path beside the paved Via Ostiensis.

They walked single file with Lupus at the front and

Aristo taking up the rear: a foreman moving three young slaves from one field to the next.

They were walking past the tombs of the rich now, and Flavia glanced at them curiously, reading the epitaphs and inscriptions. Some were long and heartfelt. Others were blunt and brief. Some were in Latin, some in Greek, one or two in Hebrew. Suddenly she stopped so abruptly that Nubia bumped into her from behind.

'What is it?' asked Nubia.

Flavia stared at the tomb and her eyes welled up again. She had never read this inscription before. Up ahead, Lupus stopped and turned and gave her his bug-eyed look, as if to say: What are you doing?

'Flavia!' whispered Aristo behind her. 'You're supposed to be a field slave. Field slaves can't read. Keep walking. *Keep walking!*'

Flavia resumed walking, but when she heard Nubia catch her breath, she knew her friend had read the epitaph, too. As Flavia felt Nubia's comforting hand on her shoulder, she began to weep.

It was Cartilia's tomb, and the Latin inscription read:

A cruel fever took Cartilia Poplicola. She lived twenty-four years, six months, twenty days and four hours. Her loving mother and sister provided this memorial to her, because she was deserving. Friend, stop a moment and remember her.

SCROLL III

Nubia was the first to hear the mule-cart. It overtook them a' the salt flats, just beyond the place where the aqueduct left the road. An old man with woolly grey hair pulled the cart to a halt and asked if they wanted a lift to Rome. Then he winked at them. Atticus had been their shipmate for the past two weeks, and although they had shared many adventures, now they had to pretend they didn't know him.

Nubia also had to pretend she didn't know Podagrosus, one of the two mules pulling the cart. She had met him two years before, and she recognised him by his peculiar limping gait.

There was not much traffic on the road to Rome, only a vegetable cart so far ahead of them that it was sometimes out of sight, and a few riders and carts coming towards Ostia. The rumble of the wheels and the clopping of mules' hooves drowned out low conversation, so Aristo finally gave Nubia permission to sit beside Atticus at the front.

'Everything going according to plan?' said the old Greek with a sidelong smile.

Nubia nodded. 'Yes. It is strange to be back in Italia after so long.'

'Six months, isn't it?'

'Yes,' said Nubia.

'Glad to be back?'

'Little bit, not so much,' said Nubia. To her left the marshy salt-beds were a sheet of dazzling brilliance in the late afternoon sun.

'You prefer Ephesus, don't you?'

'Yes,' said Nubia. She sighed as she thought of the Villa Vinea and the children still waiting to be reunited with their families. She had wanted to stay, but Flavia had insisted that they sail back to Ostia to help Jonathan save Titus and to clear their names. For once, Flavia's father had agreed with his daughter: they couldn't live under the shadow of a decree for the rest of their lives. So here they were, back in Italia, on the road to Rome.

'And you don't like Rome very much, do you?'

'No,' she said, and averted her eyes from the grisly remains of a body on a cross: a runaway slave, no doubt.

'Would you like to take the reins?' asked Atticus.

'Yes, please,' she said happily.

He handed them over and as she felt the living presences of two mules through the leather straps, joy welled up in her heart, and with it hope. Maybe Rome wouldn't be as bad as she feared.

Nubia smiled at Atticus. 'I know that mule,' she said, pointing with her chin. 'His name is Podagrosus and he is also suffering from gout, like you.'

Atticus chuckled. 'Leave it to Nubia to know every mule in Ostia, and their troubles. I have never known anyone with such a soft heart as you.'

'Try again, Aristo,' said Flavia, glancing nervously up and down the street. 'Even if Uncle Cornix is away, there should be some slaves here.'

It was dusk. Flavia and her friends were standing on the porch of a townhouse on the Clivus Scauri in Rome. Above them loomed one of the great aqueducts that carried water to a hundred bath-houses and fountains.

'All right,' muttered Aristo, 'but I can't knock too hard. I don't want to draw attention.' He lifted the bronze knocker – a woman's hand holding an apple – but at that very moment the little door in the rectangular peephole slid back and a pair of beady eyes appeared.

'Bulbus!' cried Flavia. 'It's us. It's me. Let us in!'

The eyes scowled back at her.

Flavia glanced quickly around, then pulled off her hat and ran her hand through her short hair. 'It's me. Flavia!'

A glimmer of recognition in the beady eyes, and a muffled voice: 'Miss Flavia?'

'Shhhh! Our lives are in danger and that's why we're in disguise.'

The peephole closed and Flavia heard the bolt slide back.

A moment later Bulbus held the door open. Flavia and her friends hurried into the atrium and looked around.

'Uncle Cornix?' Flavia called. 'Aunt Cynthia? Sisyphus?'

'Flavia?' cried a Greek-accented voice. 'Is that you?' A young man in a black tunic came into the atrium, holding a bronze oil-lamp. When he saw them, his kohl-lined eyes grew wide. 'What on earth are you wearing?'

Flavia took off her straw hat. 'We're in disguise. Because of the decree.'

'Great Juno's peacock!' exclaimed the Greek, and turned to Bulbus. 'Close the front door, you big onion-head! We don't want the neighbours to see. They're dangerous fugitives.' Sisyphus hugged Flavia and Nubia, shook Aristo's hand and patted Lupus on the head. Then he stood on tiptoe and looked around the atrium. 'And where's Jonathan?'

'We've been in Ephesus, and he came back a few weeks before us,' said Flavia.

'Aren't you taking an awful risk, coming to Rome?' said Sisyphus.

'We had to,' said Flavia. 'The things they say in the decree are a lie. We're innocent.'

'Of course you are. But still: why enter the lion's den?'

'We've come to help Jonathan warn Titus that his life is in danger.'

Sisyphus's dark eyes grew wide. 'But haven't you heard?'

'Heard what?' asked Flavia.

Sisyphus lowered his voice and said in a dramatic whisper: 'Titus is dead.'

Flavia and her friends stared at him in disbelief. 'Titus is dead?'

Sisyphus nodded. 'He died earlier today, at his Sabine Villa near Reate.'

'No!' cried Flavia. 'He can't be dead! Jonathan was going to warn him!'

'Warn him of what?'

'That Domitian intended to kill him.'

'I don't think Domitian did it. According to the reports, Titus died of a fever.'

'Was Domitian with him?'

'Yes. They were on their way to their Sabine villa when Titus became feverish. Domitian hurried back here to enlist the support of the Praetorian Guard – the soldiers who protect the emperor. He rode straight to their camp and said he would give them a generous pay rise if his brother died and he came to power. The moment the messenger brought news of Titus's death, they proclaimed him Caesar.'

'What about the senate?' asked Aristo. 'Doesn't a new emperor need their approval, too?'

'He does indeed,' said Sisyphus. 'They met late this afternoon but so far they've only issued an edict honoring Titus. Most senators are suspicious of Domitian and they haven't yet agreed to grant him imperium.'

'Good!' cried Flavia. 'He's evil. Where's Uncle Cornix? We have to tell him to convince the other senators not to let Domitian be emperor.'

'Your uncle is dining with some of his fellow senators tonight,' said Sisyphus. 'They're discussing the state of the empire. He told me he might not be back until midnight.'

'Oh no! We've got to talk to him.'

Sisyphus sucked his breath through his teeth. 'Not a good idea,' he said. 'When they posted the imperial decree against you . . .' He trailed off.

'What? Tell us!'

'Senator Cornix said he always knew you and your friends were devious. He thinks you're enemies of the state and he gave me explicit orders not to have anything to do with you ever again.'

'What?' gasped Flavia. 'I don't believe it. We're family!'

'You're Lady Cynthia's family,' he said. 'And recently things haven't been too good between the two of them. If the senator knew you were here, he'd throw you out. Me, too.'

'But . . . You won't . . . Oh Sisyphus! You've got to help us. We need a place to stay, just for tonight.'

'Of course I'll help you, my dear.' He patted her on the shoulder. 'You provide the only excitement I ever get in my life. How could I abandon you?' He winked at Aristo.

'Luckily the rest of the family and most of the slaves are still at the country villa. At the moment there's just me and Bulbus and the cook. I think I can convince them not to mention your presence, but you must all go to the children's wing and be quiet as mice! Don't make a sound until after Senator Cornix and I have left tomorrow morning.'

'Where are you going tomorrow morning?'

'Why to the Curia, of course. The senate will be meeting to decide who should rule Rome.'

'This is a disaster!' said Flavia later that night. 'Titus is dead. We'll never get our pardon now.' They had eaten a cold dinner of bean and bacon casserole followed by blackberry and yoghurt patina: leftovers from a dinner party Senator Cornix had hosted the night before.

Now they were sitting in a bedroom in the children's wing of the townhouse. They had lit only one small oil-lamp and they were speaking in whispers in case Senator Cornix came home early.

'It's a disaster,' repeated Flavia, batting at a mosquito. 'If only we'd arrived twenty-four hours earlier, we might have been able to warn Titus.'

Nubia frowned. 'Why did Jonathan not warn him? He departed from Ephesus more than three weeks ago.'

Lupus nodded and pointed at Nubia, as if to say: Good question.

'Maybe Jonathan's ship didn't go directly to Ostia,' said Flavia.

'Unlikely,' said Aristo. 'We know his ship was bound for Ostia. The weather's been fair these past few weeks, and there haven't been any reports of missing ships or wrecks. He should have arrived safely.'

'Then something must have happened to him,' said Flavia. 'I hope Domitian didn't catch him.'

Lupus wrote on his tablet with his right hand while raising his left.

'Yes, Lupus?'

Lupus finished writing, then held up his wax tablet: HOW DID DOMITIAN KILL TITUS? HE DIED OF FEVER.

'So far that's only a rumour,' said Flavia, irritably waving the mosquito away. 'And even if he did die of fever, it might have been caused by poison.'

Aristo frowned. 'But Domitian was back here in Rome when Titus died.'

'It could have been a slow-acting poison. Or Domitian might have hired an assassin. But we know he's behind the death of Titus. He's been plotting against him for at least half a year. Taking the emerald before we could give it to Titus was part of his plot. So was his attempt to silence us with that decree. We just need to find out how Domitian did it, before the senate makes him emperor.'

'Or we could flee back to Ephesus,' said Nubia hopefully.

'We can't!' said Flavia. 'We've got to prove Domitian's guilt.'

Lupus started to write something else on his wax tablet. DON'T THEY USUALLY DISPLAY BODY ...

'He's right!' Aristo snapped his fingers. 'They usually display the body of a dead emperor to the public!'

'We could go and examine it for signs of poison!' cried Flavia, triumphantly smacking the mosquito on her leg.

'Shhhh!' came a voice from the doorway and they turned to see Sisyphus with his finger to his lips. 'You're being very noisy mice!' he hissed. 'If Senator Cornix returns early, then he'll certainly hear you. I suggest you all go to sleep.'

'He's right,' sighed Flavia. 'We need to rest. We have a big day tomorrow. We have two mysteries to solve: how did Domitian kill Titus and where is Jonathan?'

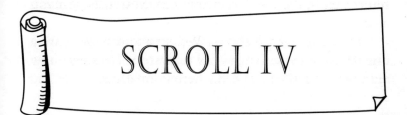

SCROLL IV

The next morning at the second hour, Nubia and her friends went to the Forum Romanum with Sisyphus. The Greek secretary had told Senator Cornix that he had forgotten his portable inkwell and had come back on pretence of getting it. Now he was leading them down the steep hill called the Clivus Scauri. Nubia looked around, remembering how she had once been borne up this same hill in a litter: a couch with poles carried by strong men. It was the first time she had ridden in such a vehicle and it had felt like floating on air. She and Flavia and Lupus had been searching for Jonathan then, too.

But they were on foot now, and as they emerged from the cool shadows of the narrow street into the brilliant morning sunshine of an open boulevard, Nubia's nostrils flared. The hot sun intensified the smells of Rome: smoke from a thousand braziers, mule manure from night deliveries and roasting flesh from the altars. Sisyphus led them to the right, towards the forum. He was wearing his umbrella hat – stained black in respect to Titus – so it was easy to follow him, even when the streets became crowded.

As they passed beneath the shadow of the great Flavian amphitheatre, Nubia shuddered. She and Flavia had faced hippos, crocodiles and man-eating bears there. She remembered the screams of the man dressed as Orpheus as the bears had torn him apart.

'Are you all right, Nubia?' asked Aristo. He was wearing one of Captain Geminus's old tunics, the kind with two vertical red stripes. The sea voyage from Ephesus had deepened his tan and brought out the gold in his hair. She thought he looked like a bronze statue of the god Mercury.

Nubia nodded. 'I am remembering the time we were in there.'

'You met Titus, didn't you?' said Aristo, glancing up at the massive amphitheatre looming on their right. 'And Domitian, too.'

'Yes,' said Nubia. 'Domitian used his bow and arrow to save my life and Flavia's.'

Aristo took her elbow to guide her around some fresh manure in the street. His touch thrilled her but she tried not to show any reaction.

'If he saved your life,' said Aristo, 'you must admire him a little.'

Nubia remembered the way Domitian had looked at her and licked his lips. She shook her head: 'No, I do not admire him, not even a little.'

'We hate him!' Flavia pulled the brim of her straw hat down to keep the sun out of her eyes. 'It was Domitian's idea to dress poor orphan girls as nymphs and throw them to hippos and crocodiles.'

'That was Domitian's idea?' said Aristo. 'But they were Titus's games.'

'Throwing us into crocodile-infested water was definitely Domitian's idea,' said Flavia with a shudder.

'Yes,' said Nubia. 'Titus was angry with him for doing that.'

'Titus wasn't just angry!' Sisyphus looked over his

26

shoulder at Nubia. 'He was furious! Remember how he rebuked Domitian in front of everyone and then told him to get out? What humiliation.'

'Yes,' said Nubia, remembering the look of pure hatred that she had seen on Domitian's face.

Sisyphus turned to walk backwards. 'I'll never forget how you came down from the sky wearing your lionskin,' he said. 'Nubia ex machina!'

'Please,' said Aristo, wincing. 'I can't bear to think about it.'

As they came into the forum – with its temples and shrines, its red-tiled roofs and coloured columns – Nubia saw that a crowd had gathered before an austere but elegant building covered with apricot-coloured plaster. Steps led up to a marble porch with eight fluted columns. Above the porch were three big windows, too lofty for anyone to be able to see inside, and above the windows was a triangular pediment. Everyone was gazing towards the bronze double doors.

'What is that building?' asked Nubia, as they reached the edge of the crowd. 'A temple?'

'It's the Curia,' said Sisyphus. 'The senate meets there. It was damaged in the fire last year, but you can see it's already been repaired.'

'Is Uncle Cornix in there?' asked Flavia.

'Yes.' Sisyphus beckoned them forward a little, until they stood beside a shrine of a god with two-faces. Nubia knew he was called Janus, the god of beginnings and ends.

'Did you tell Uncle Cornix about Domitian?' Flavia asked Sisyphus, and then lowered her voice to a whisper. 'Did you tell him that Domitian is probably behind Titus's death?'

Sisyphus lowered his voice, too. 'I didn't have a chance

to raise the subject. But most of the senators already suspect foul play. Everyone knows how much Domitian resented Titus; he never hid the fact. Furthermore, they think he's too independent. Doesn't consult them enough.' Sisyphus leaned closer. 'Senator Cornix thinks they may give the principate to Sabinus.'

'Who's Sabinus?'

'Flavius Sabinus is a cousin of Domitian and Titus. He was co-consul with Domitian two years ago. He married Titus's daughter Julia. You remember him, girls. He was in the imperial box last year.'

Nubia nodded. She vaguely remembered Julia's husband: a pleasant-looking man with reddish brown hair.

'And unlike Domitian, Sabinus has two sons. Domitian's only child died last month,' added Sisyphus. 'A little boy.'

'Poor Domitian,' said Nubia. Although she did not like him, she was sorry he had lost his child.

'So you think the senate might make Sabinus emperor?' asked Flavia.

'I hope so. And so does Senator Cornix.'

The crowds in the forum were growing every moment and a fat man in a toga pushed Nubia up against Aristo.

Aristo slipped a protective arm around her, and glared at the man.

'Excuse me,' said the man, 'I didn't mean to step on your boy.'

Nubia glanced at Flavia and hid a smile behind her hand. She kept forgetting that she was dressed as a boy, too.

The bald man mopped his forehead with a fold of his toga, and glanced at Aristo. 'Is it true?' he asked. 'Is Titus dead?'

Aristo nodded. 'The senate are choosing a successor now. It could take some time.'

At that moment the double doors opened and the crowd cheered as four soldiers appeared. Nubia could tell from their dazzling breastplates and red horsehair crests that they were special.

'Praetorian guards,' said Aristo in her ear. His breath sent a delicious shiver through her and she was glad that his arm was still around her shoulders. 'He's already won their support,' continued Aristo. 'And look: here come the senators.'

'Ah!' said Sisyphus. 'There's senator Cornix, now. I'm supposed to be waiting over there, with the other secretaries and scribes. I'll see you later.' He turned to go and then turned back and looked at Aristo: 'Make sure you aren't recognised,' he said in a low voice. 'These are dangerous times.'

He plunged into the crowd and Nubia saw his black umbrella hat moving through a sea of heads towards the Curia.

A man nearby cried: 'Caesar! Caesar!' and soon everyone had picked up the chant.

Nubia looked up at Aristo's handsome profile. 'Does this mean they are choosing a new emperor already?' she asked him.

Aristo turned his head to look down at her. His arm was still around her shoulders and at that moment the crowd surged forward so that she was pressed up against him. Their faces were only inches apart. 'What?' he murmured, gazing into her eyes.

Nubia could not remember what she had been saying. There was something about his look, about the way he was slowly lowering his slightly parted lips towards hers, almost as if he was about to kiss her.

A finger tapped her shoulder and a voice behind her said, 'Nubia? Is that you?'

And the moment was gone.

SCROLL V

'Nubia? Is that you? Is Flavia here, too?'

Flavia and the others turned to see a boy of about thirteen in a red-bordered toga.

'Tranquillus!' exclaimed Flavia, forgetting to be a slave-boy. 'What are you doing here?'

He glanced quickly around, and hissed: 'What are *you* doing here? There's an imperial edict right over there on the rostra. It names the four of you as enemies of Titus.'

'It's all right,' whispered Flavia. 'We're in disguise.' She frowned. 'So how did you recognise us, anyway?'

'I heard Nubia's voice,' he said, 'and I recognised her.' He looked Flavia up and down and gave a grudging smile: 'But I wouldn't have recognised you.'

'Flavia,' said Aristo. 'Who is this?'

'Gaius Suetonius Tranquillus. We met him last summer at the Villa Limona. Tranquillus, this is our tutor Aristo. He's pretending to be an equestrian and we're his slaves.'

Tranquillus raised an eyebrow. 'He really shouldn't have his arm around his slave-boy,' he said. 'Or people will get the wrong idea.'

Aristo flushed and withdrew his arm from around Nubia's shoulders.

Tranquillus turned back to Flavia. 'You shouldn't be anywhere near here. You shouldn't even be in Italia.'

'We know. But we wanted to warn Titus that his life was in danger.'

Tranquillus's eyebrow went up again. 'I think you're a little late.'

Flavia ignored this last remark. 'Jonathan should have warned Titus weeks ago,' she said. 'We came to the forum hoping to examine Titus's body for signs of murder.'

'Signs of murder?' said Tranquillus, his brown eyes growing wide.

'Yes!' whispered Flavia. 'We think Domitian either killed Titus or had him killed.'

'For Jupiter's sake, be quiet!' he hissed.

Lupus pretended to drink something, then clutched his throat, crossed his eyes and slumped to the ground.

'And don't do that either!' Tranquillus pulled Lupus to his feet and looked nervously around. 'Do you want to get us all executed?'

The resounding clang of bronze on marble made their heads turn towards the porch of the Curia. Flavia saw a herald standing between the columns, before the crowd of senators. He banged his bronze staff again, and the crowd grew silent.

'ROMAN CITIZENS!' he bellowed. 'AS MANY OF YOU KNOW, OUR BELOVED EMPEROR TITUS DIED YESTERDAY AT HIS SABINE VILLA.'

The crowd groaned.

Without taking his eyes from the herald, Tranquillus said, 'Have you heard how Titus died?'

Flavia nodded and opened her mouth.

'OUR BELOVED EMPEROR TITUS DIED OF A FEVER,' blared the herald, 'WHICH HE CONTRACTED ON THE ROAD. HE DIED IN HIS VILLA AT REATE. HIS BODY WILL BE ON DISPLAY THERE FOR SEVEN

DAYS, IN ACCORDANCE WITH ROMAN CUSTOM. HE WILL BE CREMATED A WEEK FROM TODAY AND HIS ASHES PLACED IN THE TOMB OF THE FLAVIANS ON THE VIA APPIA.'

'There goes your chance to examine the dead body of an overweight, middle-aged man,' said Tranquillus with a grin.

'IT IS MY HONOUR TO INFORM YOU,' cried the herald, 'THAT THE SENATE HAS TODAY GRANTED TRIBUNICIA POTESTAS AND IMPERIUM TO A MOST WORTHY SUCCESSOR, ALONG WITH THE TITLES OF AUGUSTUS AND PATER PATRIAE!'

'What?' asked Nubia.

'The senate has chosen a new emperor,' said Aristo.

Without turning her head, Flavia said to Tranquillus, 'We think it's going to be Sabinus. We have an inside source and he says . . .' Her words died away as the bronze doors of the Curia swung open to the blare of two trumpets. The senators parted and a man in a purple toga moved to the front of the porch. The man was about thirty years old, dark-haired and of medium height. He was good-looking, with large dark eyes in a square face. His full, sensual lips curved into a smile and as he lifted his hands towards the crowd he drew an enormous cheer.

'Oh no!' said Flavia and Lupus gave his 'uh-oh' grunt.

'Our new emperor is not Sabinus,' said Tranquillus drily.

'Behold it is Domitian,' breathed Nubia.

'I PRESENT OUR NEW PRINCEPS,' proclaimed the herald, 'AND MOST ESTEEMED LEADER: IMPERATOR CAESAR DOMITIANUS AUGUSTUS.'

The crowd cheered and Domitian bowed. Then his

hand went to a green medallion hanging around his neck and he lifted it to his right eye.

'It's Nero's Eye!' gasped Flavia. 'Domitian has Nero's Eye!'

'By Hercules, it *is* Nero's Eye!' said the fat man behind her, and as word passed through the crowd, the cheering grew louder.

Domitian was peering through the smooth, lentil-shaped emerald and scanning the cheering crowd, like a smiling, nodding, green-eyed Cyclops. His gaze passed over Flavia and her friends, then snapped back. His smile faded and he lowered the gem for a moment, then lifted it to his eye again.

'Great Juno's peacock!' said Flavia nervously. She tugged her straw hat down over her eyes. 'He's looking right at us.'

Lupus gave his 'uh-oh' grunt again.

'He couldn't possibly . . .' muttered Aristo.

'Don't worry,' said Tranquillus. 'They say Domitian's eyesight is rather dim.'

'That cannot be,' said Nubia. 'Domitian is a most excellent archer.'

'She's right,' said Flavia. 'His eyesight must be excellent.'

'Then why does he need Nero's Eye?'

'I think it makes far away things look closer.'

'Just as well you're in disguise,' said Aristo.

'Uh-oh,' grunted Lupus for a third time.

Domitian was leaning back and speaking to one of the red-crested guards behind him, his green lens still trained on them.

'Alas,' whispered Nubia. 'He is looking right at me.'

Flavia and Aristo both looked at Nubia.

'Your skin,' murmured Aristo, 'and your eyes. Nobody could mistake them.'

'If *I* recognised Nubia,' said Tranquillus, 'then so could he.'

'I think,' whispered Flavia. 'That we should get out of here now.'

'Great Juno's peacock!' muttered Flavia, and repeated, 'We've got to get out of here. Now!' She could see two soldiers of the Praetorian Guard coming down the steps of the Curia towards them, parting the crowd like sharks in a shoal of anchovies.

'By Hercules, I think you're right,' muttered Tranquillus, and he grasped her hand. 'Follow me,' he commanded. 'All of you. Quickly!'

Flavia did not protest as he pulled her through the packed crowd. She glanced over her shoulder: Lupus, Nubia and Aristo were close behind, looking worried. And bouncing above the heads of the crowd beyond were the curved red horsehair crests of the guards' helmets. They were getting closer.

Tranquillus and Flavia pushed their way through the people. Some cursed them, others made way smiling, most just ignored them. Flavia was dizzy with the smell of sweat mixed with the heavy perfumes used to cover the smell of sweat.

At last they emerged from the crowd and onto a side street. Still holding her hand, Tranquillus ran up it, then turned a corner. They seemed to double back, past an altar with the remains of a sacrifice still on it. Then up some sunlit steps between houses to a narrow shaded street with a wall fountain spattering water onto the cobblestones. Tranquillus's toga had slipped down around his ankles, and now it almost tripped him up. He lurched forward, cursed, pulled it off and bundled it under his left arm.

They turned another corner and came back into the bright sunshine of a crossroads. There was a gleaming basin-type fountain where the two roads met, with a marble statue of a nearly naked gauze-clad nymph pouring water into it. Tranquillus gestured for them to hide behind this fountain, crouching down on its shady side. In the distance they could hear the crowd cheering. And above it the sound of jingling footsteps coming closer and closer ... And then retreating.

'Praise Juno,' gasped Flavia. Her heart was thudding and a trickle of sweat ran down her back. 'The guards are getting further away.'

Tranquillus was breathing hard, too. 'In case we get separated,' he gasped. 'I live on the Quirinal ... on Pear Street ... Our house ... is the one opposite the biggest pear tree. It has a porch with two spiral columns.'

He cautiously stood up and looked around. Flavia and the others stood up too. They all drank from the fountain and then Tranquillus pointed. 'That way.'

He led them up a cobbled street, then turned right down a narrow sunlit back street, this one hung with washing. They stopped for a moment at the sound of footsteps, but it was only four blond slaves carrying a pink-curtained litter down the hill.

They passed some temples and walled gardens, and presently they emerged into a quiet tree-lined street, so quiet that Flavia could hear her heart beating hard. 'I've never been here before,' she said. 'Is this the Quirinal?'

'Yes. We're almost at Pear Street. This is Pomegranate Street,' he added, and tipped his head sideways. 'In case you're interested, that's the house where Domitian was born.'

'The one with the little wooden columns in the porch?' said Flavia. 'It's so small.'

'It's nice enough inside,' said Tranquillus, 'but it's not a palace. Domitian always resented not growing up in court like Titus.'

'Titus grew up in court?'

'The Emperor Claudius took him in, didn't he?' said Aristo; he was walking behind them, between Nubia and Lupus.

Tranquillus nodded. 'That's right. When Titus was a boy, he was best friends with Claudius's son Britannicus, until Nero had him poisoned.'

'Do you think Titus was poisoned, too?' asked Flavia.

Lupus clutched his throat and gave a choking noise.

Tranquillus glanced around. 'We'd better not discuss that until we get to my house,' he said. 'It's just around the corner.'

Then he caught Flavia's hand again, and squeezed it. And even though they were no longer in danger, he kept holding it.

SCROLL VI

Half an hour later they were safe in the Suetonius townhouse, munching almond-stuffed dates washed down with posca. It was still only mid-morning, but hot, so they sat on a cool marble bench in the shady peristyle which surrounded a garden courtyard.

'Where are your parents?' asked Flavia, looking around the deserted garden. She could smell thyme and hear bees buzzing.

'Pater's down in the forum,' said Tranquillus. 'I was with him and my paedagogus when I saw you.'

Flavia flushed. 'But he doesn't approve of me, remember?'

'I didn't tell him I saw you. And I don't intend to. I'll tell him I got separated from them in the crowd.'

'Why does your father not approve of Flavia?' Aristo asked Tranquillus.

Flavia felt her cheeks grow even warmer. 'Nothing, really. We held hands last summer on the beach at Surrentum.'

'In front of everyone,' said Tranquillus, looking pleased with himself.

Lupus made a loud smacking noise as he kissed the back of his hand.

'You kissed him?' Aristo raised his eyebrows at Flavia.

Nubia giggled behind her hand. 'And Flavia emerges from shrubbery with unpinned hair,' she said.

Flavia shot a glare at her friends. 'We did not kiss! At least not in public.'

Aristo glanced at Tranquillus, who was looking smug. 'Anything you want to tell me, Flavia?' he asked, taking a stuffed date from the platter.

'Of course not!' said Flavia hotly. 'Nothing happened between me and Tranquillus.'

Aristo casually examined the date. 'Besides, I thought you girls were both in love with Flaccus.'

Nubia and Flavia looked at each other in astonishment and Lupus choked on his posca, so that they all had to pat him on the back.

Tranquillus's smile faded. 'Flaccus? Which Flaccus?'

When Lupus's coughs had subsided, Flavia folded her arms. 'Nubia doesn't love Floppy,' she said. 'And neither do I! Besides,' she muttered under her breath, 'he's probably married by now.'

Aristo looked at Nubia. 'So you're not in love with him?'

Nubia shook her head and regarded him with puzzled eyes.

Aristo frowned. 'But last month Jonathan said you girls were both in love with Flaccus.'

'Last month?' said Flavia. 'When he was being tormented by evil voices in his head?'

Aristo frowned into his goblet, then gave his head a shake, as if to clear it. 'Don't you have a tutor?' he asked Tranquillus.

'Not really,' said Tranquillus. 'I'm studying rhetoric with Quintilian now.'

'Oh!' cried Flavia. 'So is Floppy! I mean, so is Gaius Valerius Flaccus. Do you have lessons with him?'

Tranquillus looked sheepish. 'When I say "with Quintilian" I mean in his school of rhetoric. I probably won't have classes with the master himself until I'm a little older.'

'What about the tutor who was beating you?' asked Nubia.

'That's right,' said Flavia. 'The one who came and dragged you away from the Villa Limona last summer?'

'He retired. I have a new paedagogus now. And ever since I caught him kissing one of mater's slave girls I can make him do whatever I like.'

'You have a mother?' asked Nubia.

Tranquillus nodded. 'Mater's staying with her sister at Alba Longa. My aunt's expecting her second child soon.' He looked at Flavia. 'But tell me about you,' he said. 'Why did Titus issue an imperial decree against you?'

'It wasn't Titus,' said Flavia. 'At least that's our theory. We think it was actually Domitian. We were on a secret mission for Titus.'

'You were?' said Tranquillus. He looked at Aristo. 'They were?'

Aristo shrugged and nodded. 'Apparently.'

'He asked us to steal Nero's Eye—'

'You stole Nero's Eye?'

'Yes.'

'Because of the Pythia's prophecy that whoever possessed it would rule Rome for a long time?'

'Yes. Titus wanted to make sure nobody else got it.'

'Then how did Domitian get it?'

'After we stole it,' said Flavia 'we gave it to Titus's agent, a man called Taurus.'

Lupus shook his head and made a thumbs-down sign.

'But Taurus was secretly working for Domitian. And

because we were the only ones who knew about it—'

'Domitian tried to get rid of you, by issuing a decree in his brother's name!'

'Exactly.'

Tranquillus nodded slowly. 'And now, at the most critical moment, Domitian has produced Nero's Eye. Great Jupiter's eyebrows!' he cried, as if struck by a sudden thought.

'What?' they all cried.

'That's probably why the senate conferred power on him so quickly. None of them would dare oppose the Delphic oracle, not publicly, at least. Domitian probably walked into the Curia this morning, held up the Eye and asked which of them wanted to call the Pythia a liar.'

'You think that's what convinced the senate to make him emperor?' asked Aristo.

'It must be,' Tranquillus glanced around, and although they were in the secluded privacy of an inner garden he lowered his voice to a whisper. 'Most of the senators dislike Domitian. They prefer Titus's cousin, Sabinus.'

'Yes,' said Aristo. 'That's what our friend Sisyphus said.'

Suddenly Flavia had an idea and she gripped Tranquillus's arm. 'Is it too late for the senate to change their minds? If we could somehow prove that Domitian stole Nero's Eye and killed his own brother, is there a chance they could appoint Sabinus instead?'

'I don't see why not,' said Tranquillus. 'Everyone knows Sabinus would be a better emperor than Domitian. Sabinus is honest and wise, and he's also related to the two previous emperors by birth and marriage.'

'And if he's honest and wise,' said Flavia, 'he might revoke the decree against us!'

'Be careful,' said Aristo. 'Times are usually turbulent in

the early days of a new emperor. In the year following Nero's death, there were four different rulers.'

'He's right,' said Tranquillus.

'That's why we must act quickly!' cried Flavia, 'Before anything gets inscribed in stone.'

'Flavia might have a point,' said Tranquillus. 'Domitian will want a proper coronation, with sacrifices and vows and pomp. But it will take a few days to get that ready.'

'And,' said Flavia, 'if we can find proof of his crimes before the official ceremony—'

'—we might have a chance!'

'I don't know,' said Aristo. 'It's a very big undertaking.'

'But I know exactly where to start,' said Tranquillus.

Flavia looked at him and he looked back, his brown eyes bright. After a dramatic pause he said: 'The place to start our quest for the Truth is the first stopping place on the Via Salaria: Eretum, the town where Titus fell ill!'

Most wheeled traffic was forbidden in the city of Rome during the day, so every gate had its stables with horses and mule-carts waiting for hire. Some of the richer families kept private carrucas in special vehicle parks outside the city wall.

'Can you just take your father's carruca and driver like this?' said Flavia to Tranquillus, as they left the Porta Collina and rode north on the Via Salaria. 'Won't he be angry?'

Tranquillus shrugged. 'I'm still on holiday for the next few days. I left pater a note saying I was going to do some research for a project. And as long as I've got *him* with me,' Tranquillus used his chin to point at his paedagogus, 'pater doesn't really mind what I do.'

Flavia glanced over at Tranquillus' paedagogus. Hilario

was a rubber-faced man in his mid-forties with goggle-eyes and dark eyebrows arched in an expression of permanent surprise. His dark hair was slicked down with strongly scented oil.

Flavia sat back and looked around. 'Your carruca is lovely,' she said to Tranquillus. The buttercup-yellow carriage had two padded benches, one along each side. Flavia, Nubia and Aristo sat on one bench; facing them were Tranquillus, Lupus and Hilario. A blue linen awning was open on all four sides, to let the breeze in, but it shaded them from the noonday sun.

As the carruca drove north along the Via Salaria, flanked by the tombs of the rich, Flavia leaned forward. 'Tell us everything,' she said to Tranquillus, who sat opposite her. 'Tell us everything you know about Titus and Domitian.'

'Everything?' said Tranquillus with a grin.

Flavia opened her wax tablet and held her stylus poised. 'Everything.'

'But not the gossip!' At the other end of Tranquillus's bench Hilario waggled his finger prissily. 'Stick to facts, not gossip.'

'Yes, Hilario.' Tranquillus sighed and rolled his eyes, then said to Flavia: 'You know about Titus's headaches, don't you? That his advisors and courtiers have been running the empire these past six months.'

'They have?' said Flavia.

'Yes,' said Tranquillus. 'Domitian in particular. They say Titus spent days on end in a darkened room. Sometimes he would get a blacksmith in to bang an anvil. Can you imagine? But it was the only thing that seemed to bring him any relief.'

Flavia nodded. She remembered the emperor suffering from headaches two years before.

43

'Then, four or five days ago,' said Tranquillus, 'Titus went to sacrifice at the Ludi Romani.'

Nubia sat up straight. 'The chariot races at Circus Maximus!'

'That's right,' said Tranquillus. 'They're on at the moment. Anyway, Titus was down on the track with his soothsayer, haruspex and assistant priests – a hundred thousand Romans all watching him intently – about to cut a bull's throat, when there was *thunder from a clear sky*.'

Lupus gave Tranquillus his bug-eyed look.

'That's right,' said Tranquillus dramatically, 'thunder from a clear sky. Everybody heard it, including Titus. He was so startled that he looked around and the bull escaped.'

'Euge!' said Nubia, clapping her hands. 'Hooray!'

'It's not euge, Nubia,' cried Flavia. 'It's eheu! When a sacrificial victim runs away it's a terrible omen. What did Titus do?' she asked Tranquillus.

'He burst into tears.'

They all stared at him.

Tranquillus looked round at them and nodded. 'Sobbed and sobbed. Big fat tears running down his face, like he'd lost his best friend. Or a child. His soothsayer led him away and the next day they set out for Sabina, a week before the end of the games!'

'And that was three days ago?' Flavia was writing on her tablet. 'Two days before the Ides?'

'That's right.'

'So,' Flavia looked down at her notes: 'Two days before the Ides, Titus botches a sacrifice and then weeps inconsolably. The next day he sets out for his Sabine Villa. At the first stopping place he suddenly takes ill, but he reaches his ancestral home, where he dies on the Ides.'

44

'Where is the first stopping place?' asked Aristo.

'A town called Eretum,' said Tranquillus. 'We should be there in about an hour.'

Flavia glanced out of the carriage. They had left the tombs behind and were now driving past potteries and tile factories.

'Anything else you can tell us?' asked Flavia. 'Anything at all?'

Tranquillus grinned and glanced over Lupus's head at Hilario. 'Only gossip,' he said.

'No gossip!' warned the paedagogus.

'Some of it might be relevant, you know,' said Aristo. 'There's usually a kernel of truth in every piece of gossip.'

Hilario looked down his nose at Aristo. 'It could also be dangerous,' he said, 'if anyone hears us repeating it.'

'Who could hear us out here on the road?' said Flavia.

Lupus glanced up at the driver, whose back was to them, and raised his eyebrows questioningly.

Tranquillus laughed. 'Don't mind him. Talpa is as deaf as a mole. Pater often uses him as a driver, to ensure he won't be overheard. So, shall I tell you what people are saying?'

'Yes!' said Flavia, her stylus poised.

Hilario puffed his disapproval. 'Gaius Suetonius Tranquillus,' he said, 'you are the biggest gossip in Rome, and no good can come of it.'

Tranquillus sighed and turned his head to gaze straight ahead. 'There they are,' he said, pointing with his chin. 'The blue Sabine hills. That's where we're going. Have you ever been there before?'

'Tell us the gossip,' pleaded Flavia. 'It might be important.'

'It rained last week,' remarked Tranquillus. 'First rain

we've had in four months. It really cleared the air.'

'Tranquillus, please?'

'It's going to be a good olive crop this year.'

'Tell us!'

Tranquillus turned back to them and grinned. 'If you insist.'

Hilario tutted, but said nothing.

Tranquillus leaned forward on his bench. 'There's a very popular pantomime dancer in Rome at the moment.'

Lupus sat up straight and looked interested. He loved pantomime.

'Narcissus?' asked Flavia and Nubia together. 'Was it Narcissus?'

Tranquillus looked surprised. 'No, his name is Paris.'

'I've heard of him,' said Aristo. 'He's supposed to be very good.'

Tranquillus grinned. 'I don't know how good he is, but he's young and very handsome. All the women in Rome swoon for him. They say that Domitian's wife Domitia is madly in love with him.'

'Domitia?' said Flavia. 'I met her once at the games and she seemed so stiff and formal. She had a wig this high.' Flavia held her hand a foot above her straw sunhat.

Tranquillus laughed. 'Well, she may be stiff in public, but apparently not in private. There is another rumour, even more scandalous than the first.'

'Tranquillus!' chided Hilario. 'I forbid you to repeat that scurrilous report.'

Tranquillus ignored his paedagogus. He leaned towards them, and even though they were driving in a noisy carruca with a deaf driver, he lowered his voice. 'They also say,' he breathed, 'that Domitia was in love with Titus!'

SCROLL VII

Nubia was doubly distracted.

Everyone in the carruca was discussing Domitian's wife and her possible love affairs. It was fascinating, but Nubia couldn't concentrate. Aristo was sitting on the bench beside her, his muscular arm next to hers. Every time the carruca swayed his arm brushed against hers, and even such an innocent touch thrilled her. A moment ago he had shifted and now his arm was pressing against hers, and she almost swooned from the feel of his warm skin.

Also, she needed the latrines.

'If Domitia had an affair with Titus,' Flavia was saying, 'that would give Domitian even more motive to kill his brother: jealousy and revenge!'

'As if Domitian didn't have enough motive already,' murmured Aristo. He shifted away from Nubia and she was able to concentrate again.

'Some people think it wasn't Domitia whom Titus loved,' said Tranquillus, 'but a Hebrew woman. They say she was a slave from Jerusalem. He set her free and realised too late that she was the love of his life.'

Nubia glanced at Flavia. She knew her friend was wondering the same thing: could the Hebrew woman have been Jonathan's mother, Susannah? She had been Titus's slave for ten years.

'And I haven't even told you about the prophecy,' said Tranquillus.

'What prophecy?' asked Flavia.

The carruca went over a bump and Nubia winced as it jolted her full bladder. Why was she the only one who ever needed to use the latrine? Didn't other people ever need to go?

'When Titus was on his way back to Rome from Jerusalem,' said Tranquillus, 'he visited Tyana, in Asia.'

'Oh!' cried Flavia. 'We've just come from Asia. But I've never heard of Tyana.'

'Tyana,' said rubber-faced Hilario, 'is nearly four hundred miles east of Ephesus. My grandmother comes from there,' he added proudly.

'That far!' murmured Flavia.

'Asia's a big province,' said Aristo. He shifted, so that he was pressing against Nubia again. Once again she felt the exciting warmth of his arm against hers. She could smell his musky lavender body oil, too. She closed her eyes and took a deep breath.

'Titus made a special detour to get there,' explained Tranquillus. 'He wanted to visit a famous philosopher named Apollonius. After conversing with him for a while, Titus was greatly impressed with the man's wisdom and insight. He asked if he had a special message for him. Apollonius looked up at the sun and said, *I swore by the sun I would tell you, even if you hadn't asked me. The gods have told me to warn you. As long as your father lives, beware his enemies, but once he is dead, beware those closest to you.*'

Lupus gave them his bug-eyed look and Aristo repeated: '*Beware those closest to you.*'

'And who was closer to Titus than Domitian!' breathed Flavia.

'Was this prophecy common knowledge?' asked Aristo.

Tranquillus grinned. 'I've heard it,' he said, 'so it must be common knowledge.'

'I've never heard that,' said Hilario with a scowl. 'How do you know something I don't?'

'My old tutor told me,' said Tranquillus dismissively. 'But listen: there's more. Titus then asked Apollonius if the gods had told him how he was going to die. And he replied: *Like Odysseus, from the sea.*'

They all looked at each other and Nubia said, 'I do not understand what this means.'

Aristo turned his head and smiled down at her. 'Don't worry, Nubia,' he said. 'Nobody understands what it means. It's cryptic.' His gaze held hers; their arms were touching and once again she felt dizzy. Any moment she was going to lose control and wet herself.

'Did Odysseus die at sea?' mused Flavia. 'How *did* he die? I can't remember.' She looked at the two tutors at the end of their respective benches. Hilario wore an expression of almost comical concentration, but Aristo was looking at Nubia with concern. 'Are you all right, Nubia?' he asked.

Nubia nodded and looked down. 'I am having to use the latrine,' she stammered.

'Me, too!' said Flavia. 'Is there a place to stop soon?'

Tranquillus reached into the leather satchel beneath the bench and pulled out a sponge-stick. He stood up, moved unsteadily forward, tapped the driver on the shoulder and showed him the spongia.

Talpa grinned, nodded and pointed ahead.

'Apparently there's a place up ahead where we can use the latrine,' said Tranquillus with a smile. He handed Nubia the sponge-stick.

'Good,' said Flavia.

It was a warm autumn day with a blue sky and fluffy clouds. At this point, the Via Salaria was flanked by plane trees, and she could see the road curving up into blue mountains. Some of the leaves on the trees were already beginning to turn yellow. They passed a tannery and an olive press and at last the cart was pulling into a semi-circular gravel drive before a buttermilk-coloured building with a columned porch. Above the columns, a sign announced in neat red letters that this was the INN OF ROMULUS. There was a hitching post in front of the inn with two mules and a horse. Another carruca stood further up the drive, near a water trough.

Talpa helped them down, then grinned and pointed to the left hand side of the building and gave them a thumbs-up. Flavia mouthed a thank you and then ran after Nubia towards the inn.

She found Nubia hesitating outside a wooden door with the word FORICA painted on it. There was also a more graphic illustration, presumably for those who couldn't read.

'I hope there are no men in here,' whimpered Nubia, hopping up and down. She held the spongia in her hand.

'If there are, we'll just have to pretend we think it's normal,' said Flavia, and made her voice gruff. 'Remember, we're boys.' She tugged her hat lower and pushed open the door. 'Oh, praise Juno,' she said a moment later. 'There's nobody else here. Nobody but some mosquitoes.'

'Ugh!' said Nubia. 'It smells.'

Despite a skylight, the wooden seven-seater latrine stank of urine. 'Better here than in the bushes,' said Flavia, hiking up her tunic and sitting on the wooden seat. She heard Tranquillus's voice and thought she saw the door starting to open. 'Stop!' she cried. 'We're in here! Wait until we've finished.'

'All right,' came Tranquillus's laughing voice from just outside, 'but remember, you're boys. Real boys don't squeal like that.'

Flavia had never been in a men's latrine before. She was amazed by the amount of graffiti on the walls. Most of the messages made her blush, but one intrigued her. CAVE REMUM it read. *Beware of Remus*. Something about it seemed familiar, but she couldn't think what.

Nubia rinsed off the sponge-stick and handed it to Flavia. Then she stepped down from the toilet bench to pick up something lying between two floor bricks.

'Nubia!' cried Flavia. 'What are you doing?'

'Behold!' Nubia held out a bronze stylus.

'Oh,' said Flavia. 'Someone must have dropped it. May I see it? Ouch!' She dropped it and sucked a drop of blood from her finger. 'Stupid thing. It's sharp as a needle.' She kicked it away, and it rolled into a dark corner of the latrine. 'Come on,' she said. 'I'm famished. Let's see if this inn serves lunch.'

Nubia did not like the Inn of Romulus on the Via Salaria. The table was sticky, the porridge was gritty and the pretty serving-girl was paying far too much attention to Aristo.

'Can I get you boys anything else?' asked the girl, looking only at Aristo. She was chewing mastic resin; Nubia could smell it on her breath.

'No, thank you.' Aristo smiled and slid two sesterces across the wooden tabletop. 'Just tell me where the latrines are?'

The girl leaned closer than was necessary and smiled

back at Aristo. She was plump and dusky with a mass of dark curls pulled back with a tortoiseshell clasp. Hilario was staring at her, his red mouth a wet 'O' of admiration.

'Just through the arch on the left,' breathed the girl. 'Be careful of spiders. A big one bit the Emperor a few days ago.'

Lupus choked on his posca and Flavia cried, 'The Emperor Titus stopped here last week?'

The girl glanced at Flavia and tossed her dark curls. 'Three or four days ago,' she said, chomping her gum. 'He and his bodyguards stopped to use the latrines and a mosquito bit him on his calf. He was shorter than I would have thought,' she added.

'Mosquito?' said Nubia. 'Were you not just saying spider?'

'Mosquito, spider ... I don't know. He just said something bit him.' The girl turned back to Aristo and fluttered her long lashes at him. 'Do you want me to go with you? To make sure it's safe?'

Hilario looked from the girl to Aristo and back.

Aristo laughed as he stood up. 'I'll be fine,' he said. 'I'll keep an eye out for biting things.'

Nubia saw the girl eye Aristo appreciatively as he walked towards the arch. Then she started as Flavia gripped her arm.

'Maybe a rabid rat bit Titus!' cried Flavia. 'And that's what killed him.'

Lupus shook his head and wrote on his wax tablet: BITE FROM RABID ANIMAL TAKES WEEKS TO DRIVE YOU MAD.

'Of course,' said Flavia. 'I should know that.'

'Don't be silly,' said the serving girl as she put the two coins into her belt pouch. 'It was just a tiny red dot. I brought his physician some vinegar and watched him apply it. Besides, everybody knows Titus died of a fever.'

'A mosquito bite can give you fever,' said Tranquillus. 'Right, Hilario?'

Hilario was still staring at the serving girl open-mouthed. 'Oh. Yes. Right,' he stuttered. 'A mosquito can give you fever.'

Flavia looked up at the serving-girl. 'How did the emperor seem to you? Healthy? Or sick?'

The girl shrugged. 'I don't know. He was eager to use the latrines, that's all. He came in with his bodyguard and a Jew. They didn't even stop to eat.' For a moment the girl stopped stacking bowls and chomped thoughtfully as she gazed up at the rafters. 'He did seem a little sad. I remember thinking that. His eyes were red, as if he'd been weeping.'

'And there was a Jew with him?' asked Flavia.

'Yes.'

'How could you tell?'

The girl shrugged. 'By his tassels and his beard. I know because the owner of this inn is also a Jew.' She winked at Hilario. 'And so am I.'

SCROLL VIII

An hour later Lupus and his three friends and the two tutors reached Eretum, the first stopping place on the Via Salaria, the spot where Titus had taken ill. Lupus was first off the carriage as it stopped before a peach-coloured hospitium with its own stables, bakery and vegetable garden.

'Titus had a bad headache and fever,' said the owner of Hector's Hospitium, as he served them lukewarm posca. 'His aides asked me for ice. I showed them the big block of ice in my storeroom. They chopped it all up, wrapped the ice chips in linen and packed it around the emperor in his litter.'

'The emperor was travelling in a litter?' said Flavia, and she frowned. 'Isn't that a very slow way to travel?'

'It's slow but smooth,' said Tranquillus. 'Much smoother than a carruca.'

Lupus nodded to himself. He had been carried in a litter once or twice. It was the smoothest ride in the world.

'There were also horses and carriages in the entourage,' said Hector, a middle-aged man with wide-spaced eyes and rabbit teeth. 'And about a dozen foot soldiers.'

'What time of day did they get here?' asked Flavia.

'Shortly before noon,' said Hector, 'the day before the Ides.'

'Assuming they set out at dawn,' said Aristo, 'that's not bad.'

Hilario nodded his agreement.

'They didn't give me half of what it cost,' grumbled Hector. 'For the ice, that is. But what could I say? He's the emperor. He *was* the emperor.'

Lupus frowned. He knew that Jonathan's father, Doctor Mordecai, always treated fever patients by keeping them warm, not cooling them off.

The same thought must have occurred to Nubia: 'Why were they putting ice around him?' she asked.

'That's right,' said Flavia. 'Aren't you supposed to burn a fever out?'

'I asked his helpers the same thing,' said the innkeeper. 'But the Jew told me it was the latest theory. Cool down a fever to save the patient.'

Lupus held up his wax tablet. IT DIDN'T WORK.

'No,' said the innkeeper. 'It didn't. All that expensive ice. And it might have killed Titus, not saved him.' He made the sign against evil.

'They didn't spend the night here at your inn?' asked Aristo.

'No. Said they wanted to make Reate by nightfall if they could. That's where the Emperor has his family estate. I heard the Jew saying they could bathe him in the cold springs there.'

'Who was the Jew?' asked Flavia.

'I don't know,' said Hector. 'A doctor.'

Lupus looked wide-eyed at Flavia. He could tell she was thinking the same thing. He made a quick sketch of Jonathan's father, Mordecai ben Ezra, and held it up for the innkeeper to see.

'No,' said Hector. 'This doctor was young, early

twenties: pale complexion, long nose, small mouth, short beard. There was an Egyptian soothsayer there, too. Asclepius, I think they called him. Thin-faced man in a long grass-green tunic. Kept repeating everything and rubbing his hands like a fly.'

Lupus looked up sharply, then wrote on his wax tablet: ASCLETARIO?

'Of course!' cried Flavia. 'Was his name Ascletario?'

'That's it,' said the innkeeper. 'Ascletario.'

'You know Ascletario, the emperor's astrologer?' Tranquillus asked Flavia as they came out of the hospitium and into the sunshine. Some chickens were pecking about their feet.

'We met him a few years ago in Rome,' said Flavia. 'We were looking for Jonathan then, too. Poor Jonathan. I hope nothing bad has happened to him.'

Tranquillus raised an eyebrow. 'You seem very fond of him,' he said.

'We're just friends,' said Flavia. 'But we've been through so much together.' She felt quite shaky and was surprised by the strength of her physical reaction.

'You're trembling,' said Tranquillus as they walked back to the carruca. 'Are you sure you and Jonathan are just friends?'

'Of course,' said Flavia. Her head was beginning to throb. 'We're just friends.'

Nubia smiled and whispered in her ear. 'Friends like you and Floppy are friends?'

The mention of Gaius Valerius Flaccus made Flavia's stomach twist and for a moment she thought she might be physically sick. She remembered how he had proposed to her nine months before, and his words: *Your arrow has pierced my heart*. She thought of his glossy dark hair and his beautiful eyes and his smiling mouth. She had rejected him, and thrown away her chance at happiness. By now he must be married to Prudentilla, the beautiful daughter of a senator. It seemed unbearably sad and Flavia began to cry.

'Oh, Flavia!' Nubia put her arms around Flavia. 'I did not mean to make you cry.'

Flavia was about to tell Nubia it wasn't her fault when her knees gave way. A moment later strong arms were holding her up.

'Flavia!' Aristo's voice seemed very remote.

'What's wrong with her?' came Tranquillus's voice, also from a distance.

Flavia felt Nubia's cool hand on her forehead. 'Alas!' came her friend's voice, the furthest away of all. 'She is hot as a brazier.'

'Whatever you do,' murmured Flavia. 'Don't pack me in ice.' And then everything went dark.

'Flavia?' It was Nubia's soft voice. 'How are you feeling?'

Flavia groaned and opened her eyes.

Nubia sat beside her. They were in a small, lamplit room with mustard-coloured panels on the red plaster walls. Flavia felt the cool cloth on her forehead and a too-firm bolster under her head. She was wrapped in three wool blankets. The inner one was damp with sweat.

'What time is it?'

'Evening,' said Nubia.

'Where am I?' murmured Flavia. She tried to lift her head, but it throbbed so she lowered it again.

'I forgot the name,' said Nubia apologetically.

'We're in Eretum,' said Tranquillus, 'at Hector's Hospitium.'

Flavia turned her head to see him standing in the doorway, holding back the striped cloth that served as a door. 'Are we still here?' she murmured. 'What about the investigation?'

'Don't worry,' said Tranquillus. 'We've been gathering more information.'

'Is she awake?' Aristo came into the room with Lupus and Hilario. 'Hello, Flavia. How do you feel?'

'As if a camel trod on my head.'

'Is she contagious?' asked Hilario.

Flavia ignored him. 'What happened?' she murmured.

'The same thing that happened to Titus. You took ill at the first stopping place outside Rome on the Via Salaria. But unlike him, you seem to be recovering.'

They all made the sign against evil and Lupus gave Flavia a thumbs-up.

'I'm so thirsty,' she groaned. 'May I have some water?'

'Here,' said Nubia. 'Drink this posca.' She lifted Flavia's head with one hand and brought a copper beaker to her lips with the other.

Flavia drank the vinegar-tinted water, then lowered her head slowly back onto the bolster, exhausted.

'Oh,' she murmured. 'I feel as if I just climbed a mountain.'

'You need to sleep,' said Nubia gently.

'No,' murmured Flavia. 'I want to hear the new information. More clues . . .'

'Well,' said Tranquillus, 'the stable-boy told us that Titus's party never intended to stop here. But as they were passing, the emperor suddenly parted the curtains of his litter, looked up towards heaven and cried out: "Alas my

life is being taken from me and I do not deserve to die!"
That was when they realised he had a fever and packed
him in ice.'

Flavia nodded, but her eyelids were very heavy, so she
closed them, just for a moment.

'Everybody go,' came Nubia's voice. 'Flavia is tired and
needing to sleep.'

'Where will *you* sleep, Nubia?' came Aristo's voice.

Flavia wanted to ask the same question but she was
exhausted and already she was drifting back into sleep.

'I will stay here with her,' came Nubia's voice, gentle
and firm. And it was the last thing Flavia heard for many
hours.

SCROLL IX

Flavia awoke to the sound of the dawn chorus and a rooster crowing and the aroma of fresh bread. She opened her eyes and frowned up at the pale light of dawn coming through a small high window. Then she remembered where she was and what had happened. She had caught a fever on the road to the Sabine Hills.

But now she felt rested and well. And ravenously hungry.

She turned her head and saw Nubia, curled up in an orange and brown striped blanket on a wicker chair, fast asleep. It was just light enough for her to see the mustard-coloured panels on the plaster walls. She was still in Hector's Hospitium, in Eretum.

Flavia could smell the bread. It must be baking nearby. Not wanting to wake Nubia, she carefully pushed back the covers and sat up. The walls of the room slowly tipped and began to spin and she sank back onto her bolster.

'Flavia,' murmured Nubia. 'Good morning! How do you feel?'

'A little lightheaded,' said Flavia. 'But hungry. I can smell bread.'

Nubia yawned and stretched. 'Yes, I am smelling it, too.' She slipped on her sandals and wrapped her blanket around her shoulders. 'I will go fetch some. You wait here.'

Soon Nubia was back with a loaf of brown bread, fresh from the oven, and a small ceramic bowl.

'There is a bakery by the stables,' she said. 'They make their own bread here. The baker gave me olive oil to dip the bread.'

She put the bowl on the little table beside the bed. Flavia saw that it was full of thick green-gold olive oil.

Nubia tore open the loaf of bread and handed Flavia a chunk. It was still hot, and Flavia had to juggle it from one hand to the other until it was cool. Then she dipped it in the oil and ate it. The bread had different grains in it and was sweetened slightly with molasses. And the olive oil was the best Flavia had ever tasted. Nubia perched on the edge of Flavia's bed, and the two girls devoured the entire loaf between them, dipping the bread in the oil and washing it all down with lukewarm posca from the pitcher on the table.

Outside, the sun was up. The birds had settled into steady cheeping but the rooster was still crowing and now a wheezing donkey was welcoming the new day, too.

The warm bread had made Flavia sleepy again, and she yawned.

Nubia put her hand on Flavia's forehead. 'Your fever is gone but you should sleep a little longer.'

Flavia lay back and snuggled down into the warm bed. Meanwhile, Nubia shivered and pulled her own blanket tighter round her shoulders.

'Do you have a fever?'

'No, I am just a little chilly.'

Flavia lifted the blanket and scooted over towards the wall. 'Come in with me, then.'

Nubia took off her sandals and slid under the blanket. Her feet were cold and Flavia warmed them with hers.

'Thank you,' said Nubia, and sighed. 'I wish we were home.'

'We can't go home until we clear our names,' murmured Flavia. 'And I also want to find Jonathan.'

'Perhaps Jonathan does not want to be found. He is making his own path in the desert.'

'What?'

'That is what my mother used to say: *Some live happily in tents, but there are others who make their own path in the desert.* It means some people like to be with other people, and some like to be alone. You and I are tent-dwellers, but Jonathan is the other.'

'You think so?' Flavia yawned. 'What about Lupus?'

'I think he was born a tent-dweller, but anger and pain made him alone. Now God is healing his heart, and he will soon live in a tent again. I hope with us in Ephesus.'

'Not Ostia?'

'I would rather live in Ephesus.'

'Why?'

Nubia was silent for a long moment. 'I was happy there,' she said at last. 'When I was with Aristo and the children. We were like a family.'

'And the Villa Vinea has its own bath-house,' murmured Flavia. 'With a hot plunge.'

'And a swimming pool,' whispered Nubia, snuggling closer. 'With palm trees.'

Flavia gave a sleepy chuckle.

'Also,' said Nubia. 'I had a beautiful dream once of us living there happily.'

But Flavia was asleep.

★

Nubia woke, two hours later, to sunshine streaming through the window and the sound of two cats fighting outside. Flavia was sitting on the end of the bed, lacing up her sandals. Nubia sat up and pressed a hand to Flavia's forehead and nodded with satisfaction. Her friend's fever was gone.

They found the others waiting at a table in a sunny garden courtyard. Their hair was damp and Aristo's cheeks were smooth, so were Hilario's; they must have all been to the baths. They breakfasted on more brown bread and Sabine olive oil, and there were black grapes, too, bursting with juice and flavour. While Aristo paid their bill, the girls used the small bath-house, and by the time the carruca set out from Hector's Hospitium it was not yet noon. Although Flavia insisted she was completely recovered, Nubia made her wrap up in a cloak and stretch out one of the carruca's padded benches with her head on her lap. Lupus went to sit beside deaf Talpa, the driver. According to Hector, the rabbit-toothed innkeeper, they had a good chance of reaching Titus's Sabine Villa in the late afternoon, or at least by dusk.

As the road began to ascend into wooded hills, Nubia pretended to look down at Flavia, but she was secretly watching Aristo through a tiny hole in the brim of her straw hat. He sat opposite her, next to Tranquillus and Hilario. He was wearing his equestrian tunic and a short red travelling cloak and he was looking forward, so that his profile was to her. Not for the first time, she thought how much he looked like a god from a red-figure Greek vase, except that his skin was not red; it was a beautiful bronze colour that was only a shade or two lighter than his hair. She longed to run her fingers through his curls.

'Mater Sabina,' said Tranquillus, stretching and smiling.

Nubia lifted her head so that she could see him properly. 'Who?' she asked.

Aristo gave her a gentle smile. 'Not who. What. This area, Sabina, is considered by some to be Rome's mother. That's why they call it Mater Sabina.'

'Why?' asked Nubia, not wanting to lose his attention. 'Why is it Rome's mother?'

Tranquillus raised his eyebrows. 'Because of the rape of the Sabine women, of course.'

Nubia frowned. 'What is rape?'

'It's when a man takes a girl or woman by force,' said Aristo. 'Although in this case the word means "kidnapping" rather than violent . . . er . . .' He trailed off.

'Who was raping the Sabine women?' asked Nubia.

'Romulus, of course,' said Tranquillus. 'Don't tell me you don't know about Romulus?'

'I know about Romulus,' said Nubia. 'He was one of the twin babies who drinks milk of the she-wolf. Rome is named for him. But I do not know about the rape.'

Hilario looked down his nose at Aristo. 'That's quite a gap in your pupils' knowledge,' he said.

'They know most of the story,' said Aristo. 'I just left out certain parts.'

'Will you tell us everything?' said Nubia to Aristo. 'About Romulus and Remus?'

'*Beware of Remus!*' cried Flavia suddenly. She sat up and the blanket slipped from her shoulders as she looked around at them. 'I knew the graffiti in the latrine looked familiar!'

At once, Nubia realised what she meant. 'Jonathan!' she cried. 'The writing was Jonathan's.'

Lupus was sitting at the front beside Talpa. Now he turned around and nodded vigorously and started to write something on his tablet. He held it up for them to see.

HECTOR'S HOSPITIUM. SAME GRAFFITI.

'In the men's latrine?' asked Flavia.

'Yes!' said Tranquillus. 'Someone wrote *Cave Remum* in the latrines of both inns we've stopped at so far, and on a tomb just outside the Collina Gate.'

'And I noticed it on the fifth milestone,' said Hilario.

'It was Jonathan,' cried Flavia. 'Jonathan wrote it.'

'Are you certain?' said Aristo.

'Yes!' said Nubia and Flavia together, and Lupus nodded

Hilario arched his heavy eyebrows at Aristo. 'Do you mean to say one of your pupils wrote some graffiti and you didn't even recognise his writing?'

'It was all in block letters,' said Nubia loyally.

'The "E" is the clue,' said Flavia. 'Jonathan makes his letter E like an epsilon.'

'That's true,' said Aristo.

From the front of the carruca, Lupus grunted and pointed at the thirtieth milestone, just passing by. Nubia saw the words scrawled in charcoal at the top: CAVE REMUM.

'Behold!' she said. 'There it is again.'

'You're right, Nubia,' said Aristo. 'That's Jonathan's hand.'

'Could it be a treasure quest?' cried Flavia suddenly. 'Like the one in Egypt?'

Tranquillus raised both eyebrows. 'Treasure quest? Egypt?'

'Yes,' said Flavia. 'When we were in Egypt this summer, we were following a trail of codes, riddles, and puzzles. It was a treasure quest. Maybe there's a clue in the story of Romulus and Remus!' she added.

'So will you tell us the story?' Nubia asked Aristo.

'Of course I will.' His beautiful brown eyes were smiling.

'Euge!' said Nubia softly, and clapped her hands.

'And while Aristo is telling us,' said Flavia to her friends, 'Let's hang on his every word and see if we can find the clue.'

Nubia gave a secret smile; she did not need to be told to hang on Aristo's every word.

At Nubia's urging, Flavia was once again lying on the padded bench of the carruca with her head in her friend's lap. As Aristo began to tell the story of Romulus and Remus, Flavia closed her eyes and tried to picture it in her mind.

'The night the Greeks burned Troy,' began Aristo, 'Aeneas escaped with his aged father and his young son Ascanius. After many adventures, he and his small band of Trojans landed in Italia at the mouth of the Tiber.'

Flavia opened her eyes and looked up at Nubia. 'In Ostia,' she said.

Without taking her eyes from Aristo's face, Nubia whispered, 'I know.'

'Aeneas vanquished the fierce warrior Turnus,' said Aristo. 'And he finally married the beautiful princess named Lavinia. Her father was called Latinus and Aeneas agreed to call his people "Latins" from then on, rather than "Trojans". This pleased the goddess Juno, and she finally stopped tormenting Aeneas.'

'Praise Juno,' murmured Flavia, and she heard Tranquillus chuckle.

'Aeneas and his princess lived happily, but now Aeneas's son Ascanius had become a man, and he wanted to found a colony of his own. So he moved a dozen miles east, to a mountain ridge overlooking a beautiful lake on one side and the sea on the other. He called this place Alba Longa. After Aeneas died, Ascanius divided his time between Latium and Alba Longa. But he loved Alba Longa best, and it was there in the lakeside woods that his son Silvius was born.'

'Silvius means "of the woods",' said Flavia without opening her eyes.

'That's right,' said Aristo. 'And from that time on most of the princes who ruled at Alba Longa bore the name Silvius. One of these was called Aventinus. He had a son who had two sons: Numitor and Amulius. Numitor was kind and wise, but Amulius greedy and ambitious. They were rivals for the kingdom.'

'Never a good idea,' observed Hilario, 'for a king to have two sons.'

Flavia opened her eyes and turned her head. 'Could that be the clue? Maybe those two rival brothers point to Titus and Domitian!'

'Perhaps,' said Aristo. 'But it's very common for two sons to struggle for power. Apart from their desire to rule, Numitor and Amulius don't bear much resemblance to Titus and Domitian. Numitor was the eldest, and should have ruled by right. But his younger brother Amulius drove him into exile and killed his sons. He also forced his brother's daughter, Rhea Silvia, to become a Vestal Virgin, so that she would never marry or have children who might claim the throne. But one day Rhea Silvia went into the woods to get water. She was very beautiful. When Mars, the god of war, caught sight of her, he fell in love with her and lay with her. Nine months later she gave birth to twin boys, Romulus and Remus.'

'Reate is named after Rhea Silvia,' remarked Tranquillus.

'What is Reate?' asked Nubia.

'The place we're going,' said Hilario. 'It's the nearest big town to Aquae Cutiliae, where the Flavians have their ancestral home.'

Flavia pushed herself up on one elbow. 'Maybe that's the clue! What happened to her? What happened to Rhea Silvia?'

'She was put in chains and thrown into prison by Amulius,' said Aristo. 'We don't know much more about her, do we?' He looked at Hilario.

'Some say she died in prison,' said the paedagogus. 'Others say her sons freed her when they overcame Amulius. I believe there is a temple dedicated to her in Reate,' he added.

'Then we're on the right track,' said Flavia. 'But there must be another clue in the story.' She rested her head back on Nubia's lap and closed her eyes. 'Tell us more, please, Aristo. Tell us about Romulus and Remus and the rape of the Sabine women.'

SCROLL X

Nubia watched Aristo with parted lips. She loved his storytelling almost as much as she loved his music. She had once composed a song about him, called 'The Storyteller.'

'After wicked Amulius imprisoned Rhea Silvia,' said Aristo, 'he commanded that her twin babies be exposed. You know what "exposed" means, don't you, Nubia?'

'Yes. It means if you leave a tiny baby on a mountainside or riverbank and it dies, then it is the gods who are guilty, and not you.'

Aristo nodded. 'Amulius's servants placed the two babies in a rush basket and pushed it out into the river Tiber, which was swollen with winter floods. The basket finally came to rest near a fording place by seven hills. In those hills were caves, and in one of the caves was a she-wolf with her newborn cubs. When she went down to the river to drink that evening, she heard the babies crying and went to them. Maybe she mistook their whimpers for the cries of wolf cubs, or maybe her maternal love overcame her savagery. Whatever the reason, instead of devouring them, she suckled them. When they had fed, she took them carefully in her mouth, one at a time, and carried them back to her safe warm cave. There she continued to feed them, along with her own cubs.'

Nubia nodded. She had once seen a bronze sculpture

of the baby boys sitting beneath the panting she-wolf and suckling from her teats.

Lupus turned and showed his wax tablet to Aristo. Nubia could see that he had written the word: MARS.

'That's right, Lupus,' said Aristo. 'The wolf is sacred to Mars. That was another indication that the twin babies were his offspring. One day, an old shepherd heard babies crying in the cave of the she-wolf. He waited until she went down to the river to drink, then crept inside. He could hardly believe his eyes when he saw two baby boys curled up with two wolf cubs in the warm den. He hesitated for only a moment, then put a twin under each arm and ran all the way home. He and his old wife had always longed for children, but never had any.'

'The poor she-wolf,' said Nubia. 'She must be wondering where the babies went.'

'Perhaps,' said Aristo. 'But the boys needed human contact by now. The shepherd and his wife were not rich in possessions, but they loved the twins and raised them as their own. The babies grew up to be strong and handsome young men.'

Nubia imagined Romulus and Remus looking just like Aristo, with his handsome face, curly hair and lean, muscular body.

'They became brigands,' said Aristo. 'They used to rob the rich and share with their parents and other poor people. They soon had a gang of other wild youths. One day they came to the attention of old Numitor, the father of their mother Rhea Silvia. He realised they must be his grandsons, so he summoned them and told them that the crown was rightfully theirs. Backed by him, Romulus and Remus made war on wicked Amulius. Victorious, they decided to build a new capital city at the place where the she-wolf had suckled them, by the hill where their great great-grandfather Aventinus was buried.'

'The Aventine Hill in Rome!' said Flavia.

'And they say,' added Tranquillus, 'that the she-wolf's cave was on the Palatine Hill next door.'

Aristo continued. 'The two brothers tried to rule together, but they could rarely agree. Finally they decided that one of them should rule, and the other step down. They would ask the gods to choose between them, by means of signs and portents. Romulus stood on the Palatine Hill, Remus took up position on the Aventine, and their followers waited in the valley below. They had not been waiting long, when a gasp went up. Six vultures were flying over the Aventine Hill, on the propitious side of Remus. What could be clearer than that? But look! Coming over the Palatine were twelve vultures, a phenomenon never seen until then. It was clear: Romulus was chosen by the gods.'

Aristo shook his head sadly. 'But Remus did not accept defeat graciously. One day he taunted Romulus by stepping over the foundations of the new city's wall. In a fit of rage, Romulus hit him with a hoe. Remus fell and struck his head and died. And so the city was called Rome, after Romulus.'

IF REMUS HAD BEEN CHOSEN, wrote Lupus on his tablet, ROME WOULD BE REME!

They all laughed and Aristo continued.

'Romulus saw that Rome needed more people, so he made the city refuge for outlaws of all descriptions.'

'Not just outlaws,' interrupted Hilario. 'But any men from the surrounding peoples – whether free, freedmen or slaves – who wanted a fresh start. *And therein lay the foundation of the city's strength.*'

'Of course,' said Aristo graciously. 'Not just outlaws, but any men who wanted to start fresh.' He paused for emphasis. '*Men* being the key word. Early Rome was a city of men, desperately in need of women and offspring.' Aristo looked at Hilario and said, '*Owing to the scarcity of women, Rome's greatness would not outlast one generation.*'

It must have been a quote, thought Nubia, for Hilario acknowledged it with a grudging nod.

'They were desperate times,' said Aristo, 'so Romulus sent ambassadors to the surrounding territories, seeking treaties and the right to intermarry.'

'But all the leaders said no,' laughed Tranquillus. 'They didn't want their daughters marrying a bunch of outlaws.'

Flavia opened her eyes and sat up. 'I've rested enough and I want to hear this part,' she said. 'Lupus, you can come sit by us.'

Lupus clambered down from his perch beside Talpa and sat on the bench beside Flavia. The carruca rumbled steadily along the sunny road.

'Romulus devised a plan,' said Aristo. 'He announced games and invited all the people who lived around Rome to attend. Many tribes accepted, especially the Sabines, the people from this region.' Aristo gestured towards the olive groves on the hills and the vineyards in the valleys. 'Entire families arrived in Rome and marvelled at the new city and enjoyed the hospitality of different houses. Then, on the day of the games they all went to watch the chariot race.'

'At the Circus Maximus?' asked Nubia.

'At the place where it is now,' said Aristo. 'In the valley between the Palatine and Aventine Hills.'

Aristo leaned forward. 'Imagine it. You've come with your family from your Sabine farm to the city of Rome.

You are going to watch the games, starting with chariot races, something you have heard about but never seen. You sit on your father's cloak on the grassy hillside with your family and wait for the horses to start racing. You love horses and you're very happy and excited.'

Nubia gazed at him in delight. It was as if he was telling the story about her.

'The trumpet sounds. The chariots burst out of the wooden gates. Suddenly a handsome young man runs up to you and pulls you to your feet. Your father and mother are startled. They smile hesitantly. Is this part of the celebration? Then the man swings you up into his arms, or even throws you over his shoulder, and now he's running down the hill. You are bumping up and down in a strange man's arms. You can smell his sweat and hear him pant for breath as he turns down a street. You hear the screams of other girls and only now do you realise what's happening: you are being kidnapped!'

Nubia and Flavia clutched each other while Lupus and Tranquillus laughed. Hilario rolled his eyes.

'One very beautiful girl was carried off by three or four men, each holding one of her limbs. They took her to the house of a distinguished senator.'

Lupus gave a mock scream and waved his legs and arms like an upturned turtle, pretending to be carried off by four young men.

Aristo looked at Nubia. 'But imagine this particular man wants you for himself and takes you to his house. You're terrified, but instead of ravishing you, the young soldier shows you to a room decorated with frescoes of cupids driving little chariots pulled by goats; a girl's room. There is a bed with an embroidered spread, and some pretty clothes laid out. There is a dressing table with everything a girl might want. There is even platter of fruit and bread. You realise he prepared it all for you.'

Nubia watched Aristo, strangely moved.

'That evening Romulus himself arrives and takes you to the inner garden. There sits the young man who kidnapped you. He has bathed and oiled himself. He no longer smells of sweat. He is quite handsome and a little nervous. You are thirteen and he is perhaps ten years older, say twenty-three.' Aristo was looking at Nubia and there was something in his look that made her heart beat fast.

'Romulus pronounces words over the two of you and declares that you are now legally married. He tells the man to be kind and gentle, to be a good husband, to provide for you and any children you might have. And he tells you that you do not have to share the man's bed until you are ready.'

Nubia felt her cheeks grow hot. She tipped her head down, so that the brim of her hat covered her face.

Aristo continued. 'You cry yourself to sleep for a few days, maybe even a week. But then you notice one or two of your friends are living nearby: other girls from the Sabine Hills. They have nice dresses and young husbands, too. But you think yours is the nicest. Sometimes you wonder where your father is. Why has he not come to rescue you?'

Aristo spread his hands. 'What you don't realise is that your father was helpless: unarmed in a strange city. He and the other fathers and brothers had to go home to fetch their weapons. And by the time the Sabine men have finally screwed up their courage to attack, a whole year has passed and you have just given birth to a baby girl and you love her more than anything in the whole world.'

Nubia and Flavia glanced at each other and giggled.

'One beautiful spring morning you are having breakfast with your husband and baby when the alarm sounds: a trumpet. Your husband puts on his armour and swings himself up onto his horse. He rides to battle and you run outside to watch. You see your husband riding down the hill with the other young Romans, so brave and handsome. Then you see your father, and the other Sabine men coming down the opposite hill. Your father looks older than you remember him, and a little frightened: he's holding a spear instead of vine-pruning-shears.'

Nubia stared at Aristo, enthralled.

'And now you realise that you love them both and don't want either of them to die. Suddenly you are running down the hill, holding your baby girl high above your head and crying out for them to stop. Your girlfriends follow, some of them hold their babies up, too, others move more slowly, because they're pregnant. You cry out for them to stop fighting and suddenly find yourself between two charging bodies of men. They rein in their horses or stop running and stare at you in amazement. You realise you have just done something very foolish but very brave. Your courage brings about a truce, so that everybody becomes friends and you,' he concluded, 'have become a Mater Sabina, a Sabine mother.'

Flavia clapped her hands. 'Euge! Aristo!' she cried. 'I love the way you told that. As if Nubia and I were young Sabine girls.'

Nubia nodded her agreement. She didn't trust her voice.

'Only one problem,' sighed Flavia. 'You told it so well that I forgot to listen for clues.'

SCROLL XI

They reached Reate late in the afternoon and stopped to lay an offering of fruit on the altar of Rhea Silvia outside her little pink and cream marble temple. Flavia prayed hard to the deified mother of Romulus and Remus, but she did not find any clues or see any graffiti. The young priestess did tell them how the imperial litter-bearers had hurried Titus through Reate, the sweat pouring off them. And she told how the townspeople had grieved after learning of the emperor's death. Titus had been well loved and they counted him as one of them, a fellow-Sabine. She then cocked her head to one side and asked why two young boys were bringing offerings to Rhea Silvia.

'She came to me in a dream,' lied Flavia, 'and healed me of a fever.'

Back at the carruca, Aristo and Tranquillus confirmed reports of Titus's litter-bearers coming through at a run, and the sound of Titus groaning within.

'So he was still alive when he reached his villa,' said Aristo. 'But he died that night. Look, Nubia.' Aristo held out a papyrus twist of dates. 'Your favourite.'

Aristo had also bought some grapes and nuts, and they shared these as the buttercup-yellow carruca rumbled on towards Titus's Villa five miles further on, at Aquae Cutiliae.

Flavia pulled her coarse woollen cloak around her shoulders. Up here in the mountains it was cooler. To the north, heavy grey clouds were already obscuring the tallest peaks and threatening to spill into the valley between.

'Aristo,' said Nubia, as they drove, 'please tell us more about Romulus?'

'There's not much more to tell. As you know, he was the first of Rome's seven kings. After him, Rome was ruled by Numa Pompilius. He was a Sabine, just, wise and peace-loving—'

'Great Juno's peacock!' cried Flavia. 'The fever must have made me stupid.'

They looked at her expectantly.

'The meaning of the riddle is obvious! Romulus and Remus *do* stand for Titus and Domitian, and by saying "beware Remus", Jonathan is warning us to beware of Domitian. And who succeeded Romulus? Numa Pompilius, a Sabine. Sabine equals Sabinus! Jonathan is telling us to be careful of Domitian, and to make sure Flavius Sabinus becomes emperor instead.'

Tranquillus raised an eyebrow. 'If you think a two-word graffito means all that, then you still are feverish.'

Nubia frowned. 'No, Flavia. I think that cannot be.'

'Why not? Isn't the handwriting Jonathan's?'

'Yes. But Jonathan does not know we are in Italia. He thinks we are still in Ephesus. Remember, he told us to stay there and not to follow him?'

Tranquillus looked at Flavia. 'He told you to wait in Ephesus?'

Nubia, Lupus and Aristo all nodded.

'Yes,' said Flavia. 'But we wanted to help him.'

Hilario looked down his nose at her. 'So you disregarded his wishes.'

'He's my friend,' explained Flavia. 'Not my master.'

Hilario tutted. 'I doubt you'd ever be obedient to any man.'

Flavia opened her mouth to say something, but Tranquillus touched her arm lightly. 'While you were ill, Flavia,' he said, 'Hilario remembered how Odysseus died.'

'You did?' said Flavia, forgetting her anger.

'Yes,' said Hilario smugly. 'Even Aristo didn't know.'

'It's true,' said Aristo generously.

And Tranquillus said, 'Go on. Tell her, Hilario.'

The paedagogus pretended not to hear and whistled a tune.

'Please, Hilario?' said Flavia. 'Please tell me?'

'Very well,' he said and stared at her with his slightly protruding eyes. 'According to one account, Odysseus was killed by a spear dipped in stingray venom.'

A pretty frown creased Nubia's forehead. 'What is stingray?' she asked.

'Yes,' said Flavia. 'What *is* a stingray?'

'The Greek word is trygon,' said Hilario. 'It's a kind of fish. It's flat and round, like a platter, not a wheel. At the back of its tail is a spine with venom on it.'

'It has a sting in its tail?' said Aristo.

Lupus nodded enthusiastically and drew one on his wax tablet.

'Eeew!' cried Flavia, when he showed it to her.

'That's right,' said Hilario, pointing at the drawing. 'It's shaped more like a lozenge than a circle. When I was growing up,' he added, 'a friend of mine was stung in the arm.'

'Did he die?' asked Flavia.

'No. He recovered. But he was very ill for many days with fever and nausea. The venom in the tail is the most powerful poison known to man, like a jellyfish, but worse. Pliny writes of it in his *Natural History*.'

'Like a jellyfish sting?' said Flavia, remembering something that had happened the previous summer.

'But worse.'

'Of course!' cried Flavia. 'Hilario, you're wonderful!' She leaned forward and gave the rubber-faced paedagogus a kiss on the cheek.

'Flavia!' cried Tranquillus. 'Why are you kissing my paedagogus?'

'He just gave me the final tessera of the mosaic,' said Flavia. 'I know how Titus was murdered!'

Nubia watched Flavia, full of admiration. How did she do it? How did she solve mysteries and puzzles so easily? Flavia's grey eyes shone and she was almost beautiful as she explained her theory:

'I think someone killed Titus using the same method used to kill Odysseus.'

'With a poison-tipped spear?' said Tranquillus. 'Don't you think somebody might have noticed? Especially Titus!'

'Not a big spear. A tiny spear with a needle-sharp tip, whose prick you'd barely feel.'

Suddenly Nubia knew the answer. 'A stylus!' she cried. 'Like the one I saw in latrines.'

'Not *like* the one. The very one itself. And I pricked my finger on it!' cried Flavia. 'Great Juno's beard. I've just realised: that's why I got the fever.'

Lupus was opening his belt pouch.

'I don't understand,' said Tranquillus.

Aristo said. 'Are you saying that Titus was murdered with a venom-tipped stylus in the latrines?'

'Yes!' cried Flavia.

Lupus held up a stylus.

'Behold!' cried Nubia. 'The stylus from the latrines at the Inn of Romulus!'

'Is that where you found it, Lupus?' asked Aristo.

Lupus nodded happily.

Aristo grinned and shook his head. 'You are such a magpie.'

But Flavia gasped: 'Be careful, Lupus! There may still be venom on the tip. That's how I got the fever.'

Lupus swallowed hard and stared at the stylus with wide eyes.

'May I see it?' said Hilario, and cautiously took the needle-sharp stylus from Lupus.

'Would a little drop of venom on a stylus be enough to kill a man?'

'Yes!' cried Flavia. 'But only if you treated the fever in the wrong way.'

'What do you mean: the wrong way?' Hilario carefully passed the stylus to Aristo.

'Did you know the treatment for a jellyfish sting is scalding water? But if you gave the victim the exact opposite treatment, it could finish them off.'

'And the opposite treatment to scalding water,' cried Aristo, 'is very cold water.'

'Or ice!' said Tranquillus. He was gazing at Flavia with open admiration.

'And you think that's what happened to Titus?' Aristo passed the stylus to Tranquillus.

Lupus nodded and pointed at his right calf.

'Yes, Lupus,' said Flavia. And to the others: 'Remember the serving girl at the Inn of Romulus?'

'I do,' said Hilario.

Flavia ignored him. 'She told us Titus was bitten on the calf by a spider when he went to the latrines.'

Tranquillus pointed at her. 'That's when they got him!'

Nubia frowned. 'But who was it? Who got Titus?'

'Someone lying in wait.'

OR SITTING IN WAIT wrote Lupus with a grin.

'But who?' persisted Nubia.

Flavia shook her head. 'That I don't know. But what I do know is this. If we get a chance to examine Titus's body, we should look for a tiny red mark on one of his calves, the part beneath the hem of the tunic and above the top of his sandal.'

Lupus took the stylus from Tranquillus and wrapped it carefully in the piece of papyrus which had held the dates. Then he put it back in his belt pouch.

Aristo pointed as the carruca rounded a bend. 'There,' he said. 'Straight ahead. That must be it.'

Flavia stood up to get a better look. Tranquillus stood, too. Before them was a green hill reflected by a small mirror-smooth lake at its foot. Half way up the hill, Flavia could see a red brick wall and part of a colonnade peeping through the beech trees.

'Is that Titus's Sabine Villa?'

'According to the directions the fruit-seller gave me,' said Aristo. 'A brick and marble villa on a hillside overlooking a lake.'

'Excellent!' said Flavia. 'Now we'll get a chance to see the body up close and test my theory.'

*

Half an hour later, Nubia and the others watched Aristo question two guards at the entrance to Titus's Sabine Villa. It was late afternoon. They had driven up to the arched gate of the villa and it had been decided that Aristo – in his equestrian tunic – should question the guards. Nubia and the others were standing beside the carruca on the green wooded hillside. Small clouds swept across the sky so that sometimes they were in shadow and at others in sunshine. Now, as Aristo turned to walk back to them, the sinking sun came out from behind a cloud. It illuminated the trees, and made the soldiers' metal breastplates flash, and painted Aristo with its golden light.

Watching him, Nubia understood how the ancient Greeks could believe the gods of Olympus sometimes walked among them. Even tired and dusty he was divinely beautiful. The familiar knife of love twisted in her heart and she had to look away.

'You won't believe this,' he said, as he came up to them. 'Titus's body is on its way back to Rome.'

'You're joking,' said Tranquillus.

'The funeral carriage set out yesterday,' said Aristo. 'It must have passed us on the road. Titus's body should be on view in the forum by now.'

'Oh, no!' wailed Flavia. 'This is my fault. Because of my fever we missed him. And it's too late to go back to Rome today.'

Aristo glanced back towards the two soldiers flanking the gate. The sun went behind a cloud and their breastplates stopped gleaming. Nubia could see the cloud's shadow sweeping up the hillside.

'The guards did give me two very interesting pieces of information,' said Aristo. 'They told me Titus's last words: *I only regret one thing.*'

'What could that mean?' said Tranquillus.

'They had no idea,' said Aristo.

'What was the second piece of information?' asked Flavia.

'The litter-bearers didn't bring Titus here first. They took him to straight to the frigidarium of the baths down at the bottom of the hill, and put him in the cold plunge. That's where he died. That's where he uttered his last words.'

'He died at a bath-house?' said Flavia. 'Is it nearby?'

Aristo nodded. 'We passed it earlier, just before you reach Lake Paternus. The locals call it the Baths of Vespasian. Hot springs, cold springs, there's even an inn nearby.' He looked around at them. 'Titus's death is the biggest news in these hills since his father died here just over two years ago. I suspect that everyone will be talking about it at the baths.'

'Good idea!' cried Flavia.

'Thank you,' said Aristo. He beckoned the two girls closer and leaned in, so that Nubia could smell the honey-sweet scent of dates on his breath. Her head was spinning but she forced herself to concentrate. 'The only problem,' whispered Aristo, 'is that the baths are only open to women in the evenings. So I suggest that just for tonight, you two become girls again.'

SCROLL XII

Nubia hated many aspects of Roman life: slavery, crucifixion, animal sacrifice. But she loved going to the baths. That night after dinner at the Paternus Inn, she and Flavia joined a dozen other women entering the luxurious Baths of Vespasian. The entry fee of a bronze *as* would buy them a marble niche for their clothes, a massage with scented oil, and a warm towel afterwards. The two friends undressed, leaving on only their headscarves to hide their short hair. Nubia found a pair of wooden clogs her size and clumped after Flavia into the caldarium. Torches burned in wall brackets and the smoke mixed with the steam to make the air thick and warm. Beneath the lofty marble dome was a large hexagonal platform of polished marble; each of the six sides was long enough for a person to lie there and be massaged. At the moment, every place was taken. But one of the smiling masseuses gestured for them to take a seat on a marble bench and wait their turn.

This bench ran around the marble-faced walls, punctuated every few feet with shell-shaped basins. Nubia clomped carefully after Flavia, admiring a dark blue mosaic floor which showed every type of sea creature. Nubia sat on the warm, slippery marble bench and looked into one of the shell basins. It was filled with steaming hot water and there was a dolphin tap which could be turned on to let in more. A scallop-shaped scoop made of tin floated on the surface. Nubia filled the scoop with water and tipped it over her head. The water was almost too hot to bear and she gasped.

'The water in my shell is cold,' said Flavia, scooping some water from her shell-basin. She tasted it. 'But delicious.' She held out her tin scoop and Nubia took a sip. The water was icy cold, with a clean metallic taste. 'No wonder this area is famous,' said Flavia. 'Hot springs *and* cold.'

Nubia was watching three young women on a nearby bench. They were mixing the water in wooden buckets and sluicing themselves. She saw one take a bucket from underneath the bench and bent forward to look underneath theirs.

'Behold!' Nubia produced two wooden buckets and handed one to Flavia. 'They are mixing the water in these.'

'Clever Nubia,' murmured Flavia.

Nubia used the dolphin tap to fill her wooden bucket with hot water. She added three scoops of the cold metallic water from Flavia's shell, then tipped the deliciously warm mixture over her head. The water cascaded over her body, splashing the bench and the blue mosaic floor. The sheet of rippling water made the mosaic sea creatures seem to quiver.

'Behold!' said Nubia again. She leaned forward and pointed. 'Could it be a stingray? That creature above octopus and below crayfish?'

'Oh, well done, Nubia!' cried Flavia. 'I think you're right. That's a stingray.' She stopped sluicing herself and sat forward to examine the mosaic.

'Behold the spine,' said Nubia, tracing its tail with the big toe of her right foot.

'Ugh!' Flavia shuddered. 'What a horrible way to die.'

'Puellae! Girls!' A large woman wearing a sage-green headscarf but nothing else clapped her wet hands. 'Time for your massage.' She gestured at two free places on the hexagonal platform. Another naked masseuse with a gap-toothed smile waited beside her.

Nubia carefully followed Flavia to the platform and stretched out on her stomach. The smooth polished marble beneath her was wet and warm. She closed her eyes and let the larger woman begin to massage her back with scented oil. It was lavender, and made her think of Aristo. She knew she should not be thinking of him now; she should be helping Flavia get information. Nubia opened her eyes and saw bare feet a few inches from her nose; Flavia was also lying on her stomach.

'I hear the emperor died in this bath-house,' came Flavia's clear voice. 'And that his last words were: *I regret only one thing.*'

'That's right!' grunted Flavia's masseuse, the gap-toothed woman. She was working her way down Flavia's legs. 'My nephew was at the games up in Rome last year, and he says Titus released two men who intended to assassinate him. I think those two men killed him and he must have realised it at the end. He regretted sparing them.'

'That wasn't it,' came the voice of Nubia's masseuse. 'It was his affair with Domitia, his brother's wife. That's what he regretted. It was nefas and he knew he'd offended the gods.'

'My father was here the night they brought the emperor in,' said another voice. Nubia turned her head so that her right cheek rested on the marble. She could see the three pretty young women on their bench. They were still sluicing themselves with water. The one with tawny hair was speaking. 'My father thinks Titus's brother killed him. My father says Titus regretted not getting rid of Domitian when he had the chance.'

'Yes,' agreed Nubia's masseuse. 'That's why Domitian killed him.'

'I heard it was that Jewish princess, Berenice,' said the thinnest girl. 'He loved her and didn't want her to go.'

'You're all wrong,' said the third girl. 'It was another Jewish woman. A beautiful captive from Jerusalem. They say she was the love of his life and so he set her free. I think that's the thing Titus regretted most.' She nodded her head wisely. 'When you find the love of your life, never let it go.'

The next morning Flavia and Nubia dressed as boys again. But despite the tight binding around her chest, the coarse brown tunic and the straw hat, Flavia felt wonderful. Her skin was soft and scented from the long session in the bath the night before and she was still elated by having deduced that the murder weapon was a poison-tipped stylus.

Nubia had gone to the stables and when Flavia came out of her room and into the courtyard, she found it empty. The grape arbour sparkled with dew and the dawn sky was palest lemon with high pink clouds, as wispy as feathers. Flavia went out the main gate and saw Tranquillus standing by the lake. He was gazing thoughtfully up at Titus's Sabine Villa, half hidden by the trees on the hill.

'Good morning!' she said brightly. 'Where are the others?'

'Aristo and Hilario are paying the bill,' said Tranquillus.

'And I think Lupus and Nubia are in the stables, helping Talpa harness the mules to our carruca.'

'Thank you for letting us use it,' said Flavia. 'And thank you for bringing your tutor. I wouldn't have been able to solve the mystery without you.'

'These have been the best three days of my life,' he said.

Flavia turned and looked at him in surprise. 'They have?'

'Yes,' he said.

The open adoration in his eyes embarrassed Flavia, so she turned and looked out over the lake. Four ducks were swimming across the opalescent surface of the water. 'Did I tell you what the women at the baths told us?' she asked.

'Yes, you told us their theories last night.'

'But did I tell you what they said about this lake? That it has no bottom? Apparently they used to have human sacrifices here,' she said. 'In ancient times.'

Tranquillus caught her hand. 'Flavia,' he said. 'I'm going to have another talk with pater.'

'About what?'

'About us.'

'Us?'

'You. Me. Us.'

'Oh.' Flavia felt her cheeks grow pink.

'I like you, Flavia. More than any girl I've ever met. Even when you're dressed as a boy.' Tranquillus took a step closer.

Flavia smiled nervously and before she could protest, he was kissing her.

His lips were wet and warm and tasted faintly of posca. The kiss was not unpleasant, but it didn't make her heart beat faster.

She couldn't help thinking of Gaius Valerius Flaccus. A

few months earlier he had given her an impulsive kiss in a crowded courtroom. It had set her heart thumping like a drum. But Floppy was married to another woman. So why was she even thinking of him? Especially at a moment like this?

Flavia put her arms around Tranquillus's neck and concentrated on kissing him back. Her straw hat fell off, but her heart continued to beat as normal.

Out on the lake a moorhen gave its squeaky call and a deep, patrician voice said: 'Flavia?'

Flavia started back with a gasp. The voice in her head had sounded so real, as if he was standing behind her. Tranquillus looked over her shoulder and his brown eyes opened wide in surprise.

'What are you doing?' came Flaccus's deep voice again.

Flavia whirled. He *was* behind her. Gaius Valerius Flaccus was here beside Lake Paternus, in the Sabine Hills.

'Floppy!' she cried, wiping her mouth with the back of her hand. 'Floppy, what are you doing here?'

'I came to find you!' he said almost angrily. 'I heard you were back in the country, and I knew you'd be trying to solve the biggest mystery of the year.' She could see a muscle clench in his jaw as he struggled to control himself. 'Flavia, I have some important news for you and your friends. Domitian is in Alba Longa. He's offering amnesty to all his enemies for three days.'

Flavia gaped. 'Amnesty?'

'Yes! Amnesty!' He still sounded angry. 'He's releasing debts and pardoning offences. It means you and your friends can live safely in Italia again. But you must go to Domitian's Alban Citadel as soon as possible. Tomorrow is the last day you can claim your pardon. Tomorrow by noon.'

'What is Domitian's Alban Citadel?' Flavia asked Flaccus a quarter of an hour later. They were in the carruca, driving south as fast as they could. Flaccus's horse was tethered to the back of the carruca; he had ridden most of the night and the black gelding was exhausted. Flaccus sat on the bench opposite her, looking tired but handsome. By letting his straight dark hair fall over his eyes he avoided her gaze.

'Domitian's Alban Citadel,' he said in his deep soft voice, 'is a palatial villa in Alba Longa. That's where he spends most of his free time.'

'Is that the place you were telling us about?' said Flavia to Aristo. 'The town that Ascanius founded?'

'Yes,' said Aristo. 'Though I've never been there.'

'I have,' said Tranquillus. 'Domitian's villa is across the lake from my aunt. We can see it from her house. He started building it five years ago and he's still working on it.'

'Why is he building a palace there and not here?' asked Flavia, gesturing at the green Sabine Hills around them.

'Domitian was born in Rome, ten years after Titus,' said Flaccus. 'His father was on campaign for most of his childhood, and his brother lived in Claudius's royal court. So he doesn't have much attachment to this area.'

'Remember I showed you the house he grew up in?' said Tranquillus. 'The house on Pomegranate Street? After his father died, he decided to build his own country retreat in Alba Longa. They say he fell in love with Domitia there.'

'His villa is being designed by Rabirius,' added Hilario, 'the finest architect alive.'

'But where is it?' asked Flavia. 'Where is Alba Longa?'

'About fifteen miles southeast of Rome,' said Tranquillus. 'On Lake Albanus.'

Flaccus glanced up at Lupus, who was sitting beside Talpa, and gave him a tired smile. 'Loan me your wax tablet?'

Lupus took his tablet from his belt pouch and handed it down to Flaccus.

Flaccus opened it. 'Look,' he said, as he drew in the yellow beeswax.

Flavia leaned forward, and he turned it so she and Nubia could both see.

'Imagine Rome is the hub of a wheel with eight spokes,' he said. 'Two vertical spokes, two horizontal and four slanting. Titus's Sabine Villa is where the angled spoke meets the wheel here, at the northeast. Lake Albanus is down here to the southeast, where other angled spoke meets the wheel at the lower right.'

'Is there a direct road from here to there?' asked Flavia.

'No,' said Tranquillus. 'We have to go back to the hub to get there, back to Rome.'

'That's right,' said Flaccus, and moved the tip of the stylus down one spoke towards the centre of the wheel. 'At the moment we're travelling south down along the Via Salaria to Rome, the hub. Once we reach Rome, we take this spoke – the Appian Way – southeast to Lake Albanus.'

'Why isn't he doing this in Rome?' asked Aristo. 'Offering amnesty, I mean.'

'I don't know,' said Flaccus, passing his hand over his face. 'I'm so tired I can't think straight. I'm going to sleep, if I can. Does anyone mind if I stretch out on the floor?'

The sun was warm and the awning rolled right back, so they all contributed their cloaks to make a bed on the floor at their feet. Flavia watched Flaccus lie down and close his eyes. She wanted to ask him a dozen questions. How had he found out they were back in Italia? Why was he helping them? What was marriage to Prudentilla like? Why had he looked so hurt when he found her kissing Tranquillus?

Flaccus's muscular forearm was over his eyes to keep out the bright sunshine. Presently he fell asleep. His arm slipped back above his head and his forehead relaxed. Although he was twenty, he suddenly looked very young.

Flavia swallowed hard. She realised she was still completely and utterly in love with him.

SCROLL XIII

Although there was a seat free on the padded bench of the carruca, Lupus remained up at the front with Talpa. He liked the steady forward motion, and when Talpa let him take the reins on a straight part of the road it made him feel capable and in control. Flaccus awoke briefly when they stopped for a midday break, and then again in the late afternoon, as they passed the eight-mile marker on the way back to Rome. They stopped again, so that Flaccus could relieve himself in the bushes. Lupus went with him. After they had done their business they both went down to the banks of the Tiber and splashed water on their faces, cold and clear from the Sabine Hills.

As Lupus began to fill his goatskin flask, Flaccus said, 'I set out in such a hurry I didn't even take a waterskin.'

Lupus held out his own dripping goatskin to Flaccus, who took a long drink and handed it back. 'How long have Flavia and that boy been together?' said Flaccus, wiping his mouth with the back of his arm. 'Are they betrothed? I didn't see a ring.'

Lupus shook his head and grunted 'no'. He wanted to tell Flaccus they had only just recently met up with Tranquillus again, and that he didn't think Flavia and Tranquillus were together. But Flaccus hadn't waited for a reply. He was already making his way back up to the road and the waiting carruca.

On the last leg of the journey back to Rome, Flavia tried to get Floppy to look at her. She told him all about their quest to find Jonathan and to prove that Domitian was behind the death of Titus. He nodded but did not raise his head. Aristo and Tranquillus helped fill him in on the mystery. He looked at them, but he would not meet Flavia's gaze.

Even Tranquillus noticed Flaccus's coolness, and he came to her rescue. 'Flavia is amazing,' he said. 'The way she can unravel a mystery.'

Flavia flushed with pleasure and looked expectantly at Flaccus.

'Yes,' he said, gazing out the back of the carruca. 'But she can sometimes be too hasty in the conclusions she draws.'

Flavia's smile faded. She needed to try a different approach. 'Enough about me,' she said. 'What about you, Gaius Valerius Flaccus? Tell us your news. How is Prudentilla?'

For a moment he looked startled. Then he said, 'Prudentilla is fine,' and turned to Nubia. 'How are you?'

'I am very well,' said Nubia. 'I am saved.'

'Saved?' he raised his dark eyebrows.

Nubia nodded and started to explain, but Flavia interrupted. 'We met a prophet in Ephesus,' she said, 'and now they've all converted to a new religion.'

'It's a new sect of Judaism,' said Aristo. 'We call it The Way. We believe God sent his son as a sacrifice, once and for all, to give us eternal life.'

'And no more animal sacrifice,' said Nubia happily. 'Also,

we try to be good and kind to each other and to do what is right.'

From his seat beside Talpa, Lupus turned and gave Flaccus a thumbs-up.

Flaccus looked surprised. 'You've all converted?' he asked.

'All except for me,' said Flavia. 'I think it's irrational. Imagine believing that a dead person could come alive again!'

'Is yours the sect that worship Chrestus?' Hilario raised one of his arched eyebrows. 'That's a subversive religion. No wonder you have no qualms about accusing the emperor.'

'We're not subversive,' said Aristo. 'We seek the Truth. And we strive to live a pure life in this world.'

Flaccus snorted. 'With the reward of immortality in the next? Good luck to you. I hope it works.'

'Wouldn't you like to live for ever in a beautiful garden, with no pain and tears?' asked Aristo.

'Actually, no,' said Flaccus in his deep voice. 'I prefer city life. Also, I think I'd go mad in a perfect world. Besides,' he stared down at the floorboards of the carruca, 'there is no such thing as life after death. The only immortality we can ever hope for is that our names be remembered because of what we write or what legacy we leave. That's why I've gone back to my epic poem,' he added under his breath.

'The *Argonautica*?' said Flavia. 'Are you still working on that?'

Flaccus nodded, but he did not look at her. 'That's the most important thing in my life at the moment,' he said, 'and I'm not going to let anything distract me from it again.'

★

They left Flaccus's horse and the tired mules at the Collina Gate stables and entered Rome on foot, just as the sun was setting.

'I suggest you set out for Alba Longa at dawn,' said Flaccus. 'Make sure you arrive by noon. Our new emperor is giving a dinner party and games later in the day.'

'Aren't you coming with us?' asked Flavia, close to tears.

'I think you have all the help you need, Flavia Gemina,' he said. And for the first time all day he looked directly at her. She saw the hurt and anger in his dark eyes and it was like a slap in the face.

'Oh, Floppy!' she whispered. 'We need you. I need you.'

But he was already walking away.

'Floppy!' called Flavia after him. 'Flaccus!'

'We don't need him,' said Tranquillus, as they all watched his retreating back. He turned to Flavia. 'Come on. We'll spend the night at my house and set out for the Alban Lake at dawn. I'll tell my father I'm visiting Mater and my aunt.' Tranquillus gave his paedagogus a meaningful glance. 'You'll back up my story, won't you, Hilario?'

'Of course, master.' Hilario rolled his eyes and sighed deeply.

'Excellent,' said Tranquillus.

'Floppy must live around here,' said Flavia to Tranquillus, as they went up the same street Flaccus had taken. 'Do you know much about him?'

'No more than the rest of Rome,' said Tranquillus. 'Just that he's accepted a junior priesthood, a good step on the cursus honorum. And that he broke off his engagement last month.'

Flavia stopped so suddenly that Nubia bumped into her. 'He didn't marry Prudentilla?' she asked.

'I don't know the name of his betrothed,' said Tranquillus with a scowl. 'Only that he ruffled a lot of feathers by calling off the wedding at the last moment. He and his sponsa had just been on a trip to Halicarnassus,' he said. 'They brought back half a dozen freeborn children who'd been sold into slavery. His position as priest is a reward for that, I think. But if he'd backed out of his engagement before the appointment he might never have received it. Come on,' he said. 'I'm hungry and tired and want to get home before dark.'

Gaius Suetonius Laetus was dining with another senator, but his son Tranquillus had the household slaves prepare the best triclinium. An hour after dusk, the friends and their tutors dined on hot leek soup followed by papyrus thin strips of cured beef and hard-boiled quails' eggs. For mensa secunda they had pears poached in honey with walnuts and creamy cheese on top. Nubia enjoyed the meal almost as much as she enjoyed reclining next to Aristo. He shared her couch, positioned slightly behind her. The autumn night was cool and when she shivered he slipped his own red travelling cloak around her shoulders. It was still warm from his body. Nubia gave another shiver, this time of pleasure.

'The slaves have heated the hot plunge,' said Tranquillus, licking honey from his fingers. 'Why don't you girls have a quick soak and then we men will use it.' He clapped twice, and a pretty dark-haired slave-girl appeared at the doorway. 'Eurydice here will assist you in the baths and then show you to your room. You girls don't mind sharing a large double bed? It's my mother's and very comfortable. A slave will wake you an hour before dawn.'

'Thank you, Tranquillus,' said Flavia. 'I don't know what we would have done without your help.'

'Don't mention it,' he said, with a wave of his hand. 'It's in times like these that you discover who your real friends are.'

The slave-girl called Eurydice led them through the torchlit garden and down a flickering corridor to a small, lamplit bath-house. Nubia and Flavia sat on a wooden bench to unstrap their sandals. Next they put their belts and belt-pouches on the bench. Finally they stood and stripped off their coarse brown tunics and undergarments.

'I will brush these and have them ready by morning,' said the girl in a pleasantly-accented voice. 'There are clogs under the bench and linen sleeping tunics there on the shelf, folded on top of your towels. Your travelling hats are in the vestibule,' she added, 'where you left them this evening.'

'Thank you,' said Nubia and Flavia together. They slipped on the wooden clogs and moved carefully into the steamy room next door. The little caldarium had a plaster dome above a small circular pool of hot water. Four torches burned in brackets on the wall, making globes of flickering orange in the steamy atmosphere.

Nubia removed her clogs and carefully descended into the deep bath. The film of oil on top smelled of myrtle. The soft slap of water echoed in the cylindrical room and when the steam parted she could see the stars through a circular hole in the top of the dome.

'Our second night-time bath,' said Nubia happily. 'This is a delicious luxury.'

Flavia gave her a half-hearted smile as she came down the steps. Nubia could see she was still upset about Flaccus.

'We are needing it after that dusty journey,' said Nubia.

'Yes,' said Flavia. 'It was a terrible journey.'

'When we have had our bath and are in bed,' said Nubia, 'I have something to give you.'

'You have something for me?' Flavia was neck deep in the bath, her eyes closed.

'Yes,' said Nubia. 'Flaccus gave it to me. He told me it was for you.'

Flavia's eyes opened. 'Something from Floppy?' she said. 'Where is it?'

'In my belt pouch,' said Nubia. 'But he told me to give it to you last thing before bed.'

'Forget that!' cried Flavia. The water slapped the sides of the pool as she moved quickly towards the steps and up them.

'Flavia, no!' protested Nubia. 'He said last thing before bed.'

Naked and glistening, Flavia slipped on her clogs and disappeared into the apodyterium. A moment later she was back, clutching the little ivory tablet that Flaccus had given Nubia in the carruca.

'Oh look!' Flavia kicked off her clogs and sat on the steps of the bath, waist deep in the warm water. 'It's bound with a sweet little red ribbon and there's tiny writing inside. What is it?'

'I do not know,' said Nubia. 'I have not opened it.'

'Pollux!' exclaimed Flavia. 'It's hard to read in this – Oh!'

There was a plop as the little ivory booklet fell from her slippery fingers into the pool.

'Oh no!' cried Flavia, and dived for the tablet. Warm myrtle-scented water splashed onto the walls and walkway of the caldarium, and a moment later Flavia held up the tablet triumphantly.

'Got it!' she cried, and then: 'But the ink is running and the message is all blurred! Now I'll never know what it said! Oh, Nubia!' she wailed. 'How could you let me be so foolish?'

SCROLL XIV

Lupus snuggled into the soft blankets on a narrow but comfortable bed in Tranquillus's bedroom. His muscles felt relaxed and warm after the myrtle-scented bath in the villa's small caldarium. Glowing coals in a bronze tripod cast a dim ruby light on the frescoed walls and took the autumn chill from the room.

'Is the bed soft enough for you, Lupus?' came Tranquillus's voice from the reddish-brown gloom.

Lupus grunted yes.

'Since my old tutor left, I have this room all to myself.' Tranquillus sounded pleased with himself.

Lupus gave another sleepy grunt; his eyelids were heavy.

'Lupus?' came Tranquillus's voice. 'Are you afraid? I mean, about going to Domitian's villa. Aren't you a little afraid?'

Lupus shrugged, then grunted yes.

'Me, too. Even though there's no edict out against me like there is against you. Have you heard the story about Domitian and the Triclinium of Death?'

Lupus grunted no.

'Last month he gave a banquet in a black-walled triclinium. All the guests had place-tags like grave-markers and Domitian served them the sort of food you usually offer to the dead: black beans, blood sausage, pomegranates. The guests all thought they were going to be murdered at any moment. They were quaking on the couches. Even on their way home they expected assassins to leap from the shadows and slit their throats. But when they got home each one found an expensive present from Domitian. He likes to play practical jokes like that.'

Lupus chuckled and rolled over to face Tranquillus. In the dim light he could only see the boy's shape on the other bed.

'It's ironic,' continued Tranquillus, 'because everyone knows Domitian is terrified of dying a violent death.'

Lupus grunted 'Why?'

'Apparently the auspices of his birth were terrible. He's obsessed with horoscopes and signs. Takes an astrologer with him everywhere. He was born when Saturn and Mars were dangerously close to the Sun and the Moon.'

Lupus gave his 'so what?' grunt.

'It's a terrible chart. It points to a sudden and violent death. Once, when he was a boy, his father Vespasian teased him for refusing to eat some mushrooms at a dinner party. He said: *Why fear poisoned mushrooms when the stars say you'll die by the sword?* Or something like that.'

Lupus grunted softly, to show he was still listening.

There was a pause, and then Tranquillus's voice came hesitantly out of the darkness: 'Lupus, do you think Flavia likes me? Or is she in love with Flaccus? I saw the way she was watching him today, when he was sleeping. I was an idiot to tell her that he broke off his engagement. Do you think I have a chance with her? Lupus?'

This time Lupus did not grunt or chuckle. He made his breathing soft and steady. He was not asleep, but he thought it best to pretend he was.

The next morning, an hour before dawn, Nubia and the others crept out of the sleeping villa into the chilly street. Nubia caught the scent of pine-pitch and smoke from the flaming torch held by Hilario. She was still looking around for Aristo when the paedagogus set off down the cobbled street with Tranquillus and Lupus and Flavia following behind.

'Wait,' cried Nubia. 'Aristo is not here yet.'

'You're right,' said Flavia, stopping and turning. 'Where is he?'

Hilario turned, too. 'He went to the forum, to investigate Titus's body for signs of prick-marks. He's going to meet us at the Capena Gate.'

'It was my idea,' said Tranquillus. 'The body is five days old now and soon it will be too swollen to spot something as tiny as the mark of a stylus.'

'Good thinking,' said Flavia, and Nubia noticed she was clutching the ivory tablet.

Tranquillus fell into step beside Flavia, 'I'm pleased that we got away without pater questioning me.'

Flavia nodded, distracted, and Nubia saw the look of hurt on Tranquillus's face.

'Will your father not worry when he finds you are gone?' Nubia asked him.

'No. I've left him a note telling him I'm taking some friends to see my mother at Alba Longa. That's almost the truth,' he added.

'Which gate are we going to now?' asked Nubia, as they turned left onto a street full of shops. Some were just beginning to open and she could smell bread from the baker's.

'To the Porta Capena,' said Tranquillus. 'The Appian

Way leads from there straight to the Alban Lake. The journey usually takes us three or four hours, so we should be there well before noon. I told Talpa to have a carruca ready by the first hour.'

Sure enough, Talpa the driver was waiting for them on the other side of the arched gate. Torchlight showed the buttercup-yellow carruca and she could see from here he had a fresh quartet of mules. The others went forward but Nubia hesitated beneath the arch, looking around anxiously for Aristo.

A few drops of water plopped onto her straw hat. She held out her hand and looked up. How could it be raining underneath a massive stone arch?

'They don't call it the watery gate for nothing,' said Aristo's voice. She turned and saw him emerging from the pre-dawn gloom. He pointed up. 'Three of Rome's biggest aqueducts pass over this gate. So I don't advise lingering underneath.' He took her elbow and looked down at her. For a heart-stopping moment she thought he was going to kiss her, but he merely directed her through the arch to the waiting carruca. 'I went to the forum to see the emperor's body,' he said. 'And you'll never guess.'

'It was gone?'

He nodded. 'Apparently it's now on its way to Alba Longa. Just like us.'

Dawn found them clipping along the Appian Way and presently the rising sun threw the shadow of one of the great arched aqueducts across their path, so that the carruca was in warm sunlight one moment and cold shadow the next.

Tranquillus was sitting next to Flavia, pointing out

monuments along the Via Appia. At the third milestone they stopped at a roadside-stand and bought hot sausages wrapped in cool grape leaves.

Flavia had been clutching the little ivory tablet, waiting for the light to be bright enough for her to decipher any traces of writing. Now she put it in her lap so that she could peel back the grape leaf from her sausage.

'Who gave you the love-tablet?' asked Tranquillus.

'What?'

'That.' He pointed at the ivory booklet in her lap.

'Why do you call it a love-tablet?' she asked, aware that all the others were watching her, too.

'Because it's a love-tablet!' he said.

'How can you tell?'

'He's right, Flavia,' said Aristo gently. 'It's a love-tablet.'

'Stop calling it that—' she spluttered. 'How can you possibly know—'

'He knows because it's small and dainty and made of ivory,' said Tranquillus. 'Did it come wrapped with a ribbon?'

Flavia nodded.

'It's the latest fashion,' said Aristo. 'For a man to give a woman he loves an ivory tablet with a poetic declaration of his feelings inside. May I see it?'

'No!' Flavia put down her sausage and closed both hands around the ivory tablet.

'Flaccus!' cried Tranquillus. 'Gaius Valerius Flaccus!'

'Where?' cried Flavia, looking around eagerly.

'He's the one who gave it to her. Great Juno's beard!' Tranquillus slowly turned his head to stare at Flavia. 'That's why he called off his engagement. He loves you, not her!'

'Don't be silly,' said Flavia, but her heart thudded at the idea.

'Let me see it,' said Tranquillus.

'No!'

'I won't open it. I just want to examine it.'

'Go ahead then!' she cried. 'Look at it. You won't be able to read it even if you tried. I dropped it in the bath last night.'

Tranquillus took the tablet and opened it and frowned. Then his eyes grew wide as he read: 'Give me a thousand kisses, Flavia, then another hundred, then a thousand, then a second hundred, then a thousand more—'

'It does not say that!' Flavia snatched the tablet back. 'You're just quoting Catullus.' She eagerly examined the two inner leaves of the tablet, but they were perfectly blank.

'You're disappointed!' cried Tranquillus triumphantly. 'You actually thought he wrote that.' Then his smile faded. 'You love him, don't you, Flavia? You love Flaccus?'

'No I don't!'

Tranquillus looked at her friends. 'She loves Flaccus, doesn't she?'

Aristo and Lupus both shrugged their shoulders and Nubia looked down at her lap.

'No, I don't,' repeated Flavia, biting her lower lip. 'Of course I don't!'

'If you say so,' said Tranquillus. He looked away.

Flavia turned her head too, and looked out the back of the carruca at the passing tombs. And for some reason the Greek epitaph came to mind: *Eat, drink, be merry and make love; all below here is darkness.*

SCROLL XV

For over an hour Hilario had been giving them a running commentary on the passing landmarks. Nubia knew he was doing it to fill the awkward lack of conversation, but something was bothering her.

So when the rubbery-faced tutor paused for breath, she raised her hand.

'Yes, Nubia?' said Aristo.

'I was thinking,' said Nubia. 'We are going to receive pardon from Domitian and then prove he killed his brother, so he will not be able to rule?'

'That's right,' said Flavia.

Nubia frowned. 'Are we doing what is right?'

'Of course we are,' said Flavia. 'We're seeking the Truth. And Justice.'

'But we are not being truthful. We are plotting against him.'

'She makes a very good point,' said Hilario. 'Is what we're doing ethical?'

'Of course it's ethical!' said Flavia. 'It's our duty to prevent an evil man from becoming emperor. And Domitian is evil.'

Tranquillus sighed. 'I agree with Flavia,' he said. 'Domitian is a sadist. They say he has a habit of spearing flies with his stylus while he's writing. He aims his needle-sharp stylus and spears them right through.'

'You Romans pierce people,' said Nubia. 'On crosses.'

'They're usually runaway slaves who deserve it,' said Tranquillus. 'The poor flies don't.'

Nubia shuddered, but Lupus chuckled.

'Domitian probably pulls the flies' wings off after he spears them,' said Tranquillus, and added, 'And he loves cruel practical jokes.'

Beside Nubia, Flavia stiffened. 'What if this is a practical joke?' she asked. 'Or worse, a trap?'

'I had that thought,' muttered Tranquillus. 'Last night.'

'What do you mean?' said Nubia.

'What if Domitian is only pretending to forgive his enemies,' said Flavia, 'in order to get them to reveal themselves?'

'That's right,' said Tranquillus grimly. 'If you want to trap a rat, you put out a piece of cheese. What if amnesty is the cheese he's using to catch his rats? Spear the fly, trap the rat.'

Hilario harrumphed. 'Shame on you two! Why can't you give our new emperor the benefit of the doubt, like this wise girl here?' He gestured at Nubia. 'If you believe a man to be honest, will he not rise to your expectations?'

Lupus grunted no, and Tranquillus snorted. 'You're a pessimist, Lupus.'

Lupus wrote on his wax tablet: I'M NOT A PESSIMIST. I'M A REALIST.

Nubia and Flavia exchanged a knowing smile. 'That's what Jonathan always used to say,' explained Flavia.

'We have no proof of Domitian's evil intentions,' said Hilario, 'only rumour. And *Rumour is a dreadful looming monster; under every feather of her body is a watchful eye, a tongue, a shouting mouth and pricked up ears.*'

Nubia knew Hilario was quoting Virgil; Flavia and Jonathan had taught her Latin by reading the *Aeneid* to her, and this was a passage she had once memorized for Aristo. Without thinking she continued the quote: *'At night she wheels in the dark and screeching sky, by day she perches on rooftops and towers, throwing whole cities into panic.'*

Flavia clapped her hands. 'Nubia, you quoted Virgil! Euge!'

Aristo gave her an approving nod and a look of such pride that her spirit soared.

'Ah,' said Hilario, raising his arched eyebrows at Aristo. 'I see you have taught your pupils something. Well done.' Then he turned back to Flavia, 'Isn't it possible that Titus really did catch a fever and die? And that Domitian is just trying to do the right thing by wiping the tablet clean?'

'Maybe,' said Flavia grudgingly. 'And I hope you're right about him wiping the tablet clean.'

'Well,' said Tranquillus, 'there's Mount Albanus now. We'll be at the lake in an hour. We'll soon know if Domitian is really pardoning his brother's enemies, or throwing them to the lions.'

Nubia closed her eyes and prayed silently. 'Dear Lord, I am not afraid to die. But please help us do the right thing. Amen.'

For the past few miles the mules had been straining, for the Appian Way was skirting the lower slopes of the Alban hills. The carruca parted a flock of goats clogging the road, and Flavia also saw cattle grazing on the grassy slopes. Just past the twelfth milestone and a large octagonal mausoleum, they passed through a pretty town with red-tile roofs and walls the colour of clotted cream. On the slopes to their left, Flavia saw some temples.

'Bovillae,' said Hilario. 'Ox Town. When Alba Longa was destroyed this colony took over the cultic duties.'

'Alba Longa was destroyed?' said Flavia.

'Yes,' said Aristo. 'Nobody knows exactly where it was.'

'They say it's under the Villa of Clodius Pulcher,' said Hilario. 'Up on the crest of the ridge. Domitian's palace is further south.'

'Where is the lake?' asked Nubia, frowning.

'On the other side of the lip of the crater,' said Hilario. 'It's quite steep.'

Tranquillus added. 'These mountains used to be volcanoes. Lacus Albanus fills the crater of the biggest one.'

Lupus looked alarmed and scribbled on his wax tablet: DORMANT VOLCANO?

For the first time since he had discovered Flaccus's love-tablet to Flavia, Tranquillus smiled. 'I hope it's dormant! It hasn't erupted in living memory.'

'Neither had Vesuvius,' said Flavia. 'Until the year before last.'

They all made the sign against evil.

'Tell us about the lake?' said Flavia to Tranquillus. She knew he was depressed and she felt sorry for him.

He shrugged. 'Nothing to tell.'

'Nothing to tell?' harrumphed Hilario, his arched eyebrows rising higher. 'What about the prophecy and the Emissario?'

'Oh, yes. That.' Tranquillus sighed.

'What is the emissario?' asked Nubia.

'Yes,' said Flavia. 'What is the emissario?'

'Euge!' Hilario sat up straight and clapped his hands. 'My turn to tell a story, a fascinating one recounted by Livy, Cicero and Dionysius of Halicarnassus.' He unwrapped a papyrus parcel of dates and offered them round.

Flavia hesitated, then took a handful. Their chewy sweetness would console her and a good story might take her mind off Flaccus. The carruca had left Bovillae behind and they were passing through chestnut woods. The bright morning sun made their leaves glow like chrysolite and cast a delicious dappled shade. Flavia popped a date in her mouth and sat back to listen.

'About five hundred years ago,' began Hilario, 'the waters of Lacus Albanus began to rise. It was the end of the summer. There had been no rain and the snows had melted long before. There was no natural explanation. And yet the level of the lake got higher and higher.' Hilario's eyes bulged and he gestured dramatically with his arms. 'The lake threatened to spill over its rim like too much wine poured into a cup. It was a prodigy!'

Flavia sat forward. She had never heard this story. The others were watching Hilario, too, and he seemed pleased by their attention.

'The senate sent an envoy to Delphi, to see what Apollo might say through the Pythia. In the meantime, on the other side of Rome, soldiers were besieging an Etruscan town called Veii. News of the rising lake reached the besieging army and even the townspeople behind the walls. One day an old Etruscan soothsayer called out that he had the answer.' Here Hilario let his rubbery face go slack and pretended to be an old man. '*I have the answer!*' quavered Hilario as the soothsayer. '*The gods have spoken to me!*'

Flavia and Nubia giggled, and Lupus guffawed at Hilario's imitation of a mad Etruscan soothsayer.

Hilario shook his jowls enthusiastically: '*When water flows out of the Alban Lake but does not mix with the sea, Rome will conquer Veii.*'

Even Tranquillus gave a grudging smile.

'But the old soothsayer was jeered at by the besieging Romans and the besieged Etruscans alike.' Here Hilario played the role of a scoffer, pointing and laughing. 'Until the delegation returned from Delphi to report that the Pythia had said exactly the same thing as the old man! And when the Sibylline books were consulted, they confirmed it, too!'

Lupus grunted and wrote on his wax tablet: HOW DID THEY DRAIN THE LAKE?

'Simple,' said Hilario. 'They drilled a tunnel in the mountain just below the rising water level. That is the Emissario. It allowed the water to come out and irrigate the farmlands here,' he gestured to the fields sloping away to their right. 'The water level in the lake returned to normal, the crops were watered, and within a year the town of Veii had been captured.'

'Oh!' said Nubia. 'They called it the Emissario, because water goes out of it.'

'Well done, Nubia,' said Aristo, and Flavia saw him give her a dazzling smile.

'What happened to the Emissario?' asked Flavia. 'Is is still there?'

'Of course!' said Hilario, and looked around at them, pleased. 'It's quite overgrown, but it's there. Tranquillus and I went to investigate its entrance last month. An old goatherd told us that it still runs all the way through. If you wanted,' he said, 'you could travel a mile through the mountain, and come out the other side. Just up ahead, on the other side of the Via Appia.'

'No, thank you,' said Flavia. 'I think that's one experience I can live without.'

SCROLL XVI

Just past the fourteenth milestone, Talpa turned the carruca off the Via Appia onto a road leading steeply up to the left. As the road curved round, Lupus caught tantalising glimpses of a magnificent villa on the hillside ahead. A high stone wall surrounded it, but he could see domes and tiled roofs peeping above the wall, and the dark tips of cypress trees, too.

'There it is,' said Tranquillus. 'Domitian's Alban Villa.'

'Great Juno's peacock!' murmured Flavia. 'Now I know why they call it Domitian's Alban Citadel.'

'It is so big!' said Nubia. 'Like a whole city.'

'And there's more outside those walls,' said Hilario. 'Two massive grottoes down by the lakeside and an amphitheatre over to the south,' he said.

Tranquillus nodded and said: 'Five years ago, when I was eight, I saw two bears fight each other in the amphitheatre.'

'As for what's inside the walls,' said Hilario. 'I've heard there are three terraces, a hippodrome, a big cryptoporticus and a small theatre. There are fountains, gardens and secret tunnels. And the palace, of course.'

'Where's the Emissario?' asked Flavia.

'It's right down by the lake,' said Tranquillus. 'You can't see it from here.'

The four mules strained, for they were still climbing. They pulled the buttercup-yellow carruca up an impressive drive, past a wall full of statues in niches. The flesh of the marble statues was subtly tinted and one or two looked so real that Lupus half expected them to turn and wave at them.

'Behold!' said Nubia, as they drove through an arch and emerged into a circular piazza. 'There is a long line of people going to that building.'

To their left was a magnificent porter's lodge. Soldiers stood either side of open doors and a queue of people stretched out from it across the piazza towards the fountain at its centre. On the other side of the fountain was the gate to the palace itself.

'Great Juno,' said Flavia. 'Look at them all.'

'I hope we are not too late,' murmured Nubia.

Talpa reined in the mules and Lupus stood up to get a better look.

'Is it true?' Aristo asked a man coming across the piazza towards them. 'Is Domitian offering free pardons and amnesty?'

The man had a cow on a leash. He stopped and squinted up at them, then his face broke into a brown-toothed smile. 'Absolutely true,' he said. 'Two years ago, my father accidentally borrowed this cow from the imperial flock. Domitian just told me I can keep her and all her offspring. But you'd better hurry,' said the man. 'The doors close at noon.'

Hilario turned to Tranquillus. 'You see?' he said. 'It's obviously legitimate. I suggest you get in the queue.'

Aristo nodded. 'That's why we came here, isn't it?'

'I'm still afraid we might be walking into the lion's jaws,' said Flavia.

Lupus held up his tablet: I'M GOING ON THE PROWL

'Not a bad idea,' said Aristo. 'Find out what people are saying. We'll save your place in the queue.'

Lupus nodded and slipped over the side of the carruca. He ran to the fountain – glittering in the mid-morning sun – and drank from one of the jets of water. He wiped his mouth, grinned at them and gave them a thumbs-up: they could depend on him.

'Are you all together?' asked the man with the tablet. His grizzled hair showed he was in his sixties, but his muscular body was that of a man thirty years younger and his keen dark eyes were full of energy. Although his short hair was grey his eyebrows were still black.

'Yes,' said Flavia, and Aristo added. 'The six of us are all together.'

The man's smile did not quite reach his eyes. 'And are you all seeking amnesty?'

'Just the three of us.' Flavia glanced at Lupus, who had come running up only moments before. Still breathless, he gave her a tiny nod and a secret thumbs-up: apparently Domitian really was pardoning people.

'Just you three boys?' the man raised a dark eyebrow. 'You are seeking imperial amnesty?'

'Yes,' said Flavia bravely. 'Just us three.'

'Then your friends here will have to wait outside. I'm sorry, but it's policy. You may sit over there.' He gestured towards a polished marble bench with lion's feet legs.

'The lion's jaws,' murmured Flavia, as Aristo, Tranquillus and Hilario walked to the bench.

'Names?' The man with the wax-tablet was speaking to her. 'May I ask your names?'

Flavia took a deep breath: 'Flavia Gemina, Flavia Nubia and Lupus.'

This time the secretary raised both eyebrows. 'Two of you are girls?'

'Yes.' Flavia took off her sunhat and ran her hand through her hair.

'Please leave your hats here, if you don't mind,' said the man, as he wrote down their names. 'Address him as Caesar, Augustus or even Jupiter. He likes that.'

Flavia's heart was pounding as she and Nubia tossed their hats to Aristo, who caught them deftly.

'Is there anyone else in there with Domitian?' she asked.

'No,' said the secretary. 'Nobody else is in with the emperor.' He smirked. 'Not even a fly.'

As Flavia led the way inside, she remembered Tranquillus's story about Domitian spearing flies with a needle-sharp stylus. She realised the secretary had been making a bitter joke.

And she remembered what Tranquillus had said about Domitian: *Spear the fly, trap the rat.*

Of course the emperor was not physically alone. Two of his Praetorian guards stood behind his desk. There could be no risk of assassination. Nubia realised this as soon as she stepped into the small, bright room. But Domitian had no secretary with him. He seemed to be dealing with the pardons by himself.

The young emperor was seated behind a marble table. Before him lay a large wax tablet, with at least six leaves. He looked up, and when his gaze locked with Nubia's it was like the shock she once had from touching a jellyfish.

'Nubia of the Colosseum!' he said. 'I wondered if

116

I would see you again. I commended your courage then, and I commend it now.'

'Caesar,' she said, her voice barely more than a whisper.

He looked her up and down, then gave a half-smile. 'Even dressed as a boy you are delectable.' With some effort he pulled his gaze from her and looked at the others. 'Flavia Gemina,' he said. 'And Vulpus?'

'Lupus,' corrected Flavia. 'His name is Lupus . . . er . . . Caesar. A few months ago we were wrongly named on a decree.'

'Of course. How could I forget? His name was on the decree. And wasn't there a fourth name?'

'Our friend Jonathan ben Mordecai,' said Flavia. 'Has he been to ask your pardon yet?'

Domitian glanced down at the wax tablet before him, and tapped his stylus thoughtfully on the marble tabletop. 'No, I don't believe he has.'

He flipped through a few leaves of the tablet, then looked up. 'So,' he said. 'Are you begging my forgiveness?'

'Yes, sir,' said Flavia in a small voice. 'Even though we don't really know why the decree was issued.'

'Because you stole a valuable gem,' said Domitian. He reached into the neck of his tunic and pulled out the large lentil-shaped emerald that had been hanging from a gold chain. Nubia recognised Nero's Eye, the emerald they had risked their lives to find. 'But as you see, it is now safely in my possession and I am feeling magnanimous. You are pardoned.'

Nubia heard Flavia swallow. 'If our friend Jonathan comes—'

'If he comes in the next half hour, then I will pardon him.' Domitian stood up. 'But pardons must be requested in person. And with suitable humility.'

He stepped out from behind his desk and came to stand before them.

Nubia caught his scent now, the smell of stale sweat overlaid with susinum, a sickly sweet and extremely expensive perfume. He was leering at her again, and licking his lips. Nubia could not take her eyes from his mouth. His lips were plump and red, the upper one protruding more than the lower.

'Kiss my feet.'

'What?' gasped Flavia.

Domitian was still staring at Nubia with his large dark eyes. He smiled. 'Kiss my feet, if you desire my pardon.'

Nubia could hear the blood pulsing in her ears. She felt hot and then cold, and her stomach churned. Once she had seen a cobra with a desert mouse. The mouse had been transfixed by the cobra's deadly stare. She felt like that mouse. She did not want to be in his presence a moment longer.

So, with all the strength in her she dropped her gaze and knelt at his feet. His toes – where they peeped out of the gilded sandals – were crooked and the joints knobbed with corns. The big toe of his left foot was the least repulsive, so she took a deep breath, closed her eyes and pressed her lips against it.

Then she stood and turned and ran out of the room.

SCROLL XVII

'Nubia? What is it?'

She heard Aristo's voice and felt his strong arms encircle her. She hugged him tightly, and felt his heart pounding against her ear. Gradually her nausea subsided. But now the tears came.

'Did he molest you?' Aristo started to pull out of her embrace but Nubia clung to him.

'Aristo!' she was sobbing. 'Don't go. Stay with me.'

'Always,' he said huskily, and she felt him kiss the top of her head. 'I knew I shouldn't have let you go in alone ... Flavia! Lupus!' He kept an arm around her as he moved towards the others. 'Are you all right?'

Nubia opened her eyes and blinked away tears to see a very pale Flavia and a grim-faced Lupus emerging from the porter's lodge. The last few people left in the queue were staring nervously at them.

'Yes,' said Flavia, catching Nubia's hand. 'I'm all right. We're just going to the fountain.'

Nubia reluctantly let herself be pulled from Aristo's embrace. She followed Flavia down the steps and across the plaza to the fountain. Once there, they both let jets of water arc into their open mouths. Lupus joined them a moment later, and dunked his entire head in the water.

'I hate him!' gargled Flavia, without taking her mouth from the stream.

'Why?' asked Tranquillus, running up to them. 'What did he make you do?' he asked breathlessly.

'Yes, tell us,' said Aristo. 'By all the gods, if he—'

Flavia came out from under the jet of water. 'He made us kiss his feet,' she gasped. 'And they're horrible; he has hammer-toes.'

'Is that all?' said Aristo to Nubia, his brown eyes full of concern. She nodded miserably, and wiped her mouth. Aristo slipped his arm around her shoulders again.

'The filthy—' began Tranquillus, but Lupus had been writing something and now he showed it to them, grinning.

AT LEAST HE DIDN'T MAKE US KISS HIS BOTTOM

'Or his big wet mouth,' said Flavia. Then she began to giggle, and despite herself, so did Nubia.

Flavia and her friends were still at the fountain, trying to wash the taste of imperial foot from their mouths, when Flavia heard an accented voice.

'Nubia? Nubia, is that you?'

Flavia turned to see an Egyptian with a narrow face and heavy lidded eyes staring open-mouthed at Nubia. He was wearing a long, grass-green caftan.

'Ascletario!' she gasped.

'Flavia Gemina!' His eyes widened. 'The voice is yours but you're taller, and you're dressed like a boy!'

'Yes,' said Flavia ruefully. 'I know.'

'And Lupus,' said Ascletario. 'My little mute friend.'

Lupus narrowed his eyes at the Egyptian and nodded warily.

'This is a very good disguise for you,' said Ascletario to

Flavia. He was rubbing his hands nervously together. 'But not so good for Nubia. Her unique beauty is most difficult to hide.'

'So true,' murmured Aristo.

Flavia smiled. 'It's good to see you again, Ascletario,' she said.

'*The* Ascletario?' said Tranquillus. 'Titus's astrologer?'

'I humbly bow,' said the Egyptian, and did so.

'Ascletario,' said Flavia, 'this is our tutor Aristo, our friend Tranquillus and his tutor, Hilario.' Her smile faded as a thought occurred. 'Do you work for *him* now? For Domitian?'

'I hope to, hope to, hope to,' said Ascletario. 'He is choosing his amici this week.'

'His amici?' said Nubia.

'His inner circle,' explained Aristo. 'Advisors and stewards. They're called his amici, his friends.'

Ascletario bowed and rubbed his hands. 'And I hope to become one of them. I am his servant, his servant, his servant.'

'Why?' said Flavia.

'Because he is powerful,' said Ascletario. 'It is better to be with him than against him.' The Egyptian glanced around nervously. 'You are here for Jonathan, Jonathan, Jonathan?'

'What?' gasped Flavia.

'Jonathan, Jon—'

'Yes!' interrupted Flavia. 'We heard you the first time. But do you know where he is?'

And Nubia whispered: 'Have you seen him?'

Ascletario glanced towards the soldiers guarding the columned porch. Only a few petitioners still waited outside; it was almost noon.

'I will tell you,' he said, rubbing his hands together nervously. 'But we must walk back to your cart and you must pretend to drive back towards Rome.'

Flavia nodded and as they started towards the yellow carruca, Ascletario spoke in a low voice. 'A few days ago, some guards caught Jonathan outside Reate shortly after the emperor became ill. Domitian had him arrested and brought here.'

'Here? To Lake Albanus?'

'Yes,' said the Egyptian. 'He has been . . . interrogating him.'

'Alas!' whispered Nubia. 'Poor Jonathan.'

'Jonathan would never hurt Titus!' hissed Flavia. 'He was trying to warn him.'

'Are you certain?' said Ascletario. They had reached the carruca and he turned to face her. 'Flavia Gemina, are you most certain that Jonathan was trying to save the Emperor and not assassinate him?'

'Yes!' cried Flavia. 'If anyone killed Titus it was Domitian. Maybe Jonathan found proof of his guilt. Maybe that's why Domitian arrested him.'

'Ascletario,' said Aristo, 'you were with Titus on the road. Don't you know what happened?'

Ascletario glanced over his shoulder at the porter's lodge. Flavia could see that one of the guards was watching them with narrowed eyes.

Ascletario smiled and nodded, as if bidding them farewell. 'At the first stopping place, Titus caught a chill, which soon became a fever. We treated him as best we could.'

'Who?' hissed Flavia. 'Who was travelling with him?'

'Apart from me? Domitian and his slaves, and Titus's,

too, of course. Also the Praetorian Guard, a Jewish doctor and Crispus, the secretary you just met.'

'A Jewish doctor?' said Flavia sharply. 'Was it Doctor Mordecai?'

'No. It was a man called Ben Aruva. Pinchas ben Aruva. He recently began treating the emperor's headaches, headaches, headaches.'

'Titus destroyed Jerusalem,' said Aristo quietly. 'And yet he put his trust in this Jewish doctor?'

'They say he is the best,' said Ascletario.

'Packing Titus in ice was probably what killed him,' said Flavia.

'On the contrary,' said Ascletario, still grinning and nodding for the sake of the guard. 'Packing him in ice saved Titus twice before.'

'It did?'

'Yes. He had a fever three months ago. Many doctors tried to help. But only Ben Aruva's cure succeeded.'

'He packed him in ice?'

'Yes! And the emperor was instantly cured. That's why Titus put such trust in him.' Once again, Ascletario glanced over his shoulder. 'I think the guards will be getting suspicious of my talking to you. Jonathan is being held at the mouth of the Emissario. Do you know what that is?'

Flavia and Tranquillus exchanged a surprised glance, and Hilario said: 'We know.'

'Then you must go there now,' said Ascletario. 'I do not think Jonathan can stand another night of interrogation. Good luck and be careful, be careful, be careful.'

It was noon. Tranquillus and his tutor Hilario were taking them down to the Emissario via a steep gardener's footpath winding through the woods.

At the top of the path Flavia and her friends had seen the vast oval of Lake Albanus for the first time. Lying four hundred feet below them, it filled the volcanic crater like blue wine in a green kylix.

Now, going down the path, she could still catch glimpses of the lake's sparkling surface through gaps in the trees.

'Are you sure this is the way to the Emissario?' she asked Tranquillus.

'Yes,' he said grimly. 'This is the way.'

'Why do you think Domitian has taken Jonathan there?'

'I don't know. Probably because he doesn't want anyone to hear his cries. It's off the beaten track. Only swineherds and fishermen ever come down here.'

'Master Gaius,' said Hilario, 'you cannot do this. If our new emperor has imprisoned someone in the Emissario, it would be foolishness to try to free them.'

'But Jonathan's our friend!' said Flavia, close to tears.

'He's not Master Gaius's friend,' said Hilario. 'He's *your* friend.'

'He was caught doing something brave. He was trying to warn Titus about Domitian's plot,' said Flavia.

'Well, he obviously didn't succeed,' said Hilario. 'And as your Egyptian friend has just said, Domitian is now the most powerful man in the Roman Empire. If Jonathan is his prisoner then there will be guards, chains and locks. If you are caught they could execute you.' He looked at Tranquillus. 'Master Gaius, I forbid you to take part in this scheme. Up to now you may have used blackmail to bind me to your wishes,' he said. 'And you may use it again to get me dismissed, but I will not allow you to be captured and killed. This is madness.'

Tranquillus stopped walking and turned to look at Hilario. 'You're right,' he said.

Flavia turned to Tranquillus. 'You agree with him?'

Tranquillus stared at the ground. 'Yes. I think I do. I don't know why I'm doing this. It's madness.'

SCROLL XVIII

'Tranquillus,' pleaded Flavia. 'You've got to help us.'

'I *have* been helping you! I've been driving you around for three days in my family's carruca, helping to pay for meals and rooms. I let you stay at our house. And all because I thought ...' He stopped and took a breath. 'Tranquillus is right. I draw the line at marching into a dungeon without a plan. Think about it, Flavia. There must be a better way. Let's all go to my aunt's house. We'll send a message to pater and find out if he can help us save Jonathan.'

'But what if they're torturing him?' cried Flavia. 'We don't have a moment to lose!'

'If they're torturing him,' said Tranquillus, 'that means he's definitely being guarded. How will you get past them? How will you get him out of here without anyone seeing?'

'We've done things like this before,' said Flavia, 'and we can do it again. Can't we?' She looked at her friends. Nubia and Lupus nodded, but Aristo frowned and opened his mouth. Before he could speak, Flavia said: 'At least show us where the Emissario is. Then go back to your aunt's house and send word to your father. Maybe there is something he can do to help. But I can't wait. *We* can't wait.' She looked at Aristo and this time he nodded, though his face was grim.

Tranquillus sighed and glanced at Hilario. 'All right,' he said. 'I'll show you where it is. But no more.'

Hilario shook his head at the sky, but followed as Tranquillus resumed his descent. They continued down the steep, wooded hillside. Along the way, they passed a sow and her piglets browsing among the oaks and, later, a donkey tethered to an olive tree.

At last they emerged onto a hard-packed earth road.

'They call this road the Via Corona,' said Tranquillus, 'because it rings the lake like a garland. Follow me.' He turned left onto the road. Flavia and the others followed.

Presently Hilario pointed. Flavia could see that a section of the road up ahead was made of grey stone. 'That's where the water goes under the road,' said Hilario. 'Those blocks of peperino form a bridge over it.'

Tranquillus beckoned them on: 'Follow me,' he whispered. 'Quietly.' He moved off the road and into a copse of oak trees. He beckoned them to follow him, then parted the branches of a shrub. Flavia peeped over his shoulder. She could see a wall of massive grey stone blocks built against the lower slope of the mountain. There was a gap in the wall – presumably for the channel of water – and a curving iron fence in front of it, to keep out animals. Through the bars of the fence, she could see the statue of a naked goddess on one side of the gap and a statue of a soldier on the other. And something like an iron door in between.

Then the statue of the soldier turned his head.

'Pollux!' cursed Tranquillus, pushing Flavia down. 'It isn't usually guarded. But I don't think he's seen us,' he added a moment later.

'If there's a guard,' whispered Flavia, 'that must mean Jonathan is there!'

'Is that the Emissario?' asked Nubia softly.

Tranquillus nodded. 'You can see there's not even a lock on the gate in the fence. There's nothing to steal in there. Just a channel leading from the lake through the mountain. See the sluice gate?'

'The thing like a door frame with the plate on top?' said Flavia, 'like a toga press?'

'Yes,' said Tranquillus. 'You turn the wheel and a screw makes the gate go down or up. According to my aunt they only need to use the sluice gates once every few years.'

'Is the channel going all the way through?' asked Nubia in disbelief.

'Yes,' said Hilario. 'Farmers on the other side of the Via Appia use the water to irrigate their fields.'

'You're absolutely sure the tunnel goes all the way through?' persisted Flavia.

Tranquillus looked at Hilario, and they both nodded.

'Then all we have to do,' said Flavia, 'is get rid of the guard, rescue Jonathan and escape through the tunnel!'

'If Jonathan is really there,' said Flavia, 'then we'll set him free, and escape through the Emissario.' She looked at Tranquillus. 'Can you and Hilario wait for us on the other side of the mountain, by the Via Appia? At the place where it comes out?'

Tranquillus frowned. 'I'm not sure that's such a good idea,' he said. 'You'd have to go nearly a mile through a channel full of cold water in the pitch black. Also, there are sluice gates at the other end, to let the water out. Some of them might have teeth.'

'Gates have teeth?' whispered Nubia and Lupus gave Tranquillus his bug-eyed look.

He nodded. 'Teeth, bars, whatever. To regulate the flow

of the water. I've only seen the ones at this end.'

'If there is just one guard,' said Aristo to Flavia. 'Then maybe we could escape along this road.'

'Yes, that would be better,' said Tranquillus. 'But you can't go north. The harbour is there and the hill isn't as steep. People would be able to see you. You'd have to go that way.' He pointed back in the direction they had come.

'Wouldn't they be able to see us from Domitian's Citadel?'

'I don't think so. Most of the palace is on the western slope of the ridge. It will take you two or three hours to reach the village on the other side of the lake. But then you can go up to our house. We'll wait for you there.'

Lupus was writing on his tablet: THAT CAN BE OUR ALPHA PLAN

'All right,' said Flavia. 'Plan alpha: we escape around the south side of the lake. Plan beta: we go through the tunnel. We don't have time to make rafts,' she said. 'But if the current is with us, then we can float. But how do we get rid of that guard?'

'I have a suggestion,' said Hilario.

They all looked at him in astonishment.

'Master Gaius and I will stroll casually along the road, past the guard. When we're out of sight, Master Gaius will utter a bloodcurdling scream. The guard will run to help and when he gets there he'll see me beating my unruly pupil with a cane; a logical and innocent explanation.'

Tranquillus looked at Hilario. 'You'd do that?'

'With great pleasure,' said the paedagogus drily.

'Wait,' said Aristo. 'What if there are more guards inside?'

'I don't think there will be,' said Tranquillus. 'The entrance doesn't go back very far.'

'When we get there,' said Flavia, 'we'll peep inside and see. If there are more guards then Nubia and I will cause another diversion while you and Lupus can knock them on the head. But with any luck, Tranquillus is right and we'll only have to distract that one guard.'

Aristo closed his eyes and shook his head. 'Dear Lord, what am I doing?'

'You're doing what is right and just,' said Flavia, and to Tranquillus: 'Are you ready?'

He sighed and nodded.

'Wish us luck, then!' She smiled, even though she felt sick with excitement and dread.

'Good luck,' said Tranquillus. 'My aunt's house is called the Villa Dorica; it's the villa with the Doric columns. If you're not there by nightfall we'll know you've taken the Emissario route or that . . .' He trailed off.

'That we've taken the Emissario,' she said bravely.

'Just in case I don't see you again . . .' Tranquillus leaned forward and before Flavia could turn away, he kissed her quickly on the mouth. 'Goodbye, Flavia.'

'Goodbye for now, Tranquillus.'

Tranquillus shook hands with Lupus and Aristo and gave Nubia a kiss on the cheek.

'Good luck,' he said again. 'May Fortuna be with you.'

Then he and Hilario stepped back onto the road.

A few moments later Flavia saw them come into view. The guard saw them, too, but they appeared to be arguing and did not even look at him. In a few moments they passed out of sight, heading towards the lake harbour.

The sun was at its zenith and for a moment all was

peaceful. The wind sighed in the trees and a bird sang sweetly.

Then a scream pierced the air. Flavia knew it was coming, but it made her jump nonetheless. The guard outside the Emissario jumped, too. He ran to the gate in the fence, opened it, and a moment later he was clanking down the road in the direction of the cries. The screams were still coming and Flavia gazed at her friends in horror.

'Do you think he's all right?' she whispered. 'Those cries sound so realistic.'

Lupus chuckled and gave her a thumbs-up. And the moment the guard had passed out of sight, he led the way to the Emissario, running at a crouch.

As they crept towards the gate in the iron fence, ferns brushed Nubia's face and the fresh smell of damp, green plants filled her nose. The retaining wall was built of massive blocks of the grey stone which Hilario had called peperino; she wondered if that was because it was the colour of pepper. Above her, where the wall turned a corner to pierce the mountain, an ancient oak tree dangled its roots down the side, groping for nourishment in thin air. The twisting roots seemed to reach out for her and she shivered.

And now she saw something even more extraordinary. Sunk into the mountain was a lofty vault of the same blocks of pepper-coloured stone. Its entrance was screened by a living curtain of vine tendrils.

Nubia could hear the rush of water and as she moved closer she saw the channel cut into the peperino, its edges green with moss, and the dark lake water flowing in it.

Lupus crept forward, still in the lead. A marble statue of

a nymph representing the lake sat guarding the entrance. Lupus gave her a pat on the thigh, and then parted the screen of hanging vines. Nubia held her breath as he peeped inside, then she released it as he beckoned them on. She glanced back at Aristo, who gave her a grim but reassuring nod, then followed Flavia. Once through the tendrils, the light was emerald green.

As Nubia's eyes adjusted, she saw that the lofty stone vault only went back about a dozen feet into the mountain, before ending in another grey stone wall. There was a door-shaped hole piercing this wall with another sluice gate, and the channel of water entered below it. On either side of the channel was a ledge about four feet wide.

Suddenly something like a small glittering bird whirred out of the dark interior straight at Nubia.

With a cry she started back, and felt Aristo's warm hands steady her shoulders.

'Only a dragonfly,' he whispered, and released her.

Nubia closed her eyes and whispered a prayer. 'Dear Lord, please protect us and help us find Jonathan.'

'Amen,' murmured Aristo behind her.

In front of her Lupus grunted and Flavia whispered: 'Jonathan?'

Beside the second sluice gate was a pile of rags. Flavia and Lupus were staring down at it.

Then Nubia realised that the pile of rags beside the gate was not a pile of rags at all, but a crumpled boy.

He lifted his head. And although his hair was very short and his beaten face almost unrecognizable, she knew it was Jonathan.

SCROLL XIX

'Jonathan?' cried Flavia, rushing forward. 'Oh, Jonathan!'

'Flavia?' His voice was muffled and she saw that his lips were swollen and his jaw bruised. 'Nubia? Lupus? Don't hug me!' he wheezed, 'Think I have some cracked ribs. Hurts when I breathe.'

Lupus was on his hands and knees in the cramped space behind Jonathan, trying to find a way to release him. Now Flavia could see her friend was chained to the inner sluice gate. Aristo had jumped across the channel to the ledge on the other side and was examining the iron frame. Flavia saw that the tongue of this inner gate was down, and that it had bars. The black water gurgled as it passed through into the dark tunnel.

'He's chained to the frame,' said Aristo. 'We can't free him without a key.'

Flavia crouched on the narrow ledge. 'Jonathan. What happened?'

He hung his head. 'Domitian's men.' Flavia noticed he was wheezing; the cold and damp here couldn't be good for his asthma.

Nubia had taken the sea-sponge from her belt pouch and had managed to wet it in water from the channel. She squeezed past Flavia and began to gently dab the cuts on Jonathan's face.

He winced but did not draw back.

'We heard they caught you outside Reate,' said Flavia. 'Were you trying to warn Titus about the murder attempt? We've just been to the Sabine Hills, looking for clues, but we came back to receive a pardon from Domitian.'

'A pardon?'

'Yes! Domitian was offering a free pardon to anyone willing to kiss his foot.'

Jonathan gave a bitter laugh. 'It's probably just a trick,' he wheezed. 'You shouldn't have come.'

Behind Jonathan, Lupus stood up, defeated by the chain. Aristo was examining the cracks between the massive blocks of stone. 'Who has the key to your manacles?' he asked.

'A blind man named Messallinus,' wheezed Jonathan. 'He's Domitian's torturer. He comes and beats me while the Egyptian watches.'

'Egyptian?' said Flavia. 'Which Egyptian?'

'You know!' muttered Jonathan. 'The one who repeats everything three times and rubs his hands together like a fly.'

'Ascletario?' said Flavia. All the blood in her body seemed to sink to her feet.

'Yes. Ascletario. He likes to watch.'

Flavia stood up. 'Aristo!' she cried. 'It's a trap. We've got to get out of here.'

But as she turned, she saw she was too late.

Three men stood on the other side of the vine curtain. She could only see their silhouettes but she could tell that two of them were soldiers and that the man in between wore a caftan. It was the traitor who had betrayed them: Ascletario.

★

It was an hour past midday. Golden Helios beamed down on silvery-green olive trees and a sparkling blue lake, as if nothing bad could ever happen. But Flavia knew that Helios was wrong: she and her friends were Domitian's prisoners, and Jonathan was still chained to a sluice gate in the damp mouth of the Emissario.

They were being escorted north along the lakeside road, in the direction Tranquillus and Hilario had gone. One guard led the way, one took up the rear, and Ascletario walked beside Flavia.

'Why?' she turned her head to look at the Egyptian. 'Why did you betray us?'

'I am sorry, sorry, sorry,' said Ascletario. 'But your friend Jonathan was acting suspiciously and the emperor believes that you also are plotting against him.'

Flavia had no answer for that. Ascletario was right. They had been plotting against the emperor.

'I told you to go, but you would not listen,' added the Egyptian under his breath.

Flavia secretly scanned the trees on the left, looking for Tranquillus or his tutor. Had they lingered? Or were they already back in the buttercup-yellow carruca, on their way to his aunt's villa across the lake? She thought she saw movement up on the hillside among some oaks, but it was only a sow and her piglets rooting for acorns.

'You should not be defying Caesar Domitian,' murmured Ascletario.

'How can you serve a murderer?' hissed Flavia. 'He killed Titus.'

'Please do not call my master a murderer,' said Ascletario. 'If you say that again I will take you back to the Emissario and chain you beside your friend. Domitian did not kill his brother. It was Titus's time to die.'

'What do you mean?'

'I mean that his death was from the gods. His horoscope proves it.'

'Where are you taking us?' said Flavia suddenly. 'Isn't Domitian's palace up there?' She looked back over her shoulder at the wooded ridge high above them.

'I am taking you there,' said Ascletario.

Flavia saw a harbour up ahead, with opulent barges and other colourful pleasure craft moored there. But Ascletario was not looking at the harbour. He was pointing to the mouth of a vast cave, partially screened by ancient oaks and shrubs. 'The nymphaeum, nymphaeum, nymphaeum,' he announced.

Two guards stood on either side of the arched opening in the steep hillside. They both saluted Ascletario as he led his prisoners inside.

'Great Juno's peacock!' gasped Flavia as they entered a vast, cool space. Directly before them was a large sculpture showing Odysseus and his men about to put out the eye of the sleeping Cyclops. In the dim, green light the painted marble figures seemed almost real. To the right, statues gazed out from rectangular niches in the wall, to the left a smaller cave held another sculptural group. What lay at the back of the cave, Flavia could not tell. But she could hear water splashing and the eerie sound of a flute, both sounds magnified by some strange acoustic quirk of the cavern. The space reminded her of the great octagonal room of Nero's Golden House, only much more mysterious.

A plump bald eunuch in a long black shift stepped forward.

'This way,' he said in a soft voice, and led them to the left. The smaller cave contained a sculpture of a terrifying sea-monster with seven snarling heads: Scylla. A hidden light well illuminated a small niche with a bench.

The bald eunuch took some long black shifts from the bench. 'Put these on,' he said. 'They go over your own clothes.'

The tunics were made of black silk. They all had to put one on, even Ascletario. Flavia looked at her friends and made the sign against evil. Dressed all in black, they seemed like the spirits of the dead. Lupus's oversized tunic reached almost to the floor, making him appear small and pale and vulnerable.

The eunuch beckoned them out past the snarling marble Scylla and back into the vast cavern. There he bowed to Ascletario and gestured with his right arm, as if to say: please proceed. Ascletario led the way deeper in. As they passed the sculptural group in the centre of the cave, Flavia glanced at it. The hairy Cyclops Polyphemus was shown fast asleep on his back, unaware that he was about to be horribly blinded. Flavia shuddered and averted her eyes. Why had Domitian brought them here? What did he intend to do?

As they moved past the sculpture of the doomed Cyclops, Flavia saw two more dark arches sunk into the very back of the cave, on a slightly higher level. A cascade of running water poured out of the arch on the left: no doubt a natural spring.

The arch on the right was covered with a heavy black curtain.

The flute music must have come from behind that curtain. It had stopped now but as Flavia followed Ascletario up some steps, she thought she could hear someone reciting. She couldn't make out the words, but she caught the distinctive rhythm of dactylic hexameter.

The muffled voice – deep and patrician – made her think of Flaccus, though she knew it couldn't be him.

When they reached the upper level, Asceltario hesitated for a moment. Then he took a deep breath and pulled back the black curtain to reveal the innermost room.

It took a moment for Flavia to register what she was seeing before her: a completely black triclinium. Dimly lit by a few bronze oil-lamps, it had black walls, a black floor and a black vaulted ceiling. The coverings on the three low couches were black and all seven diners were dressed in black, too. The emperor, reclining alone on the central couch, wore a black synthesis and a garland of dark green leaves. And the muscular young poet who had stopped reciting to look over his shoulder at them wore black, too.

It was Gaius Valerius Flaccus.

SCROLL XX

Flavia almost cried out Floppy's name, but stopped herself just in time. She mustn't let on that she knew him. He had obviously come here in order to rescue them. So why did he look so astonished to see her? And how had he managed to get an invitation?

Ascletario was addressing Domitian: 'Your Excellency, you told me to bring the children and their tutor if they tried to rescue their friend . . .'

'I did indeed,' said Domitian. He patted the couch beside him. 'Come, Nubia of the Colosseum. Recline beside me. You others may sit on the floor at our feet.' And to Flaccus he said, 'Please continue.'

'I'm sorry, Caesar,' said Flaccus. 'I can't remember where I was.'

'You were reciting a passage from your new epic, a passage about the underworld, as I requested.' Domitian was talking to Flaccus but looking at Nubia. 'Today,' he said, 'we are dining in honour of Hades.'

'Oh. Yes,' stammered Flaccus. He resumed his recital: '*The palace of Tartarus lies deep beneath us, cut off from the concerns of man and from the toppling sky . . .*'

Flavia heard Ascletario hiss: 'Go, Nubia! Recline beside Caesar. The rest of you: sit on the floor, the floor, the floor.' And she felt him give her a little shove from behind.

As if in a nightmare, Nubia slowly walked into the terrifying black room to join Domitian on the central couch. She glanced over her shoulder at her friends. They were lowering themselves to the black marble floor, at the foot of one of the couches furthest from the Emperor.

'*Twin doors lead to the darkness below,*' Flaccus was saying. '*The first lies open to kings and commoners alike.*'

Nubia saw that Domitian was patting a spot on the couch in front of him and slightly to his right. Reluctantly, she climbed up and stretched out on her left side. He was behind her now, so at least she didn't have to look at him.

'*The other gate to Hades is barred, it only opens to the warrior who has died bravely in battle . . .*'

Nubia realised she was trembling. Hades was the god of the underworld. And this seemed like the underworld. Would she ever see sunshine again? Was Domitian planning to kill them all? She stifled a gasp as Domitian laid his hand on her upper arm and she heard the couch creak as he leant forward. 'Thank you for joining me, Nubia.' His breath was hot in her ear.

'* . . . this other gate only opens to the woman who has given her life for others, or the children who have conquered fear . . .*'

Flaccus seemed to put a slight emphasis on this last phrase and she shot him a grateful look.

'*. . . or the priest whose conscience is as spotless as his robe.*'

Domitian's hand came away from her shoulder, as if he had been burnt. Nubia remembered that the emperor was also the pontifex maximus – the high priest – and that Flaccus had just taken up a position as some kind of priest, too.

'*Torch in hand, Mercury guides the righteous forward until they reach a path that gleams with its own divine light. This path leads to woods and meadows full of eternal sunshine, where they will dance and sing for ever.'*

Flaccus was looking at Nubia and she wondered if he was speaking about her paradise. A flicker of movement pulled her attention away from the young poet. Lupus was sitting beside Aristo, making his thumbs-up sign, trying to tell her it would be all right, and Aristo was giving her an encouraging smile, too.

Nubia tried to smile back.

'Thank you, Valerius Flaccus,' came Domitian's voice from behind her. 'You may be seated.' He clapped his hands. 'Pueri! Boys! Bring in the oysters!'

There was a smatter of polite applause as Flaccus went back to his couch. He climbed up and reclined between a fat man and a man with long, dark hair pulled back into a ponytail.

A moment later, the heavy curtain was pulled back and three beautiful serving boys with shoulder-length black hair came into the room. They wore short, sleeveless black tunics and they carried bronze tripods, one for each of the couches.

Nubia saw that the bronze bowl of each tripod was filled with crushed ice. On the ice lay oysters, prawns and lobster claws.

Nubia started as the emperor clasped her shoulder again.

'Pass me an oyster, would you, my dear?'

Nubia reached out a trembling hand and picked up one of the oysters on its half-shell and brought it up to him. He took it with his right hand, the one which had been clasping her shoulder, and he held the oyster before her face.

'Open your mouth,' he said, pulling her gently back

with his forearm. 'Open your mouth and tip back your head.'

In this strange embrace, Nubia had no choice but to obey. She tipped back her head until it touched his chest. Then she closed her eyes and opened her mouth. The sharp edge of the shell scraped against her bottom teeth and then the cold, slimy oyster filled her mouth. It tasted of seawater and she tried not to gag as she choked it down.

'Was that good?' He tossed away the shell, and it clattered onto the marble floor.

Nubia's eyes were watering but she nodded bravely.

'Excellent. Now give me one.'

Nubia leaned forward and picked up another oyster from the bed of ice. She turned to see Domitian looking at her, heavy-lidded and with parted lips. He closed his eyes and tipped his head back.

For a heartbeat she considered how easy it would be to slash his detestable throat with the razor-sharp edge of the oyster shell.

But she did not have the courage, so she brought the shell carefully to the imperial mouth and tipped out its contents and watched him swallow it down.

'Mmmm.' He licked his lips. 'Montanus,' he said, opening his eyes to look at the fat man on Flaccus's couch. 'They say you can tell the provenance of an oyster with one bite. Imagine your life depended on it. Where would you say these oysters came from?'

The fat man began to choke so Flaccus slapped him on the back. When the man had recovered, he stared at Domitian with horror-stricken eyes.

'Come, Montanus,' said Domitian. 'Don't be modest. Are they from the Lucrine Lake, perhaps? Or from the sea-beds of Massilia?'

The fat man reached out a trembling hand and took an oyster and brought it to his mouth and tipped it down. He chewed for a moment, swallowed hard and gazed at the emperor imploringly.

'Go on,' chuckled Domitian. 'Try one more.'

With a queasy smile, Montanus dropped the empty shell onto the floor and took another oyster from its bed of ice. His three chins wobbled as he chewed. Some oyster juice dribbled down his chin and he mopped it with his napkin. He mopped his perspiring forehead, too.

'I think,' stammered Montanus, 'that is, I believe . . .'

'Yes?'

'Are the oysters from Rutupiae in the far province of Britannia?'

There was a terrible pause and then Domitian clapped his hands. 'Euge!' he cried. 'Well done, Montanus. You are a true epicure.'

Nubia realised she had been holding her breath. She let it out as quietly as she could, aware that her whole body was trembling again.

'Now,' came Domitian's voice from behind her, 'while we finish off these delicious oysters, who else would like to recite something on the theme of Hades?'

There was another deathly pause, then a small voice said. 'I will.'

Nubia gasped.

The small voice had been Flavia's.

How in the world could her friend find the courage to speak up in a company of Rome's most powerful men, in this terrifying place? Nubia closed her eyes and prayed again. 'Please Lord, give her the words to say . . .'

SCROLL XXI

Flavia's heart was pounding so hard she thought it would burst. Her mouth was dry and her palms were damp. But she knew this was her only chance. The Emperor would not dare refuse her request in front of all these men. If he did, he would look foolish.

Domitian raised an eyebrow in surprise, then beckoned her to rise. 'The person standing before us,' he proclaimed, 'may look like a boy, but it's really a girl in disguise. Or perhaps it's a trained monkey.'

There was nervous laughter in the black triclinium.

'I don't usually allow trained monkeys to perform in public, but I think this might amuse you all. Proceed!' he said to Flavia. 'Recite something about death.'

Flavia glanced at Flaccus. His head was down; he was examining an oyster. A stab of anguish was replaced by a surge of hot anger. Could he not even give her one look of encouragement? Her anger gave her courage. She lifted her chin and turned to Domitian.

She would paraphrase some lines of Ovid she had once memorized for Aristo: the passage where Orpheus asks Pluto to give him back his wife Eurydice. Flavia took a deep breath.

'*I do not come down here, O Deity of Darkness, to see the gloomy realms of Tartarus or to chain up three-headed Cerberus, but because of my wife,'* Flavia paused and corrected herself: *'Because of my friend. I was convinced by Love, a god well known in the world above. I cannot say if he is known down here, but I suspect that even you, O Pluto, have been touched by Love.'*

'Well spoken, Little Monkey,' said Domitian. 'For that I decree that you shall be reunited with the *friend* you were seeking. Guards!' he cried, and clapped his hands. When two guards appeared in the doorway a moment later, he said: 'Take the children and their tutor back to the Emissario. They can join their Jewish friend.' He put a hand on Nubia's shoulder. 'But not this one. This dusky beauty can stay with me.'

'No!' Nubia heard Aristo cry. 'I won't let you touch her again!' He had scrambled to his feet and he was rushing towards Domitian.

But the man with the ponytail had leaped off his couch and now he tackled Aristo. For a moment the two grappled on the black floor among discarded oyster shells. One of the bronze tripods clattered to the floor. Two guards rushed in and pulled out their swords.

'No! Aristo!' cried Nubia, and she began to get off the couch. But Domitian caught her and pulled her roughly back into his arms.

Nubia gasped as one of the guards struck Aristo's face with the butt of his gladius. 'Aristo!' she sobbed. 'Don't fight them. They'll hurt you.'

Aristo raised his head. His mouth was bleeding and his eyes were dazed. 'Nubia,' he said. 'Nubia, I love you.'

'Ha!' cried Domitian, squeezing Nubia tight in his excitement. 'This is better than anything I had planned.'

The other guard began to kick Aristo.

'Stop!' Domitian laughed. 'Don't harm him! Take him

to the theatre. This is too good an opportunity to miss.'

The guards nodded and manhandled Aristo out of the black triclinium.

Nubia heard the smile in Domitian's voice. 'I was just about to put on a little gladiatorial show and a beast-fight,' he announced to the astonished diners, 'and I hope you will all attend.' Then Nubia felt his breath hot in her ear as he whispered. 'Especially you, my dear. Your handsome Greek lover is going to be the main attraction.'

'Oh, Jonathan!' said Flavia as she finished telling him what had just happened. 'This is the worst situation we've ever been in.'

Jonathan looked at her from his swollen eyes and gave a single nod. He was wheezing from his asthma.

Two guards had used vines to tie Flavia and Lupus to the other side of his sluice gate. Outside, the sun had passed its zenith and the dark shadow of the mountain combined with the overhanging oak and the screen of vine tendrils made the light in the vault a gloomy green.

'And Nubia is alone with Domitian. Oh, I can't bear to think about it. Oh, Jonathan, Lupus, what are we going to do?'

Lupus nodded down towards his waist. He was still wearing his long black tunic and his hands were tied behind his back, just below hers.

'What? What do you want? Oh! Our belt-pouches are underneath the black tunics. The guards didn't see them!'

Lupus nodded excitedly.

'You want something from your belt pouch?'

Lupus grunted yes.

'Your wax tablet?'

Lupus grunted no.

'The needle-sharp stylus?'

Lupus shook his head.

'You have to move a little,' said Flavia. 'That's right . . . So I can roll the outer tunic . . . up enough.' After several attempts Flavia got her fingers under the tunic and found his belt. 'Suck in your stomach,' she grunted, 'so I can pull the belt around . . . and there! I think I can open it . . .' She closed her eyes and concentrated on trying to undo the tie. 'Opened it!' she grunted at last, and then felt inside: 'An oyster shell. Lupus, you're brilliant! You took one from off the floor! And it's–ow! It's razor-sharp! I don't think I can do it. My fingers are getting numb.'

Lupus grunted and squirmed until she felt his fingers take the oyster shell carefully from hers. Awkwardly, he began to saw at the vine binding her hands.

As Lupus worked away at her bonds, Flavia told Jonathan her theory about how the murder had been committed. She wasn't sure he was listening, but she knew if she kept talking she could keep the panic at bay. She had just finished explaining about how stingray poison was deadly if treated with cold water, when Jonathan cut her off.

'Why did you come here?' he said angrily.

Flavia looked over at him in surprise. 'To save you.'

'I'm not asking you why you came here to Alba Longa.' Jonathan's chains clinked as he shifted a little. 'I'm asking why you came back to Italia after I told you not to follow me. I told you it would be dangerous. So why did you come?'

'To help you,' said Flavia in a small voice. 'To see home. To clear our names.'

'I told you I would try to do that. Now you've ruined everything.'

Flavia felt Lupus stop sawing the vine.

'It's what we do,' she said. 'We solve mysteries. We're trying to prove Domitian killed his brother. We needed more evidence.'

Behind her, Lupus resumed work with his sharp oyster shell.

'That's what I thought,' wheezed Jonathan. 'You don't really care about people. All you care about is solving mysteries.'

'But Jonathan, the Truth is important. It helps people.'

'Who says?'

Flavia was speechless.

'Who says the Truth ... is always good?' persisted Jonathan. He was wheezing.

'Jonathan, if we can prove Domitian killed Titus, then the senate will appoint a better man: Flavius Sabinus. And then the world will be a safer place.'

'Who's to say ... the man they appoint ... will be better than Domitian?' wheezed Jonathan.

'Because ...' Flavia spluttered, 'Because anybody would be better than Domitian. He's evil. He made us kiss his feet. He killed his brother. He's probably going to molest Nubia and to throw Aristo to the lions, and if Lupus doesn't cut this vine soon he's going to kill us, too.'

Nubia sat in an upper room of Domitian's Alban Citadel weeping tears of joy and anguish. Joy, because Aristo loved her, and anguish because now he was going to die. And now she wanted to die, too.

She heard the squeak of a door opening behind her and a man's voice said: 'Undress.'

Nubia turned around. The man was wearing a patrician's tunic rather than a black one and his face was in shadow, but she thought she recognised him from the banquet.

'Did the emperor not tell you to put on a gold shift and to paint your face?'

Nubia sniffed and nodded.

'I can hear you sobbing and I'm guessing you have not done so.'

Nubia frowned through her tears. She was still wearing the black tunic. Couldn't he see that?

'Domitian sent me,' said the man, 'because I am blind.' He stepped forward and she saw that his heavy-lidded eyes were clouded. He had a short, blunt nose, a cleft chin and pockmarked skin. His face was devoid of humour or kindness. Nubia shivered.

'My name is Messallinus. Lucius Valerius Catullus Messallinus. This is Domitia's dressing room. Do you see the wooden chest?'

Nubia nodded.

'Answer me!'

'Yes,' stammered Nubia.

'Go to it.'

Nubia stood and went to a gilded cedarwood chest. The lid was open and it was full of shifts and stolas in jewel-coloured silks.

'The emperor wants you to dress in gold, to match your eyes. Find something suitable and put it on, or I will do it for you.' His voice sent a chill through her and she remembered Jonathan saying that a blind man named Messallinus had enjoyed whipping him.

Nubia searched through the clothing and found a simple gold shift.

'Have you found it?'

'Yes.'

'Put it on.'

Although he claimed to be blind, Nubia turned her back to the man. She tugged off both tunics and hastily slipped on the gold shift. It was gossamer light and silky smooth.

Nubia used the brown tunic to dry her tear-streaked face.

'Put on the gilded belt and sandals,' said Messallinus.

Nubia rummaged among the silky tunics until she found a belt in the form of a gold snake. It took her a moment to realise that the clasp was the mouth of the snake biting the tail. She put it on. The gilded sandals were under the table. She sat on the couch. They were a little too big so she laced them up tightly.

'Now go to the table,' commanded Messallinus. 'Put colour on your lips and cheeks. And make up your eyes in the Egyptian style. Blue or green for the lids and black eyeliner around. Can you do that?' His voice was cold. 'Or shall I do it for you?'

'I will do it,' stammered Nubia.

The window was near a small west-facing window, and a beam of slanting sunshine fell on a selection of gold, silver and ivory hairpins, making them glitter. A silver one was particularly long and sharp.

'Are you ready?' he asked, as she applied some shimmering coral powder to her lips.

'Almost.' Nubia carefully took the silver hairpin from Domitia's table and slipped it into the neck of her tunic, between the bandages binding her breasts. Then she stood up and turned to face the blind man.

'Now I am ready.'

SCROLL XXII

Nubia emerged blinking into the brilliant afternoon light.

Surrounded by a crowd of courtiers, Domitian stood on a lawn that glowed like chrysolite. He looked up as Nubia and Messallinus approached.

'Ravishing,' he said. 'You look ravishing, as I knew you would.' He had changed into a purple toga but still wore the dark-leafed garland.

Domitian held out his hand. 'Come.'

She took his hand and kept her face impassive, a trick she had learned when she had first been enslaved, two and a half years before.

'We don't even have to leave the grounds of my villa,' he said. 'There is a charming theatre at the other end of the terrace.' In the harsh light of day, she could see his face was powdered in an attempt to cover some spots on his chin. He also wore a beauty patch on his forehead. She knew such patches were the latest fashion among high-class men and women, but she suspected it covered a boil or a wart.

'Walk with me,' he said. 'The theatre is not far.'

They began to walk along a path between low box hedges, splashing fountains and flowerbeds in different shapes. The sea glittered far to the west, and a soft breeze carried its scent.

Nubia's heart was full of a terrible fierce joy. Aristo loved her. He had said it in front of everyone, and she had seen the passion in his eyes. But now he was going to die. Before she could tell him she felt the same way. Before they could experience one kiss. Before they could share one embrace.

She reached up her free hand and quickly touched the place where she had hidden the silver hairpin. It was safe. She allowed herself a secret smile of triumph. She would not give Domitian the pleasure of making her watch Aristo die. She would kill herself first.

Nubia entered Domitian's private theatre by means of a hidden corridor beneath the cavea. He had sent most of his courtiers ahead and stopped for a moment in the dim corridor to adjust the folds of his purple toga. For a moment Nubia considered running away, but she could see two guards at the opening, silhouetted against brilliant daylight. On the frescoed wall behind Domitian, a satyr seemed to be laughing at her plight.

Then Domitian took her hand and led her blinking out into the brilliant daylight. She felt like Persephone on the arm of Pluto, emerging from her six months in the Underworld.

Every seat in the small marble theatre was taken, mostly by men. They had risen to their feet and were applauding, and Nubia saw many of them were looking at her. She scanned the faces hopefully, especially those in the rows closest to the front. She saw some of the men from the banquet. But Flaccus was not there, and Ascletario was nowhere to be seen, either.

Now Domitian was guiding her to the front seats and she saw a large marble throne with griffin armrests. To her relief, he indicated that she should sit on a footstool; the throne was obviously meant for him alone.

Nubia sat trembling at the emperor's feet, anxiously scanning the stage and its backdrop for some sign of Aristo. She did not see him, or anyone else, but she saw that the circular part of the theatre below the stage – the orchestra – had been covered with sand and fenced off to make it an arena. The fence was not high, but guards stood every three paces, and they held spears and nets.

Now that she was sitting still with time to reflect, another strong mixture of emotions swept over her. Elation that Aristo loved her. Helpless despair that he was to be thrown to the beasts. Loathing of the Romans for their love of blood sports. She was also aware of the sharp pin hidden in her breast band.

She took a deep breath. She wasn't afraid of death – she knew where she was going – but she was afraid of dying. Would it hurt? Would a single pin in her heart even kill her?

Behind her, the theatre erupted into fresh cheers as a man walked out onto the stage above the arena. It was one of the men from the banquet, the one who had tackled Aristo. Most of Domitian's courtiers looked the same to her, but this one was recognizable by his long, dark hair tied back in a ponytail.

'It is my honour,' said Ponytail, 'to welcome you to this intimate show for our new emperor. The emperor has much to do; he has already spent three mornings granting amnesty and wiping tablets clean.' More cheers. 'In the weeks to come he will rebuild temples and restore altars. He will repair aqueducts and pipe water to thirsty places.

He will reduce taxes and increase benefaction.' This last statement got the biggest cheer of all. 'But today,' continued Ponytail, 'he craves your indulgence in a small private celebration of his accession to the seat of power.' The man glanced quickly down at a sheet of papyrus. 'In a short time we will have two pairs of gladiators to fight for your pleasure. But first, for your amusement, a battle of strength and grace. All the way from Crete, your new emperor presents Theseus and the Bull!'

Nubia's heart was pounding so hard she thought she might be sick. They were going to match Aristo with a bull.

The crowd gasped as an enormous bull burst into the sandy orchestra beneath the stage. Nubia was so close that she could see the bull's eyes, long-lashed and bloodshot. She could smell his fear and rage and she could hear him perfectly: his deep grunts and snorts. The bull was so big, so angry. How would Aristo ever defeat it?

The crowd cheered as a long-haired youth in a sky blue loincloth vaulted over the wooden barrier and did a backflip. Nubia almost fainted with relief. It was not Aristo.

She had never been this close to such a contest; she was only feet away, close enough to see the concentration in the young man's dark eyes and the sheen of oil on his slim torso.

The bull pawed the sand, then charged the acrobat called Theseus. He let it come and at the last moment he stepped casually aside, leaving less than a handsbreadth between him and the massive creature. The crowd gasped, and applauded. Again the bull charged, again the youth let him thunder past, this time turning his back to the furious creature and smiling at the crowd with his kohl-lined eyes.

For a few moments, Nubia forgot everything else. The battle of boy and beast was enthralling. The youth avoided each charge with a different manoeuvre: he knelt, he twirled, he did a backflip.

Now Nubia could see that the bull was tiring, and she knew the youth could see it, too: there was a slight change in his expression. Although he was still smiling, his eyes narrowed a fraction in concentration. The bull charged and this time the youth took a deep breath and then ran towards it. Nubia gasped as the boy grasped the bull's horns and did a high somersault over the charging beast, twisting in the air and landing lightly on the sand a moment after the bull thundered past.

Nubia was on her feet cheering and clapping. So was every man in the theatre, Domitian included.

They remained on their feet and cheered as the youth did it again, and again. On his fourth jump the acrobat seemed to do the impossible: he landed lightly on the bull's back and rode him around the arena. The boys' arms were outstretched and his long dark hair flew behind. He wore a huge smile of triumph. The crowd was wild with delight. Nubia was cheering and clapping, too.

Suddenly she felt hands on her shoulders, turning her, and Domitian was pressing his full wet lips against her mouth. He released her before she could protest and she whirled away in horror.

For a moment Nubia stood breathing hard, overcome with fear and revulsion. Then, with trembling hand, she reached into the neck of her tunic. Before she killed herself, she would kill him. While the crowd was still distracted and cheering, she would drive the silver pin deep into the pulsing artery of his thick and loathsome neck.

'Titus Flavius Domitianus!' came a woman's imperious voice. 'What do you think you're doing?'

Nubia started, and the pin fell onto the marble step at her feet. She turned to see a middle-aged woman in a tall, elaborately-curled wig.

'Domitia?' said the emperor. His smile stiffened as he addressed his wife. 'What are you doing here? I thought you were in Rome.'

The crowd was still applauding and Domitia gestured towards the arena. 'I think your attention is required.'

'What?' said Domitian. He turned just in time to see the acrobat cut the throat of the kneeling bull and then raise a bloody knife triumphantly aloft. Nubia saw the blood gushing from the bull's severed throat, and the dying animal gasping its last. The panting boy wiped the knife on the bull's back, replaced it in its sheath and smiled up at the emperor.

'Oh,' said Domitian. 'Yes, of course.' He held out his hand and one of his courtier's put a small but heavy leather pouch in his palm. Domitian tossed the bag of gold to the youth, who caught it deftly and bowed. Then Domitian took a proffered wreath and spun that to the boy. The boy caught the wreath and placed it on his head. The crowd cheered as he did a backflip onto the stage, then disappeared through a door in the scaena.

Without a pause, three dwarves ran onto the stage, while attendants used hooks to drag the bull's body out of the arena.

'Who is this?' said Domitia, looking Nubia up and down. 'Why is she wearing my clothes?' She bent down and picked up the silver hairpin. 'Why is she using my hairpins?' She glared at Domitian. 'What did I tell you last week?'

'It's not what you think,' stammered Domitian. 'My dear, I knew you were coming and I ... er ... I planned this especially for you.'

'What? You planned what?'

Domitian turned away from her and patted his right hand, like an orator motioning for silence. He was saying something in Ponytail's ear. The courtier nodded and went to the chief guard at the perimeter of the arena. Nubia saw them exchange words and then the guard disappeared backstage.

The crowd was applauding the three dwarves, who had just finished their juggling act.

And now Ponytail was stepping back on stage.

'Please welcome our empress Domitia!' he cried. 'Straight from the Palatine Hill.'

The crowd cheered. The Empress turned and bowed, then sat on Domitian's throne and pulled him down beside her.

'For you, O exalted one,' bellowed Ponytail, 'your princeps and emperor has prepared a special amusement: Aristo and the Beast!'

SCROLL XXIII

In the mouth of the Emissario, Lupus had almost cut through Flavia's bonds when someone parted the screen of tendrils to enter the vaulted chamber. Lupus immediately dropped the shell and wriggled around to see who it was. Beside him Flavia hurriedly did the same.

Two men stepped into the green gloom of the Emissario vault on Jonathan's side of the channel.

As they came closer, Lupus saw that one of the men wore a long grass-green caftan. It was the Egyptian astrologist, Ascletario. The other man wore a toga over the tunic of a patrician, with its two vertical blood-red stripes. He held a whip in one hand and a plate of food in the other. Ascletario's hand was on the patrician's elbow; he was guiding him. As they came closer, Lupus saw the milky film on the man's unseeing eyes.

Lupus's blood grew cold, and he exchanged a worried look with Flavia. He knew she was thinking the same thing: the patrician was the blind man called Messallinus who enjoyed whipping Jonathan.

'Good afternoon, Jonathan,' said Messallinus. 'It's dinner time again. What will you have today? Cold chicken, apples and bread? Or the whip?' Messallinus made a gesture with his chin and Ascletario moved forward to unlock Jonathan's manacles. He darted an apologetic look at Lupus and Flavia. Lupus glared back.

Jonathan slowly stood up, wincing and rubbing his raw wrists. He was wheezing a little.

'Ox tread on your tongue?' said Messallinus to Jonathan. And to Ascletario: 'Tie him to the wheel.'

Ascletario pulled off Jonathan's tattered tunic and turned him to face the sluice gate. Then he began to bind his hands to the horizontal iron wheel that raised and lowered the grille.

Jonathan was now bent over awkwardly, wearing only a grubby loincloth. Lupus swallowed hard as he saw the weals on Jonathan's back. Some were still bloody.

When Ascletario finished tying Jonathan's hands, he backed away and stood behind the blind man.

'All you have to do to get the dinner,' said Messallinus, 'is to tell me the truth. Not lies. The truth.'

Lupus heard Jonathan mutter something under his breath.

'What?' said Messallinus. 'I didn't hear you over the sound of the water.'

Jonathan looked over his shoulder. 'I said I *have* been telling you the truth.'

'No.' Messallinus smiled. He held out the plate. Ascletario took it and backed hastily away. Messallinus was caressing the whip with his free hand. 'No, I don't believe you have. Let me ask you again. Who killed Titus?'

Jonathan was silent.

The blind man drew back his right arm and let fly with the whip. Its crack and Jonathan's cry of pain came at the same moment.

Lupus winced. *Please God*, he prayed silently. *Please help Jonathan.*

'Who killed Titus?' said the blind man.

'I don't know!' wheezed Jonathan.

Again the crack of the whip and this time Flavia screamed along with Jonathan. Lupus looked at her and saw that the tip of the whip had caught her across the cheek, leaving an ugly red weal.

'Who was that?' asked the blind man sharply.

'The girl, the girl, the girl,' said Ascletario. 'One of the children who tried to rescue him. I told you they were here.'

'What is your name, girl?' asked Messallinus.

'Flavia Gemina,' she said. Lupus could feel her trembling.

'The mute boy is there, too,' said Ascletario. 'His name is Lupus.'

'Lupus and Flavia,' said Messallinus. 'You are friends of Jonathan?'

'Yes,' said Flavia in a small voice.

'Excellent. Ascletario, take down the boy. Tie the girl up instead.'

'No!' cried Flavia. 'Please!' She was sobbing.

Lupus gritted his teeth and stared down at the rough stone floor. If only he'd been able to cut through Flavia's bonds. Or if only she had cut his.

But his hands were still bound and he was helpless.

Nubia sat heavily on the stool at Domitian's feet and stared bleakly at the small circular arena. Aristo and the Beast. What creature was Domitian going to pit against Aristo? A rhino? A tiger? A bear?

The world swam around her as a door opened in the backdrop of the stage and two guards brought out Aristo. They had stripped and oiled him and dressed him in a red leather loincloth. His eyes were lined with kohl to make them stand out, and his lips were stained pink. He also had a belt with a small dagger, like the Cretan youth's.

The crowd cheered and Nubia heard Domitia purr: 'What a beautiful young man. He looks like a Greek god.'

'Just wait until you see what I have in store for him,' said Domitian with a chuckle.

Nubia took a deep breath. She must stay alive long enough to tell Aristo how she felt; to tell him that she loved him, too. Then she would kill herself. Domitia had taken her pin, but she could throw herself into the arena with him. They would die together and be united in Paradise this very day.

The guards pushed Aristo off the stage and into the arena. He fell on his hands and knees, then picked himself up and looked around. Nubia knew he was looking for her, so she stood up. He saw her at once, and his kohl-lined eyes widened. She remembered she was wearing Egyptian eye-paint, too, and a golden shift. What must he think?

Before she could call out to him, a woman's hand on her shoulder pressed her firmly down. 'Sit down, girl!' hissed Domitia. 'You're blocking my view.'

Then the animal gate rattled from the other side, as if something big had rammed it. Aristo tore his eyes from Nubia's. She saw him catch sight of the trail of blood on the sand left by the bull and his eyes widened in horror as he followed the trail to the gate.

'Yes,' whispered Nubia. 'That is the gate the Beast will enter.'

Aristo pulled out his dagger and faced the gate. He crouched slightly, waiting, alert, silent.

The crowd gasped as the gate burst open. Then the entire theatre burst into roars of laughter.

A small black rabbit hopped out onto the sand, and its pink nose twitched as it stared up at Aristo.

'Kill the fierce beast, Pretty Boy!' called a nasal patrician voice behind Nubia.

'Yes!' cried several other men. 'Kill the Beast!'

Nubia's face went cold, and then hot.

The crowd was laughing at Aristo. They were mocking him. They thought he was just a beautiful young Greek, probably a slave. They didn't know he was a gifted musician and a wonderful teacher.

'Use your bare hands!' jeered the nasal voice again.

'No!' rasped someone else. 'See if you can capture the beast alive!'

The whole theatre burst out laughing again.

Without taking his eyes from the rabbit, Aristo slowly replaced his knife in its scabbard. Suddenly he dived for the rabbit. He caught it, but his arms must have been too oily, for the rabbit slipped away and hopped a few paces behind him.

The crowd was in pandemonium.

Nubia glanced behind her and saw the emperor doubled over, helpless with mirth. Domitia was crying with laughter, too, the tears making tracks down her powdered cheeks.

Aristo scrambled to his feet, sand sticking to his oily skin. He whirled around and crouched, ready to leap. But the rabbit hopped away a moment before he landed, and he ended up face-first in the sand.

The crowd roared with laughter. Nubia's eyes filled with tears of embarrassment and outrage.

He stood up again, coated in sand; shaking it from his hair, spitting it out of his mouth.

Nubia hid her face in her hands.

She peeped through her fingers in time to see him leap for the rabbit yet again. But this time he succeeded in keeping hold of it.

This drew a standing ovation, and now the men were throwing coins at him, and the chant arose: 'Pretty Boy! Pretty Boy! Pretty Boy!'

Domitian rose majestically to his feet, using the corner of his purple robe to wipe the tears from his cheeks.

He faced his delighted audience and gestured for silence. Presently they were quiet.

'Thank you, pretty boy Aristo!' he proclaimed, nodding over his shoulder. 'For giving us the best performance of my short reign.'

'Hear, hear!' shouted the crowds. 'Euge!'

Aristo's smooth, muscular chest was rising and falling with exertion or fear, or both. He was clutching the rabbit tightly and he was looking at Domitian. Nubia knew he was wondering what this sadistic emperor had in store for him next.

'Pretty Boy Aristo!' proclaimed Domitian. 'I have a very special reward for you!'

Now the blood drained from Aristo's face and for a moment Nubia thought he might faint. This might be her last chance to tell him how she felt about him. So she took a deep breath and rose trembling to her feet.

'Aristo, I love you!' she called out. 'I love you!'

'I am sorry, I am sorry, I am sorry,' muttered Ascletario, as he bent to untie Flavia's hands. Flavia felt him pause and she knew he must have seen the cuts in the vine made by Lupus's oyster shell. But he made no comment. He resumed fumbling at her bonds. In a moment she would be free. Her mind was racing.

She knew this was their best chance for escape. Ascletario had unchained Jonathan from the sluice gate, and although he was bruised and beaten, he was mobile. In a moment her hands would be free, too. If she could just push Ascletario into the channel of water, they could easily elude the blind man. Or maybe push him in, too.

Then she would untie Lupus, and together they could take Jonathan across the lake to Tranquillus's house. Then they would rescue Nubia and Aristo.

At last the vine fell away from her wrists. As Ascletario helped her up, Flavia lowered her head and charged at his stomach.

But the Egyptian twisted away and now his hand was like a vice on her wrist. 'If you try this again I will throw you in the water,' he said, and for the first time he sounded really angry. On the stone wall were some metal brackets for torches. Ascletario tied her wrists to one of these, so that her arms were above her head and her back to the channel.

'It's too tight,' she said, fresh tears filling her eyes. 'And my cheek hurts, too.'

'Do you hear that, boy?' said Messallinus. He had manacled Jonathan to the sluice gate again. 'We're hurting your little girlfriend.'

Flavia twisted to look over her shoulder at Jonathan. He stood swaying on his feet and shivering. He wore only a soiled loincloth and she could see all his ribs. They must have been starving him as well as beating him. He was so weak they had not bothered to tie him up.

'Jonathan!' she pleaded. 'If you know something, tell them.'

Jonathan did not reply.

Across the channel, Messallinus drew the whip through his hand and gave it an experimental crack. 'I can tell where you are by the sound of your whimpering,' he said. 'Let us discover if this whip is long enough to reach you.'

Flavia turned and faced the cold, unfeeling rock and cringed. 'Jonathan. Please.'

The whip cracked and Flavia screamed. Even through two tunics she felt a searing stripe of pain flash across her back.

'All right!' wheezed Jonathan. 'I'll tell you . . . who killed Titus . . . It was me!'

SCROLL XXIV

'I killed Titus!' gasped Jonathan. 'I am the guilty one.'

Flavia opened her eyes and turned to stare over her shoulder at Jonathan.

'You?' said Messallinus. 'I find that hard to believe.'

'I killed him!' cried Jonathan. 'I killed him because he destroyed Jerusalem and ruined my life. He was a monster!' wheezed Jonathan. 'That's why I killed him.'

Flavia felt sick.

Now she understood why Jonathan had not wanted her to follow him.

Now she understood why he had been angry when they appeared.

Now she finally understood why he had said the Truth was not always a good thing.

'Tell me how,' said the blind interrogator Messallinus. 'Tell me exactly how you killed the emperor.'

'I used poison,' said Jonathan.

Even above the gurgle of water Flavia could hear his teeth chattering.

'The truth at last,' said Messallinus. He laid the whip on the ground and moved closer. 'What kind of poison did you use, Jonathan?'

'Venom of a trygon,' said Jonathan through his battered lips.

Although Flavia's hands were still tied above her head, she managed to twist her whole body to see him.

'I don't know what that is,' said Messallinus.

'A sea creature,' wheezed Jonathan. 'Also known as stingray. Trygon is the Greek word. Its poison is deadly.'

'Yes,' said Ascletario. 'Yes, that fits the prophecy. *Like Odysseus from the sea . . .'*

Messallinus nodded, took off his toga and wrapped it around Jonathan's bare shoulders. 'See? That wasn't so difficult.' Then he held out his hand. 'Give me the dinner, Ascletario.'

Ascletario picked the plate up from the stone ledge and put it in Messallinus's outstretched hand. The blind man took a piece of chicken from the plate and sniffed it. 'What puzzles me,' he said to Jonathan, 'is that the emperor always had a taster.' Messallinus took a bite of the chicken and chewed it thoughtfully. 'Mmmm. Seems all right.'

'The poison wasn't in his food,' said Jonathan. Flavia saw that his eyes were fixed on the piece of chicken. 'I used another method.'

'You must have,' said Messallinus. 'His tasters were very capable.' He held up the piece of chicken. 'Would you like some?'

Jonathan nodded and took the chicken and tore at it ravenously.

Messallinus put the plate on the floor. 'Tell me, Jonathan. How did you administer the poison?'

'I couldn't get at Titus when he was on the Palatine Hill,' said Jonathan through a mouthful of chicken. He swallowed. 'So I waited until he left for the Sabine Hills. Everybody knew he was going home.' Jonathan devoured the last shreds of chicken, then broke the bone in half and sucked out the marrow.

'Excellent, excellent,' said Messallinus. He bent and groped and took an apple from the plate and held it out. 'Tell me more.'

Jonathan snatched the apple and bit into it. 'When the emperor left Rome,' he said through his mouthful. 'I was waiting outside the gate. I followed behind the cortege, disguised as a charcoal-seller.'

'Yes?' said Messallinus. 'Go on.'

'When the cortege stopped at a roadside tavern, I had my chance. I heard Ascletario asking where the latrines were. I got there first, and when the emperor came in I was already there, sitting on the bench with my hood up. I had some of the venom on a sharp object and as I stood up, I gave him a quick prick on the leg.' Jonathan ate the core of the apple. 'He thought he'd been bitten by a spider.'

'What sharp object?' said Messallinus. 'A dagger?'

Jonathan reached out a hand. 'May I have that piece of bread?'

Messallinus bent and groped for the piece of bread. When he had it he said again: 'I repeat the question: what sharp object?'

'Um ... I used ... a quill,' stammered Jonathan. 'The quill of a sea-urchin.'

Flavia stifled a gasp.

Messallinus turned and cocked his head at her. 'Yes?' he said. 'Do you have something to add?'

'My wrists hurt,' she whimpered. 'I can't feel my hands. Please untie me?'

He looked at her with his terrible blank eyes, then said to Ascletario: 'Unbind her. And the mute boy, too. The Emperor will want to hear this. And I don't want to bring him here. It's damp.'

Messallinus pressed the piece of bread into Jonathan's hands and turned to Ascletario. 'Get this one bathed and dressed,' he said. 'He smells. The Emperor will want to interview him and I don't want him to have to endure a stinking murderer.'

An hour later, Jonathan sank down into the scented water of a hot plunge in the baths of Domitian's Alban Citadel and tried not to cry out as the wounds on his back sang with pain. Presently the agony subsided to a bearable throb and he closed his eyes. The steam helped him breathe a little easier.

He had done it. He had confessed to the murder of Titus. Would his execution be swift or lingering?

He let himself sink right under the water, until he was completely submerged. The thought occurred to him that he himself could choose the manner of his going, as the philosopher Seneca always urged. All he had to do was open his mouth and breathe in water. Then the pain in his back would be gone and the pain in his spirit, too. He would be in a better place: a place with no pain and no tears. He would be in the Garden.

A hand closed around his neck and pulled him up out of the bath. Jonathan choked and spat out water and opened his eyes to see a muscular guard in full armour.

'Emperor would be very angry if I let you drown,' said the guard, shaking drops of water from his arm. 'I might end up drowned, myself. Get out. Go dry yourself. There's a doctor waiting to put balm on your stripes.'

After Jonathan's confession, Ascletario had taken Flavia and Lupus up to Domitian's Alban Citadel, to a room on the third floor. The room was flooded with the golden light of late afternoon. Flavia went to the window and looked out. She could see the flat coastal plain far below her, and beyond it the Tyrrhenian Sea. A path of dazzling gold led from the coast to the horizon; the sun would soon be setting. She knew her beloved Ostia was only twenty miles away as the crow flies. She tried to make out the thread of smoke from the lighthouse at Portus. But she couldn't find it, so she turned to look at Lupus, who was investigating the room for means of escape.

'Lupus,' she said. 'Do you think Jonathan really killed Titus?'

Lupus looked at her, pursed his lips in thought, then shrugged and nodded.

'I don't understand it. I thought he had changed. In Ephesus he seemed so calm. He seemed full of ... something. Peace. Contentment. Purpose. I don't know.'

Lupus unflipped his wax tablet and wrote: HIS REASONS MADE SENSE

'I know,' murmured Flavia. 'But something about his story doesn't make sense.'

Lupus sat on a purple-cushioned ivory couch and shrugged, as if to say: what?

'He was so detailed about the poison he used and how he administered it. But then at the last moment he said he used the quill of a sea-urchin.'

Lupus nodded, then raised his eyebrows and turned up the palms of his hands: And?

'But we found that needle-sharp stylus in the latrines. Do you still have it?'

Lupus nodded and reached under the black silk tunic and fished in his belt pouch. A moment later he produced the stylus in its papyrus wrapping.

Flavia carefully unwrapped the bronze stylus and let it

roll onto the inlaid wooden surface of a side table.

'This has to be the murder weapon,' murmured Flavia. 'I pricked my finger on it and that's what gave me the fever. Great Juno's peacock!' exclaimed Flavia suddenly. 'Do you realise what this is?'

Lupus frowned and shrugged.

'This stylus is proof,' said Flavia, 'that Jonathan *didn't* kill Titus!'

SCROLL XXV

Jonathan lay naked on his stomach, on towel spread over a couch in the apodyterium of Domitian's private baths. Presently he heard the swishing robes of the doctor and felt gentle hands smooth a cooling balm on his wounds. The cream hurt as it went on, but then the pain subsided and he felt a delicious numbness.

'That's good,' he wheezed.

'Sit up,' said a voice in Aramaic.

Jonathan twisted to see who it was. He saw a thin young man with curling sidelocks and a turban: a Jew. The man had large dark eyes in a pale ascetic face. His small mouth was curved into a smile. 'I'll wrap your ribs in strips of linen soaked in aloes,' said the doctor, 'and I want to put some salve on your face, too. I'm just brewing a beaker of ephedron for your asthma.'

'Ben Aruva,' said Jonathan. He wrapped the towel around his waist and sat up.

The Jew's smile faded and his eyebrows went up. 'You know my name?' And then he said, 'Of course you do. You preceded us all the way from Rome to Reate.'

'I'd heard about you before that,' wheezed Jonathan. 'In the Jewish quarter in Transtiberim they talk of you.'

'I don't know Rome very well,' said the young doctor. 'I was born and raised in Alexandria. Here, let me put some balm on your cheekbone for that bruise.'

The doctor's touch was gentle but firm, and the cream soon took away the pain of his bruise. Ben Aruva put the ceramic pot of balm on a table and took a metal pan from the brazier. He poured some steaming liquid from the pan into a ceramic beaker and handed it to Jonathan.

Jonathan took the cup. It smelled like ephedron but there was another unidentifiable smell. He hesitated.

'Drink the brew,' said Ben Aruva, as he turned away to roll up the unused bandages. 'If the emperor had wanted you dead then he would have killed you before your bath, not after.'

Flavia and Lupus gazed out a window of Domitian's Alban Citadel. The sun was setting, sinking into the Tyrrhenian sea, bathing the room with cherry-red light.

'Ever since Vesuvius erupted,' murmured Flavia, 'every sunset in the world is blood-red.'

Beside her Lupus nodded, then turned as the door behind them opened.

'Jonathan!' cried Flavia. She was going to embrace him but Lupus caught her wrist and shook his head, and she remembered that Jonathan's body was bruised and beaten, and his back raw.

'Are you all right?' she asked him. 'I see they gave you some fresh clothes.'

He nodded. 'I had a bath. And a doctor put balm on my back and bandaged my ribs. Is that food?'

'Yes,' said Flavia, as he went to the table. 'But we didn't taste any, in case it's poisoned.'

'It won't be poisoned,' said Jonathan, taking a handful of dark blue grapes. 'If they wanted us dead, they'd have killed us back in that water channel.'

'Jonathan,' said Flavia, 'thank you for what you did back there in the Emissario. Confessing it was you who murdered Titus. I know you did that to protect me.'

Jonathan was at the table and his back was still towards her.

'What do you mean?' he said, his mouth full.

'I know you didn't kill Titus.'

He turned slowly and looked at her. He had a piece of cheese in his hand.

'Yes, I did.'

'Why do you keep saying that?'

His eyes flickered around the room, wary and nervous. 'I keep saying that because it's true.'

'No, it isn't. You didn't even know what the murder weapon was. And I think the murderer would know a thing like that.'

Jonathan stepped forward and lowered his voice, 'What are you talking about.'

'The murder weapon was a needle-sharp stylus,' said Flavia. 'Like the one Domitian uses.' She went to the side-table and carefully picked up the stylus. 'We found this in the latrines of the Inn of Romulus. There was venom on the tip. If you had been the one who killed Titus, you would have known that. But you didn't know. You guessed a sea-urchin's quill. Ergo: you didn't murder Titus.'

Jonathan was staring at her, his face pale.

'The stylus was my first choice,' he stammered. 'But I dropped it, so I had to use the sea-urchin's quill as a back-up.'

'No,' said Flavia softly. 'I know you changed in Ephesus. I saw it in your eyes. You came back to help Titus, not to harm him. Unless you discovered something terrible about him, and I doubt that because we already know the worst of what he did. Or unless . . . Eureka!'

He stared in dismay.

'You're protecting someone!'

'Be quiet, Flavia.' He had begun to wheeze again.

'You know who the real murderer is!'

'Shut up!' he cried.

'You know who the real murderer is and you're protecting him and that means . . . Great Juno's beard! I know who did it!'

'Do you indeed?' came a voice from the wall. The three friends turned to see a panel in the wall sliding open. The emperor Domitian stood there, along with Ascletario, Vibius Crispus, two guards and a pale young Jew in a turban.

'If you know who really murdered my brother,' said Domitian, 'I would be most obliged if you would tell me.'

Flavia stared at Domitian in dismay. His dark eyes burned with a cold anger.

'I knew it!' cried Jonathan, rounding on Flavia. 'I knew this was a trap. That's why they let me go. That's why they put us together in the same room.'

'Oh, Jonathan. I'm sorry. I'm so sorry.'

'If you do not tell me,' said Domitian, 'I will see that your deaths are long and painful and public.' The red light of the sunset gave the emperor's face a ghastly sheen. 'If you do tell me, then I promise to spare the lives of you and your friends.' He turned to Crispus. 'Bring in our newlyweds.'

Without turning, blind Crispus beckoned.

Nubia and Aristo came into the room, hand in hand. Nubia wore a gold silk shift, Aristo a red-leather loincloth and red boots, but very little else. Both wore eye-make-up.

Flavia stared in disbelief. 'Newlyweds?' she gasped. 'What do you mean?'

'I had them join hands in my little theatre an hour ago,' said Domitian. 'They exchanged vows. Two hundred men witnessed their marriage, as well as my wife, the empress Domitia. She was so pleased. She cried tears of happiness. You see, Nubia here was Aristo's prize for vanquishing a fierce beast.' He giggled and then stopped, his face serious again. 'The newlyweds will die first,' he said, 'without even having shared a kiss, unless you name the person who killed my brother.'

Flavia looked at Nubia and Aristo, holding hands and gazing back at her anxiously. She looked at Jonathan, his eyes pleading her not to tell. She looked at Lupus, and saw understanding dawn on his face. He looked at her and set his jaw and gave a small nod.

Flavia turned back to Domitian. 'If I tell you, will you promise to let us go back to Ostia and live there?'

Domitian shook his head. 'No. The most I can promise is twenty-four hours to depart this country and never come back. If you do that, then I swear by Minerva – the goddess I hold most dear – I will not pursue you or take any further action against you. And I have already revoked the decree.' He looked at Jonathan. 'Against all of you. My brother and I disagreed on many things,' he added. 'But I did not murder him. For justice's sake, I need to punish the man who did.'

Flavia nodded and carefully picked up the needle-sharp stylus from the little wood-inlaid table. She held it out. 'Be careful,' she said, as Domitian took it.

'Is this a joke?' he asked.

'No. It's the murder weapon,' she replied. 'We found it in the latrines at the Inn of Romulus, where Titus went to relieve himself. Less than an hour later he was stricken by fever. The stylus had been dipped in a poison made from the spine of a stingray or trygon. That way the prophecy would be fulfilled that Titus would die *like Odysseus from the sea . . .*'

'You knew of that prophecy?' said Domitian.

'Lots of people knew about it,' said Flavia, 'including the killer. Stingray venom causes fever and paralysis. The killer knew that Titus had a new doctor, one who practiced the use of ice to take down a fever. But with this poison, cooling the body is the worst thing you can do.'

'Caesar!' cried the young Jew. 'I didn't know! I had no idea.'

Without looking at him, Domitian motioned for silence. 'I believe you, Ben Aruva,' he said, and to Flavia. 'Continue.'

Flavia glanced at Jonathan. 'The murderer had to hate Titus. There are many people who hated Titus and wanted him dead. The whole race of Jews, just for a start. The murderer also had to be someone,' she continued, 'who knew that Titus's doctor liked to treat a fever with ice. And someone with enough medical knowledge to know which poison is more deadly if the victim is cooled. And finally,' she said, 'the murderer also had to be someone whom Jonathan would die to protect.'

Behind her Jonathan groaned, and she heard a chair creak as he sat down.

Flavia took a deep breath: 'There is only one person I know who fits all those categories,' she concluded. 'Mordecai ben Ezra. Jonathan's father. I believe he is the one who murdered Titus.'

SCROLL XXVI

'This boy's father was the one who murdered Titus?' said Domitian.

Flavia nodded. 'All the clues point to that fact, Sir. I mean, Caesar.'

'Crispus, I want a proclamation issued on him immediately. No, wait! That will just alert him that we know what he did. No decree, but send out all the agents we have. Find this Jew . . . what is his name?'

'Mordecai ben Ezra,' said Crispus, referring to his wax tablet.

Jonathan's head was down and his shoulders were shaking.

'Find this Ben Ezra and bring him here.' Domitian stood up and stared coldly at Flavia. 'You and your friends conspired against me. But I am a man of my promises. You have twenty-four hours to depart Italia. If you are still in the country by dusk tomorrow, I'll have you all sent to the Sicilian mines.'

Then he turned and swept out of the room, followed by everyone except Ascletario and two guards.

Flavia looked at Jonathan. His head was still down and he was muttering to himself.

'Jonathan, I'm sorry—' began Flavia.

He raised his battered face and glared at her. 'Why did

you have to interfere?' he cried. 'I was ready to die for my father.'

'Because he was the guilty one,' said Flavia. 'Not you! It's not fair that you die for him.'

'That's my decision, not yours! I tried to save Titus and I failed. I deserve to die!' He stood up and ran out of the room, shoving Ascletario as he did so. One of the guards strode after him.

The Egyptian stood hanging his head and rubbing his hands together. 'It would not be wise of you to linger. You should leave quickly, quickly, quickly. Follow me.'

Ascletario led Flavia and her friends along the middle terrace and out into the circular piazza. It was dusk and starlings were wheeling in the sky above. 'I am sorry, sorry, sorry,' said Ascletario, hanging his head. 'Domitian is the emperor; I could not disobey him. You must leave now. It would not be wise of you to linger.'

'What about Jonathan?' asked Flavia.

'If I see him, I will urge him to leave also.'

'Poor Jonathan,' whispered Nubia, rubbing her upper arms. With the setting of the sun, the air had grown chilly.

'You must go!' cried Ascletario.

'How?' said Flavia miserably. 'It's almost dark and we don't have any transportation.' She nodded at Nubia's thin gold shift. 'We're not really dressed for travel.'

'No, we're not,' said Aristo. He looked down sheepishly at his red loincloth and boots.

'Walk,' said Ascletario. 'Or run. But go!'

'Come on, then,' said Flavia to the others. 'Let's start walking. That should warm us up. And I want to get out of here,' she added.

They left the piazza and went out through the arch.

'Flavia!' A deep voice from the dusk. 'Flavia, is that you?'

Flavia's heart skipped. 'Floppy?'

'Over here,' he said. And she saw him coming out from behind some tall cypress trees, his shape a flat black silhouette against the deep blue sky.

'Oh, Floppy!' she ran to him and threw her arms around his waist. 'Praise Juno, I'm so glad you're here!'

He hugged her and began to say something but she cried out as his arms pressed the weal on her back.

'What's wrong? Are you hurt?' He held her at arm's length and looked down at her. 'Your cheek. What happened?'

Flavia put her hand up to her cheek and winced as it touched the cut from the whip.

'I just got whipped a little,' she said. 'Once on the cheek and once on my back. Nothing like as bad as Jonathan. Floppy, how did you find us?'

'I went to the Emissario. I saw the chains, and drops of blood. I feared the worst. Then a swineherd told me the guards had taken three children up to the villa. What happened? Has Domitian pardoned you?'

'Yes, but he's exiled us, too. But Jonathan ran off and we can't see him anywhere.'

'Exile?' said Floppy. He looked sick.

'You must go!' said Ascletario, who had followed them out through the arch. And to Flaccus: 'Before Domitian changes his mind.'

Flaccus ignored the Egyptian. 'Exile?' he repeated.

Flavia nodded. 'Domitian has given us twenty-four hours to leave Italia.'

Flaccus shook his head slowly, then caught sight of Aristo, shivering and practically naked.

'You look cold, friend,' said Flaccus. He unwrapped his toga and handed it to Aristo. 'Better take this.'

'Thank you,' said Aristo. He pulled Nubia close and swung the toga over both of them.

Flavia saw Floppy's eyebrows go up but he only said, 'I saw your young friend Suetonius Tranquillus driving away around noon.'

'Praise Juno,' breathed Flavia. 'I'm glad he's safe. His scream was very convincing.'

'I presume he won't be coming to rescue you?'

'No. He's at his aunt's house across the lake.' She turned to Ascletario. 'Please will you do us one favour?' she asked. 'Will you tell Gaius Suetonius Tranquillus what happened? He's staying at the Villa Dorica, across the lake.'

'I will tell him if you will go, go, GO!' said Ascletario.

'They're going,' said Flaccus. 'They can come with me.' He pointed at a two-wheeled plaustrum parked behind the umbrella pines. It was hitched to a pair of patiently waiting oxen.

'An ox-cart!' cried Flavia. 'Praise Juno!'

'I traded my gelding for it,' said Flaccus with a sigh. 'You'll have to share with a cargo of grapes, but with the help of the gods you could be in Ostia by dawn.'

'Oh, Floppy,' said Flavia and she burst into tears.

Nubia would never forget her wedding night. She spent it wrapped in Aristo's arms and a woollen toga, lying on clusters of plump black grapes in a plaustrum pulled by two white oxen.

The Via Appia was so smooth and straight that the stars gave just light enough for them to drive slowly back towards Rome. Flavia and Lupus sat up front, either side of Flaccus. Their backs were turned and the night was dark and the low rumble of the wheels muffled all but the loudest sounds. So the rocking, grape-scented cart under its canopy of stars became their chaste marriage bed, giving them a strange, almost magical privacy. Between kisses they told each other all the thoughts and feelings they had never dared to share before.

'I first knew I loved you the Saturnalia before last,' whispered Nubia. 'When you played music and your music described perfectly what was in my soul. It swept me away.'

'You've loved me for nearly two years?' he whispered. His warm breath was grape-scented. 'Why didn't you say anything to me?'

'I was shy. Also you loved Miriam.'

He groaned. 'That was infatuation. I didn't even know her. Not like I know you.' He kissed her. 'I love your spirit, Nubia. You have the gentlest, loveliest, bravest spirit I have ever known.' He kissed her again. 'I love the music you make, too. Your music shows your soul.'

'When did you first know you loved me?' she asked, dizzy with happiness and the scent of grapes.

'In Halicarnassus,' he said. 'I thought Jonathan said you loved Flaccus. I felt as if a rug had been pulled out from under me. I think I must have loved you for a long time. But I didn't realise it until then.'

'Oh, Aristo.' They kissed.

'I tried to tell you one night in Ephesus,' he said. 'In the palm-tree courtyard. But you ran away.'

'I tried to tell *you* once,' she said. 'In the Cave of the Furies. But then I fainted.' She giggled from pure happiness and they kissed again.

They spoke for hours, laughing and crying and kissing, then fell asleep in each other's arms.

★

A drop of cold water on Nubia's forehead brought her awake with a start. It was night and dark. Had it all been a dream?

Then she felt Aristo's warm strong arms pull her closer and his lips on her forehead, kissing away the wetness.

'Don't worry, my love,' said Aristo. 'It's only the Capena Gate. We're back in Rome.'

Flavia woke with a start, her neck stiff from leaning her head against Floppy's muscular shoulder. He smiled down at her. 'You fell asleep,' he said. 'Lupus, too.' He turned his head and she saw Lupus curled up on a bed of grapes in the back of the cart, wrapped in a hemp bag. Nubia and Aristo were still wrapped up in Floppy's grape-stained toga but they were sitting up now, their backs against the inner wall of the plaustrum.

The cart had stopped in a quiet, residential street, silver in the light of a crescent moon. After four hours of rumbling wheels, it was the silence that had woken her.

'What time is it?' said Flavia, yawning.

'It's about midnight. And this is my house.'

'You live here?' Flavia blinked at the marble-columned porch and the other wealthy townhouses either side. Somewhere a dog was barking. One of the oxen snuffled and then was quiet again. 'I know this street.'

He smiled. 'Some people call it Pomegranate Street.'

'Didn't Domitian grow up over there?' She pointed. 'In that house with the little wooden columns.'

'That's right. That's how I know him. We first met when I was four and he was fifteen. That's one reason he invited me to his luncheon.' He gave her a tired smile. 'Flavia, I want you to wait here for a few moments.

I'm going inside to get some money and some cloaks for you. Then I'll put you on a fresh cart to Ostia.'

'Aren't you coming with us?'

'I can't, Flavia.' In the faint moonlight, his handsome face looked tired and pale.

'But Floppy, I thought you could come to Ephesus with us. I thought we could . . .'

'What?' His voice was very deep and very soft.

'You proposed to me once. You said you loved me.'

'And I do. You're the reason I broke off my engagement to Prudentilla. When I discovered you were living, not dead . . .' He looked down at his feet. Flavia could hear an owl hooting from a garden somewhere. The night air was cool and damp.

'Then can't we get married and live in Ephesus? We have a beautiful villa there.' She looked down at Aristo and Nubia, sitting up in the plaustrum and wrapped in a grape-stained toga. They smiled back.

Flaccus turned her chin with his finger, so that she was looking at him again.

'Flavia, listen. The emperor might make me his court poet.'

'Domitian? But he's evil.'

'Is he? You unjustly accused him of fratricide and plotted to overthrow him, but he spared your lives. Is that evil behaviour? Poor Domitian. All he ever wanted was his father's approval. And his brother's.'

'How can you say "poor Domitian" after what he did to Nubia?'

'What?' said Flaccus. 'Domitian joined her publicly to the man she loves and he let them go, too.'

'Well, then, what about the edict? He tried to have us killed.'

'He may have issued the edict against you in his brother's name but can you prove he tried to kill you? The way you "proved" he killed Titus?'

Flavia began to cry and he put his arm carefully around her.

'Flavia. If Domitian makes me court poet, I could finish my version of the *Argonautica*. I could write epigrams and letters. I could be as famous as Virgil. Don't you see? It's my life's dream. It's my chance at immortality.'

'You could write in Ephesus . . .'

'If I left all my responsibilities to come with you, I'd bring disgrace on my family name. Nobody would read my writings. Flavia, my life is here in Rome. I've just been given access to the Sibylline books. I'm a priest now, and I'll be helping to supervise foreign cults. I'm studying rhetoric with Quintilian. I've become good friends with Pliny. I have a household full of servants. A sister.'

'I didn't know you had a sister.'

'I have a dog, too. That's him you hear barking.'

'You have a dog? What's his name?'

'Argos.'

'My dog is called Scuto.'

'Yes. I know.' He kissed her forehead and then jumped down off the front of the plaustrum. Behind him the front door opened and she saw his body-slave Lyncaeus yawning and holding an oil-lamp.

'Floppy,' she whispered. 'I love you.'

'I love you, too, Flavia Gemina. But I can't go into exile with you.'

SCROLL XXVII

Flavia was too miserable to speak as Flaccus drove them through the sleeping streets of Rome to the Via Ostiensis. She wanted to plead with him to reconsider, but how could she ask him to give up everything for her? That would be unspeakably selfish.

If only she had listened to her father that winter day half a year earlier. If only she had agreed to marry Floppy when he first proposed. If only she had never gone on the quest for Nero's Eye, which had resulted in the edict against them, and had failed anyway. If only she had not fancied herself as a detectrix.

If not for her truth-seeking, she could be betrothed to Gaius Valerius Flaccus, and in a few years she might be living with him in his town house on Pomegranate Street, watching him plead cases in the law courts, helping him write poetry, raising fine sons and daughters. But that would never be.

She bravely fought back the tears as Flaccus helped her down from the back of the ox-cart. She stood beside her sleepy friends in the torchlit arch of the city gate and watched miserably as he negotiated another lift with an empty bread cart on its way back to Ostia after a night delivery.

She could not even bring herself to look at him as he

said goodbye, and it was all she could do not to burst into tears when he took her face in his hands and gently kissed her forehead.

He had given them warm woollen cloaks and the bottom of the cart was padded with empty grain sacks. Lupus curled up and went back to sleep almost at once. Beside him, Nubia and Aristo lay in each other's arms, the two of them speaking softly together. But Flavia sat cross-legged at the back of the cart and watched Flaccus, a solitary figure in the arched gateway, silhouetted against the smoky torchlight behind him, one hand lifted in farewell.

Tears were running down her face now, but she didn't bother to wipe them away until he was out of sight. Then she used the cloak he had given her to dry her cheeks. The cloak smelled of him – of musky cinnamon – and she began to cry again.

The cart passed between tombs of the dead and tall, thin cypress trees. The moon painted the world silver and black, beautiful but bleak. As the cart crested the hill and began to descend, Flavia knew Rome would soon be out of sight. She might be seeing it for the last time.

'Goodbye, Sisyphus,' she whispered. 'Goodbye, Aunt Cynthia and Uncle Cornix. Goodbye, Floppy.' The tears welled up and spilled over again. 'Goodbye, Rome. I loved you and I hated you, but mostly I loved you. And I only tried to do what was good for you.'

They reached Ostia an hour before dawn, and the cartdriver had to shake them all awake.

As if in a dream Flavia and her friends climbed down off the cart and stumbled along the moonlit Decumanus Maximus.

They turned left down Bakers' Street and left again at Green Fountain Street and at last they stood before Flavia's front door, so familiar and yet so strange. Lifting the bronze knocker of Castor, she rapped it urgently against the brass plaque of Pollux. A chilly pre-dawn breeze skittered some dry leaves along the pavement, and she pulled Flaccus's cloak tighter around her shoulders. Something about the sound of the dry leaves brought a chill of foreboding.

Flavia knocked again, and heard the rapping echo in the atrium. Some of the neighbourhood dogs had begun to bark, but there was an ominous silence from within her house. She glanced at the others – bleary-eyed and shivering in their cloaks – and then knocked a third time. 'Oh please, Castor and Pollux,' she whispered. 'Please let pater be home.'

But although she knocked and knocked and knocked, no one answered.

Lupus stood in the deserted nighttime street and wondered if he was dreaming.

In the moonlight, the place looked both familiar and strange.

Flavia sat on the cold pavement, weeping silently. Nubia was next to her, with her arm around Flavia's shoulders.

Aristo stood before them, wearing a toga and very little else. His head was turned in profile. In the moonlight he looked like the marble statue of an athlete with a spotted blanket draped around its shoulders.

Then a dog barked somewhere and Aristo turned his head. Lupus realised he was back in Ostia and he remembered how he had got there.

Nubia was looking up at Aristo. 'We must try Jonathan's house.'

He nodded. 'Yes.'

'We can't go to them!' wailed Flavia. 'I betrayed him and informed on his father.'

'I know,' said Aristo. 'But we're cold, tired and hungry. And we have to tell his mother what's happened. I'm knocking.'

'No!' cried Flavia, pulling out of Nubia's arms and standing up. But Aristo was already rapping on the front door of Jonathan's house. Lupus pulled his cloak tighter around his shoulders. It was a good cloak – warm and woollen – but he couldn't remember where he had got it.

After a short time the door opened and Lupus heard Aristo speaking and a woman's low voice answering.

Then the slim figure of a young woman came out onto the pavement. Her fluffy hair was unpinned and floated like a cloud around her shoulders. 'Come in, my friends,' said Hephzibah. 'I will give you hot mint tea and warm blankets and a soft divan to rest on.'

Flavia sat on the red and orange striped divan of Doctor Mordecai's study, wrapped in a cumin-scented blanket. She listened to Hephzibah telling them what had happened in the past six months. They were sipping mint tea and it reminded Flavia of the first time she had been in this room. She had twisted her ankle and Doctor Mordecai had carried her to the divan and served her mint tea, hot and sweet. She still could not believe that gentle Mordecai had killed the emperor.

Hephzibah sat on the divan, stroking Tigris's head. 'When the four of you disappeared at the end of February,' said Hephzibah, 'we were shocked. Then in June, we heard the news that you had died in a shipwreck. We were devastated. Almost immediately there was another wave of kidnappings, and Popo went missing. One tragedy after another.'

She looked up at Flavia. 'Your father became obsessed with finding Popo; I think it gave him a reason to keep living. But Doctor Mordecai nearly died of grief. He was always in a stupor of poppy tears and wine. Susannah, Priscilla, Delilah and I made sure Soso was safe. One of us is always with him. He is all we have left.'

'Where is Ferox?' asked Nubia. She was sharing a blanket with Aristo at one end of the divan, curled up in his arms.

'Poor old Ferox died last month,' said Hephzibah. 'He was old but I believe he died of grief.'

Nubia nodded sadly and laid her head on Aristo's shoulder.

'Captain Geminus set off to find Popo,' said Hephzibah, 'so he didn't see the notices about you go up. But as soon as we read the decree, we realised that you were still alive and that you were probably somewhere in Egypt.'

'That's when I went to Alexandria,' said Aristo, 'to try to find you and warn you not to come back here.'

'Did Jonathan's parents do anything?' asked Flavia.

'Susannah began to spend all her time in prayer,' said Hephzibah. 'She became very devout, as devout as Mordecai once was. She is devoted to Soso and spends all her free time helping the poor and doing good works. She attends the synagogue here in Ostia.' Hephzibah looked at Lupus. 'I know she remembers you every day in her prayers,' she said.

Lupus nodded from his place on the divan; he was cocooned in a blue and green striped blanket.

'And Doctor Mordecai?' said Flavia. 'What happened to him?'

'It was quite extraordinary,' said Hephzibah. 'When he realised Jonathan and the rest of you were alive and wanted by the emperor, he stopped mourning. He got up, went to the baths, dressed in clean clothes and shaved off his beard, which had grown long and straggling. Then he set out for Rome, telling Susannah he was going to petition the emperor on your behalf, or at least try to gain an interview. But we never saw him or heard from him again.'

'How long ago was that?' asked Aristo.

'About six weeks,' said Hephzibah.

At her feet, Tigris pricked up his ears and gave a single bark.

'And you haven't seen him since?' said Flavia, leaning forward, 'Not even in the past day or two?'

Tigris trotted out of the study, towards the back door.

'No. Why do you ask?'

'Mordecai didn't go to Rome to ask help of the emperor,' said Flavia with a sigh. 'He went to kill him.'

Hephzibah's brown eyes grew wide. 'Mordecai?' she said. 'He killed Titus?'

'Yes,' said Flavia. 'Jonathan found out what his father had done. He tried to take the blame himself, but I couldn't let him do that. And now he hates me for it!' She began to cry.

'I don't hate you,' said a tired voice.

Flavia looked up and through her tears she saw Jonathan swaying in the doorway. Tigris panted happily at his feet, gazing up at his beloved master. Jonathan's mother Susannah stood behind him, a sleeping baby in her arms.

'I'm sorry I got angry with you, Flavia,' said Jonathan. 'You were only doing what you do. Trying to solve a mystery. Trying to find the Truth. You deserve to hear what happened. You all do.'

SCROLL XXVIII

As Jonathan limped into the study, Nubia gasped. In the lamplight, he looked terrible. He had a black eye and his lower lip was cut and swollen.

'Behold your face!' she cried. She and Aristo both sat forward and the blanket fell from around their shoulders.

'Not a pretty sight, am I?' said Jonathan.

'Are you all right?' asked Flavia.

'Did they beat you again?' asked Aristo.

'No. These wounds are just getting ripe.'

'How did you get here?'

'I stole a donkey. I left it out in the necropolis.'

Susannah handed Popo to Hephzibah and said something to Jonathan in Aramaic. She clutched his arm and tried to pull him out of the room.

'I can't rest now, mother.' He pulled his arm free and eased himself carefully onto the divan. 'There's no time. We've been exiled and we have to leave Italia by this evening.'

'No!' wailed Susannah, throwing her arms around his neck. 'Don't leave me!'

Jonathan winced. 'Mother, you're hurting me. Please!' Susannah pulled away from him and began to moan and scratch her cheeks.

'Don't do that either,' he said in Latin. 'You can mourn

me later. I have to tell you what happened.' He added something in stern Aramaic.

Susannah stopped scratching her cheeks and sat up straight, as if preparing herself for a blow. Her black hair fell loose to her shoulders and Nubia saw there were strands of silver among the black.

'Tell us, my son,' said Susannah. 'Tell us what happened.'

Nubia moved away from Aristo's side to pour Jonathan a beaker of mint tea. He took it with a grateful look but winced as he took a sip.

'Is it too hot?' asked Nubia.

'No,' he said. 'My lip is just swollen. It's good. The tea is good.' He looked around at them. 'I left Ephesus secretly,' he said, 'because I saw you were happy there. I wanted to make things right so that you could come back to Italia. So that we could all live here again.' He turned and looked at his mother. 'When we were in Asia, I started having visions.'

'Visions?' she said. 'Like the prophets?'

'I suppose.' Jonathan said something to her in Aramaic and then continued in Latin. 'The dream that I kept having over and over was of warring brothers, like Cain and Abel, Esau and Jacob, Romulus and Remus. I remember the words: *Dark against Light. Good against Evil. Ice against Fire.*'

'What did it mean?' asked Hephzibah.

'At first I thought it was something to do with Flavia.'

'With me?' cried Flavia. 'Why?'

'Castor and Pollux are your family deities.' He picked up his beaker and warmed his hands on it. 'But one night I realised my dreams were more about fighting brothers, like Romulus and Remus. I had a vision of a howling she-wolf, and I knew it was about Titus and Domitian.'

'Because they were brothers struggling for power,' said Flavia. 'Like Romulus and Remus who were suckled by a she-wolf.'

'Yes. I thought God was calling me to Rome to warn Titus that his brother was about to act against him somehow. I thought it would be my chance to atone for the fire ...' Jonathan frowned. 'But there was a problem. The last time Titus saw me, he told me to go away and never come back. Still, I hoped he would see me if I told him I had a message of life and death.'

Jonathan sipped his mint tea, and Nubia drank some of hers, too. Its sweetness gave her strength.

'When I got to Ostia,' said Jonathan, 'I went straight to Rome, to the Palatine Hill. But Titus's secretaries and bodyguards told me the emperor was too busy to see me. The guard told me to wait. I waited outside the palace door for three days, me and a small group of other petitioners, but they wouldn't let us in.'

Jonathan stared into his beaker. 'Nothing went right. I should have known,' he murmured, then looked up and continued: 'I caught a chill and managed to find a room in the Jewish quarter across the Tiber before I passed out. I had a fever for a week. If it hadn't been for the innkeeper's kindness nobody would have fed me or looked after me ... I must have been delirious at one point, because right before I left, he told me not to worry. He said the doctor would take care of Titus.'

'The doctor?' said Flavia.

Jonathan nodded. 'At the time I thought he meant Ben Aruva. The innkeeper was always telling me how "one of our own" was Titus's doctor and all about the miraculous ice-treatment. But now I know: he didn't mean that doctor. And he meant "take care of" in a different way.'

Jonathan drained his beaker and put it on the divan beside him. 'When I recovered, I thought, What would Flavia do?' He looked at Flavia. 'Do you remember the Jew who was working for Titus, writing a history of the war against Judea?'

'Josephus!' said Flavia. 'Titus's freedman. The scholar we met the last time we were looking for you.'

'That's right. I went to the baths and ate some food and then I went to look for him. I found him in the Greek section of the library in the Temple of Apollo, where you told me you'd seen him once before. I told him about my visions, and that I thought Titus's life was in danger. I think he believed me, because he told me Titus wasn't too busy to see me: he was too ill. His headaches were almost constant and he was always depressed and weeping. He also told me about the prophecy of Apollonius of Tyana, that Titus would *die like Odysseus from the sea*. Josephus said he and some other scholars thought the prophecy might refer to the poison of the sea-hare.'

'What is sea hare?' asked Nubia.

'It's a kind of sea-slug. Its poison is deadly. But Josephus said the poison couldn't be in Titus's food because his tasters try everything.'

Nubia leaned forward again and poured the last of the mint tea into Jonathan's beaker.

'Josephus had to go prepare his booth for Succot. We agreed to meet the next day. I was still in the library, trying to find some more information about sea-hare venom, when someone said that Titus was about to leave Rome early, before the end of the games. They said Domitian was going with him to their Sabine farm. I still hadn't figured out how Domitian would poison Titus. I only knew he would. I ran all the way to the Porta Collina and hired a donkey and bought a bag of charcoal. Because Titus wasn't feeling well they were carrying him in a slow-moving litter, so I managed to keep ahead of him. I scrawled graffiti anywhere I could: *Beware Remus*. I hoped Titus would see that and understand.'

'So you were on the road ahead of Titus?'

'Yes. At first just a few minutes ahead of him. I wrote my message on gravestones and on the walls of every public latrine along the way.'

'Then it wasn't an elaborate code?'

'No. Just the simplest warning I could think of. But I know now it was foolish. I must have been suffering after-effects from the fever because when I saw my father outside the Inn of Romulus I didn't even stop.'

'You saw your father?' gasped Susannah.

'Yes. He was wearing a hooded cloak. I thought it was him and almost called out, but then I told myself it couldn't be him. I told myself it must be the fever. So I carried on up the road, scribbling my pathetic warning on the wall.'

'Mordecai didn't recognise you?' asked Flavia.

'I don't think he even saw me.'

'And the emperor's litter hadn't passed by yet.'

'No, but I heard the sound of the Praetorian guard, marching fast. You always hear them before you see them,' he added. 'If only I'd stopped. If only I'd said something to him.'

He rested his bruised face in his hands for a moment, then took a deep breath and looked up. 'That afternoon, I was writing the warning on the city gate outside Reate when a man grabbed me. He was one of the emperor's courtiers, I think. He'd been riding ahead with the news that Titus had a dangerous fever. A few minutes later the litter-bearers came running past. I presume Titus was inside. Domitian and some mounted guards were following on horseback. When Domitian saw his courtier holding me there by the side of the road, he commanded the cortege to halt and he rode over to us.'

'This was outside Reate?' asked Aristo.

'Yes. The man holding me told Domitian that I was obviously part of a plot to murder Titus and maybe even overthrow the government. Domitian thought for a moment, then announced that he was going straight back to Rome to stop any attempt by his enemies to seize power. He sent the litter-bearers on with orders to keep Titus chilled. A group of us rode back to Rome.'

'So you're the reason he returned to Rome in such a hurry,' said Aristo.

'And that's why Domitian tortured you,' said Flavia. 'He thought you were part of a conspiracy against him.'

'Yes. He sent me straight on to his Alban Villa in a chariot with two fresh guards.' Jonathan closed his eyes and leaned back against the cinnabar-red wall. 'On the way there, I had time to think. I realised the man I saw going into the Inn of Romulus must have been my father and not a hallucination. That was when I realised what the Jewish innkeeper in Transtiberim meant when he said a doctor would take care of Titus. By "doctor" he meant my father. By "take care of" he meant kill.'

'No!' cried Susannah. 'No, it cannot be!'

Jonathan shook his head and looked at Flavia. 'I didn't even realise how Titus was killed until you explained it to me, Flavia. That's how stupid I am.'

'You're not stupid,' said Flavia. 'You just didn't have as many clues as I did.'

'Why did you say that you killed Titus?' asked Nubia, even though deep down, she knew the answer.

'Because if they thought I did it they wouldn't hunt down father,' Jonathan looked at his mother, who was weeping silently. 'If I hadn't gone looking for you two years ago,' he said to her, 'I'd never have discovered that you were alive and that Titus loved you. I don't think father ever forgave Titus for having kept you as his slave for ten years. That's why he killed him. In a way, it was all my fault.'

Jonathan's mother closed her eyes and she began to tug her hair again. This time Jonathan did not try to stop her.

For a long time they were silent, watching Susannah weep, lost in their own thoughts.

'Great Juno's peacock!' said Flavia. 'I just had a terrible thought. What if Domitian hired Mordecai to kill his brother?'

Jonathan nodded miserably. 'I've been thinking that too. He knew my father hated Titus. They had that in common.'

'I wonder where your father is now?' said Flavia.

'Titus died six days ago,' said Aristo, 'so Mordecai is probably long gone.'

'Mother,' said Jonathan softly. 'Have you seen him?'

She shook her head. 'No. I have not seen him.'

'Will you come with us to Ephesus?'

'No, my son,' said Susannah. 'I will wait here in case he returns. I will stay here to raise my grandson.' She looked at Hephzibah. 'I have Hephzibah and Priscilla and Delilah. And our community.'

The first birds were beginning to twitter sleepily in the garden courtyard and Flavia knew it would soon be dawn. 'We have to leave Ostia by sunset,' she said, twelve hours from now.

'Where will you go?' Hephzibah asked them.

'Ephesus,' said Nubia and Aristo together, then looked

at each other and smiled. Lupus nodded and gave a sad smile, too.

'Yes,' said Flavia. 'We have a beautiful villa there.'

'And children who need us,' said Nubia.

'I can be a teacher,' said Aristo, he slipped his arm around Nubia's shoulder. 'And in time, a father, too, God willing. Nubia and I were married yesterday,' he explained.

'Oh, I'm so happy for you!' said Hephzibah.

'I also,' said Susannah. And to Aristo: 'She has loved you for many years.'

'I know,' said Aristo, and kissed the top of Nubia's head. 'I have a lot of catching up to do in Ephesus.'

'And there's a beautiful harbour for the *Delphina*,' said Flavia. 'So pater can come and live with us and go on his travels. Right, Lupus?'

Lupus nodded.

'But I need to tell pater what's happened,' said Flavia. She turned to Susannah. 'Do you know where he is? We knocked just now but there was no one there.'

Susannah and Hephzibah exchanged a quick and knowing glance.

'What?' cried Flavia. 'What is it?'

'Your father doesn't live next door any longer,' said Hephzibah gently. 'He had to sell the house to pay his debts. He was searching for Popo and not pursuing his business.'

'But pater never told me!' cried Flavia. 'When we met him at the family tomb a few days ago. And he gave us all that gold.'

Hephzibah glanced at Susannah. 'Probably the last of his money. He didn't want you to worry.'

'Then where is he?' cried Flavia.

Susannah glanced at Hephzibah. 'He's with his wife,' she said.

Flavia's jaw dropped. 'His wife?'

'His wife?' echoed Aristo and Nubia together and Lupus gave his bug-eyed stare.

Jonathan opened his eyes. 'Flavia's father is married?'

Hephzibah and Susannah looked at each other and for the first time all evening they smiled. 'Yes,' said Hephzibah. 'Yesterday Flavia's father married someone you all know, and of whom I think you'll approve. They're living aboard the *Delphina*.' She looked out the open doorway to the inner garden. 'It will be light soon,' she said. 'I'll make you some breakfast and then you can go see him.'

'But not you,' said Susannah to Jonathan. 'You must rest.'

An hour later, Lupus and his friends left Jonathan sleeping in his old bedroom, and made their way through the streets of Ostia. As they passed beneath the arch of the Marina Gate – on the lookout for Captain Geminus – early-morning fog swirled around their ankles. The fishmarket ahead was already busy and seagulls circled overhead, alert for scraps or tidbits. On the docks, men were loading and unloading crates, barrels and amphoras.

Suddenly Lupus found himself surrounded by half a dozen boys.

'Are you Lupus?' said one of them, and pointed to a boy with tawny hair. 'He says you're Lupus.'

Lupus stopped and stared and the circle of eager faces. He nodded warily.

The tawny-haired boy stepped forward and held out his hand. His tunic was a hemp bag with a hole for the head and a belt made of twine. 'I'm Threptus,' he said. 'Thank you for not being dead.'

Lupus shook the boy's hand and gave a little bow. The boys laughed.

'You used to be one of us,' said Threptus, his eyes shining. 'Is it true you own a ship?'

Lupus nodded.

'You're our hero.'

Lupus stared at them. Flavia and Nubia giggled. Aristo put his hand on Lupus's shoulder and said, 'I'm afraid your hero has to leave Ostia this evening. We all do. You should say goodbye to him now.'

'Eheu!' cried the boys, and looked at each other in dismay.

Lupus took out his wax tablet, wrote something on it and showed it to Threptus.

'I can't read,' said Threptus, hanging his head. 'None of us can.'

Aristo looked at it. 'He says: CARRY ON MY GOOD WORK.'

'We'll try,' said Threptus.

Lupus added something and held it up for all the boys to see.

'AND LEARN TO READ AND WRITE!' said Aristo.

On impulse, Lupus gave Threptus his wooden wax tablet and the bronze stylus.

Threptus took the objects as if they were pure gold and looked questioningly at Aristo.

'Don't worry,' said Flavia. 'Lupus has at least half a dozen wax tablets.'

Lupus pointed at her and nodded.

'Thank you!' said Threptus. He and his friends ran off.

As Lupus followed his friends out of the fish market, he saw the masts and sails of the ships in the Marina Harbour.

And there was his ship, the *Delphina*. The sight filled him with a mixture of sadness and joy. Her sail was grey and patched, and the painted dolphin hung limply. She carried many memories – both good and bad – along with her cargo of salt and wine.

'Salvete, shipmates!' cried someone from the rigging. 'Where have you been?'

It was Atticus, the woolly-haired Greek who had driven them into Rome. He was sitting on the yardarm doing something with a rope.

Lupus grinned and waved. The others waved, too.

'Is pater on board?' called Flavia.

Atticus grinned and shook his head. 'He and his new bride have gone shopping. You'll find them in the fish market, I'd wager.' He pointed for good measure, then called down to Lupus. 'I know she looks battered and old,' he said. 'But don't worry: I intend to give her a new coat of paint after the festival.'

Lupus frowned and Aristo grinned. 'I think he's talking about the ship, Lupus, not Flavia's new stepmother.'

Flavia saw them first. Her father, tall and fair-haired, was standing at the oyster-stall, haggling for a barrel.

The woman standing next to him was slim and of medium height. She wore a long, nutmeg-coloured tunic and a sage green palla around her head and shoulders. She turned her head and Flavia saw her profile: grave, intelligent, beautiful.

'Cartilia?' she whispered. 'Cartilia Poplicola? It can't be ...'

Then Aristo groaned and covered his face with his hand.

Flavia turned and looked up at him. 'How can it be Cartilia? She died two years ago of the fever!'

'Ah!' breathed Nubia and she gave Aristo a laughing glance. 'It is not Cartilia. I think it is her younger sister, Diana.'

SCROLL XXX

'Diana?' gasped Flavia. 'Pater married Diana? The girl with the short hair and even shorter tunics? The girl who used to run around the woods pretending to be a huntress? The girl who was madly in love with—'

Flavia clapped her hand over her mouth and stared bug-eyed at Aristo, who was blushing furiously.

Nubia was giggling behind her hand. 'It does not matter,' she said to Aristo. 'The past was yesterday. Today we are husband and wife.'

'And you're a wonderful wife,' he said. He bent to kiss her on the lips and Lupus made a protracted smacking sound.

'Stop it, Lupus!' Nubia giggled and gave him a playful slap on the arm.

'Pater!' called Flavia, waving. 'Pater! We're here!'

'Flavia!' Her father turned and pushed through the crowd and embraced her. 'Where have you been?' he cried. 'When we heard of Titus's death we thought you would come straight back here. I rode up to Rome to see Senator Cornix and he told me he hadn't seen you in months. I've been sick with worry. And then the bailiffs came for the house. Are you all right?'

Flavia nodded. 'Domitian revoked Titus's decree against us.'

'Praise Jupiter!'

'But we have to leave Italia by nightfall. We've been sent into exile. Oh, pater!' She burst into tears and he gave her another hug. 'Pater, did you really have to sell our house?' Her face was pressed against his cloak and her voice was muffled.

'I'm afraid so, my little owl. It was the only way.'

'But what about Alma and Caudex and the dogs?'

'On board the *Delphina*,' he said. 'For the time being.'

'Oh, pater, will you take us?' She pulled back and looked up at him. 'Will you take us to Ephesus and live there with us? The villa is huge.'

He smiled and gave her his handkerchief. 'Of course I'll take you to Ephesus,' he said. 'But I'm not sure yet if we'll . . . I mean if I—'

He paused and then turned to Diana, who stood anxiously beside him. 'Flavia, I have something to tell you. Diana Poplicola and I were married yesterday in a very quiet ceremony. I hope you will love her as you loved her sister.'

Flavia looked at Diana and swallowed hard. How could her father be so callous? How could he marry someone without telling her? For all he knew his only daughter could have been languishing in Domitian's dungeon.

Diana caught her hand. 'Flavia,' she said. 'Don't be hurt. My mother died and a relative inherited everything. I had nowhere to live and Marcus . . . Your father invited me to stay aboard *Delphina*. We didn't think there was any point in us waiting . . . We're not getting younger,' she said.

'I'm not hurt,' said Flavia bravely, and tried to smile. 'I'm glad there will be someone to look after pater. Will you come and live with us in Ephesus?'

Diana looked up at Flavia's father. 'Marcus has

promised to show me the world,' she said. 'I can't wait to see Ephesus.' She looked back at Flavia. 'But I also want to see Corinth, Alexandria and Rhodes.'

Flavia glanced at Nubia and Lupus, and then smiled. 'Well, I hope you have a less exciting time than we did in all those places.'

Diana nodded. 'I can't wait to hear all about it.'

'And about how you gained a pardon and exile,' said her father.

'You'll never believe it,' said Flavia.

Her father clapped his hands and rubbed them briskly together. 'Well, if we have to leave Italia by this afternoon there's a lot I must do to get the *Delphina* ready. Pack what you most want to bring. Your things are at Jonathan's house,' he said to Flavia and Nubia. 'I'll send Caudex to bring your luggage around noon and we'll set sail at the sixth hour after noon. Go to the baths, if you have time. It may be your last chance for a week or two.'

Jonathan woke to the sound of his mother singing a Hebrew lullaby.

He opened his eyes. He was at home in Ostia, in his old bedroom. He looked at the familiar walls with their mustard-yellow panels and the wood beams in the ceiling. The light slanting through the latticework window showed him it was late: perhaps the third hour after noon.

He knew he would never see this room again and so he lay quietly, listening to his mother's song and savouring the bittersweet moment.

Presently he sat up, then winced at the pain from the throbbing weals across his back and his aching, cracked ribs. It would be several weeks before he would be totally healed. And he would always have the scars. Carefully he got up and went to Lupus's empty bed and picked up the tunic laid out there. It was woven of the finest wool and dyed a soft cinnamon colour. He could not see the stitching and he realised it was woven in one piece, so that there were no seams. He had heard of such tunics, but never seen one, much less owned one. He carefully stripped off the tunic they had given him at Domitian's Alban Citadel and he put on the new one. As it slipped over his face he caught the faint scent of lemon oil. He belted it and went out of the room, in the direction of his mother's singing.

She was in Miriam's old room, sitting in a wicker rocking chair, holding Soso in her arms and crooning a lullaby. When she saw him, she stopped singing and smiled. 'Do you like your new tunic?' She spoke in Hebrew rather than Aramaic, and it reminded him that his father had always insisted they speak Hebrew around the house, so that they would remain fluent.

'Yes,' he replied in the same language. 'It's beautiful.'

'I wove it myself,' she said.

'You wove this?'

'Yes. Over the past six months. And with every sweep of the shuttle I offered up a prayer for you.' Jonathan could tell she had been weeping, but she was smiling now as she stood up. 'Happy Birthday, my son.'

'What?' He stared at her.

'It was your birthday three days ago. You are thirteen now, and a man in the eyes of God.' She kissed his bruised cheek and gestured to the chair. 'Sit. Hold Soso for a moment.'

Dazed, he sat in the wicker rocking chair she had just vacated and received his baby nephew. Three days ago he had been tied to the sluice of the Emissario, beaten and half starved. That had been his thirteenth birthday. Soso gazed up at Jonathan with solemn grey eyes. Jonathan tried to smile but his lip hurt too much.

Susannah went to a table and opened a small box. She came back to him and handed him a gold signet ring with ruddy-brown sardonyx. There was a dove carved into it. 'I had this made for you,' she said. 'The dove is to remind you that your grandfather was a priest named Jonah.'

'Yes,' said Jonathan. He was about to slip it on when Soso reached up and grasped the ring in his tiny fist.

'Oh!' cried his mother, 'Do you think it's a sign?'

'What kind of sign?'

'That he will be a great priest, too, when the Temple is restored to us?'

'I think it probably means he likes shiny things,' said Jonathan.

Soso unclenched his hand and the ring fell into Jonathan's palm. He quickly put it on. Soso regarded him gravely from clear grey eyes.

'Will his eyes stay that colour?' Jonathan asked his mother.

'Yes. He's ten months old now; his eyes will always be that colour. He has his father's eyes and his mother's black hair,' she added.

'I hope he doesn't have her curly hair,' said Jonathan.

Soso smiled and gurgled up at him.

'It's no laughing matter,' said Jonathan softly, 'If you have curly girly hair all the boys will beat you up. Trust me.'

Soso gripped Jonathan's finger with his tiny hand.

'He seems happy.'

'He is much loved. But I think he misses his brother.'

'I'll try to find Popo. When I'm better.'

'I know you will, my son.'

'Mother, are you sure you won't come with us to Ephesus? It's a huge villa with over two dozen bedrooms and its own swimming pool and bath complex. And gardens.'

'No. I will stay here in case your father returns.'

'But he killed Titus.'

'I do not believe he could have done such a thing. He was never that kind of man.'

'Jonathan?' They both turned to see Flavia standing in the doorway.

'Is it time to go?' he asked.

'Not quite. But there's someone here to see you. To see *us*. It's Titus's doctor, Ben Aruva. And he says he has something very important to tell us.'

SCROLL XXXI

Ben Aruva was sitting in the triclinium. There were floor cushions rather than couches and a single hexagonal table in the centre. Delilah was putting small bowls of delicacies on this table: green almonds, pistachio nuts, dates, dried figs and mulberries. Jonathan knew that the two small pitchers contained wine and vinegar, and that the big jug was for water.

The doctor got up as Jonathan entered the room.

'Peace be with you,' said Jonathan.

'And with you,' said Ben Aruva, with a small bow. 'How are your wounds?'

'Sore, but they'll heal.'

'Please, sit,' said Hephzibah. 'Wine or posca?'

'Wine, please,' said the doctor, sitting cross-legged. 'Well watered.'

Jonathan sat on a cushion near the door, with his back to the bright garden courtyard. His mother sat on one side of him and Flavia on the other. Nubia was sitting next to Aristo, holding Soso in her arms and smiling down at him. Lupus squatted on his haunches near Ben Aruva, watching the young doctor with wary eyes.

'I've come to share some extraordinary news,' said Ben Aruva. 'After you left the Alban Citadel, I convinced Domitian to perform an autopsy on Titus.'

'An autopsy?' said Flavia.

'Yes. A test done on a body to determine the cause of death. When I studied in Alexandria I watched many and performed a few myself.'

'Isn't that unusual here in Rome?' said Aristo.

'Almost unheard of. But I convinced Domitian. I told him we had heard some incredible conjectures about how Titus died but that there was only one way to be sure. Domitian agreed, almost at once. He had his men bring the body to a well-lit room in one of the towers and he summoned a handful of Rome's most respectable men, including two priests.'

Ben Aruva looked at Flavia. 'I began by examining the body for marks on the legs or lower arms. Marks that might have been made by a poisoned needle or stylus. I found nothing.'

'Nothing?'

'Nothing. No mark at all, apart from a few mosquito bites. And they look quite different from a puncture by a man-made implement.'

Jonathan and Flavia exchanged a puzzled glance.

'Next I cut him open and carefully examined his internal organs. One of the men present was an augur, used to examining the innards of bulls and sheep. He agreed that Titus's organs were in perfect condition.' Ben Aruva took a small sip of his well-watered wine and replaced the cup on the table. 'Finally, I split open his head.'

'Oh!' cried Flavia. 'How horrible.'

Ben Aruva ignored her. 'And there we finally found something. In his brain.'

'What?' said Jonathan.

'It looked like a mosquito, but it was the size of a sparrow.'

'Oh!' cried Flavia and Nubia together, but Susannah looked puzzled. 'What did you find?' she asked Ben Aruva in Aramaic.

'Yattush,' he replied, in the same language. 'A mosquito or gnat. But it was this big.' He indicated its length with finger and thumb.

'Dear Lord,' murmured Aristo.

'How did it get there?' asked Jonathan.

'I have two theories,' said Ben Aruva. 'As I'm sure you know, many rabbis say that after Titus destroyed Jerusalem and our Holy Temple, the Lord – blessed be he – cursed Titus. Perhaps he sent a mosquito up Titus's nose to plague him, and it lived in his brain for ten years, tormenting him with headaches and depression until it finally killed him.'

Jonathan and his friends stared at Ben Aruva. Even Flavia was speechless.

The doctor took another small sip of his wine. 'As you might imagine, Domitian was not pleased with this particular theory. So I offered him another. Several years ago I saw an autopsy being performed in Alexandria. My teachers were trying to determine the cause of death of a woman who had suffered headaches so terrible that she took her own life. They found something like a crab in her brain. Only it was not a crab, it was just fleshy matter. One of our teachers – a very wise and experienced physician – said he had seen other such growths from time to time. He called such growths "tumours" because they often caused parts of the body to swell. He said that people affected by blindness, madness and depression often were found to have tumours in their brains.'

Jonathan stared at him. He had heard of tumours in the belly or breast, but never in the brain.

'What causes them?' asked Aristo.

Ben Aruva gave a small shrug. 'We don't really know,' he said. 'A tumour is an illness. Like a boil on the skin, or a bunion on the toe. Sometimes they are harmless, sometimes they are deadly.'

'And they can cause depression, madness and headaches?' asked Flavia.

'According to my wisest teacher. Yes.'

Jonathan felt sick as he realised what Ben Aruva was saying. 'Are you telling us that Titus wasn't murdered?'

'That is exactly what I am telling you.'

Flavia and Jonathan looked at each other.

'I don't believe it,' said Flavia. 'We had proof.'

'What proof?'

'Well, first of all,' she said, 'there was the prophecy given by Apollonius of Tyana, that Titus would die at the hand of someone close to him.'

'No. Apollonius merely told Titus to beware of those close to him.'

'All right,' Flavia stuttered. 'But when Titus asked by what means he would die, Apollonius said that death would come to him from the sea. *Like Odysseus, from the sea.*'

'Perhaps it did. Perhaps he merely caught a chill from the sea air.'

'But he was in the Sabine Hills, fifty miles from the sea.'

'Four days before he died, he spent the afternoon in Portus. The sea breeze was quite stiff that day. I know. I was with him.'

'But Odysseus was killed by the spine of a stingray, a trygon,' persisted Flavia.

'According to one account of several. You know how fluid myths can be. Besides, none of this is proof.'

Jonathan looked at him. 'There was no mark on his calf?'

'Just a few mosquito bites.' Ben Aruva pointed at Flavia's leg. 'Like that one.'

'But what about the needle sharp stylus in the latrine? I pricked myself on it and the venom nearly killed me. I came down with a fever an hour after I touched it.'

'Coincidence, or another cause. The bite of a mosquito can cause fever, you know. Your whole theory was no more than that,' said Ben Aruva. 'An elaborate and complicated theory.'

Flavia and Jonathan exchanged another look. She was very pale.

'Titus had something in his brain?' said Jonathan's mother in Hebrew, as if she had only now grasped the fact. 'Something the size of a sparrow?'

'Yes,' replied Ben Aruva in Hebrew.

'And it could have been the cause of his headaches and his depression?'

'Yes.'

'So my husband didn't murder him? Mordecai is innocent?'

'I do not believe Titus was murdered,' said Ben Aruva in Hebrew, and then repeated it in Latin: 'Titus was not murdered. He died of a mosquito in the brain, which means his killer was either God or fate, depending on your beliefs.' Ben Aruva looked into his wine glass. 'If anyone is to blame, it is me. I insisted on the ice treatment, which helped him so much in the past. But he hadn't long to live, in any case. Such a tumour . . .' Ben Aruva looked up at Susannah. 'Your husband is innocent.'

'Then it wasn't father I saw,' said Jonathan slowly. 'It was all my imagination. Master of the Universe, what have I done?' He looked at Flavia. 'What have we done?'

'What have we done?' repeated Jonathan, looking at Flavia. 'Between the two of us we convinced everyone that father killed Titus.'

'Don't worry about your father,' Ben Aruva said to Jonathan. 'Domitian has called off the hunt. He realises your father is not to blame. But he is still angry with you.' Ben Aruva was looking at Jonathan. 'Because of you, he panicked and rode back to Rome and was not with his brother when he died.'

Jonathan hung his head. He felt sick.

'I was Titus's doctor,' continued Ben Aruva. 'And I do not know Domitian well. But I believe he loved his brother. Yes, he was bitter and jealous. Yes, he occasionally conspired against him. But I do not believe that he would ever have killed him.'

Ben Aruva stood up, so everyone else did, too. 'And now I must go back to Rome and prepare Titus's body for the funeral tomorrow. The citizens of Rome would be horrified to know that a Jew cut open the deified Titus. I have to make it look as if nothing has happened.'

'Then Domitian isn't going to tell people how Titus really died?' said Aristo.

'No,' said Ben Aruva with a sad smile.

'But people will talk!' cried Flavia. 'They'll jump to conclusions, just like we did.'

'Yes,' said Ben Aruva. 'They probably will.' He picked his way through the cushions to the doorway of the triclinium. Here he turned and faced them. The bright green garden was behind him so Jonathan could not see his expression clearly.

'Power is a dangerous thing,' said Ben Aruva in a quiet

voice. 'Any kind of power. If you have it, be careful to use it for good.'

'Jonathan, do you realise what this means?' said Flavia after Ben Aruva had gone.

He looked up at her and she saw that one of his eyes was almost swollen shut.

'What?'

She hesitated, wondering if this last blow would be too much. But they were all looking at her, so she said, 'Domitian never planned to kill his brother. The autopsy proves it. Why cut his brother open unless he really wanted to know the cause of his death? Unless he was really concerned? Don't you see? We were completely wrong about Domitian.'

Jonathan nodded bleakly. 'I thought I had a vision from God. My vision of Romulus and Remus. It seemed so real. Maybe I have a tumour, too,' he said miserably.

Nubia sat up straight. 'Maybe your vision was being from God,' she said. 'But maybe it was not concerning Domitian.'

'She's right,' said Flavia. 'Titus and Domitian weren't twins. But all those other pairs you named were.'

'I thought of them more as brothers who fought each other.'

'Not Castor and Pollux,' said Flavia. 'They never fought because they had different skills and they alternated being mortal and immortal.

Lupus grunted and wrote on his wax tablet: POPO AND SOSO?

'Yes!' said Flavia. 'Lupus is right! They're twins and they're related to you. Maybe your vision was telling you to save Popo, not Titus.'

Jonathan stared at her like a boxer who has received too many blows but is still swaying on his feet. 'You mean I went through all this for nothing?'

'Not nothing,' said Aristo. 'You came back to Italia to clear your names, and you've done that.'

'But we're exiles,' said Flavia. 'We have to leave Ostia, and we can never come home again.'

SCROLL XXXII

Flavia and her friends set out dejectedly for the Marina Harbour at the fifth hour after noon. They took the back streets to avoid being seen, but when they approached the Marina Gate, they found the road clogged with people.

Jonathan tightened his grip on Tigris's leash.

'What's happening?' Flavia asked the Old Woman of Ostia as they passed the Hydra Fountain for the last time.

'You'll see,' said Lusca, and her one good eye twinkled.

As they passed through the marble arch of the Marina Gate they were met with a cheer.

People were lining the streets, as they did when a victorious gladiator emerged from the arena. Some were waving, others were clapping. One or two even held palm branches, the sign of victory.

'Maybe a famous athlete is in town,' said Jonathan.

'Or charioteer?' Nubia looked eagerly behind them, but the people were closing in.

Lupus looked around warily.

Then Flavia began to notice familiar faces in the crowd: Oleosus, the door slave at the Forum Baths, Brutus the butcher and Fabius the fuller. They were smiling and looking at her.

'Flavia,' said Nubia. 'I think they have come here to see us.'

'Great Juno's beard,' muttered Jonathan behind her. 'You're right.'

'They shouldn't be cheering us,' said Flavia wretchedly. 'We botched this whole investigation.'

'I know,' said Jonathan.

'But you helped return many children to their families,' said Aristo. 'Like Porcius there. You brought him back from Rhodes.'

'Behold!' cried Nubia. 'Porcius! And his sister Titia with Silvanus!'

'Silvanus!' Flavia rushed forward to greet the handsome youth. 'The last time we saw you was on that island, when you went for water. We thought we'd never see you again.'

'I made it home,' he said. 'Titia and I were married in July.' The two of them smiled at each other.

'Thank you, Flavia,' said a shy voice. 'May Fortuna bless you.'

Flavia turned to see Pandora, a poor freeborn girl whose gold coin she had once found. Behind Pandora stood Feles – the cat-faced cart-driver – and his girlfriend Huldah. Flavia also recognised the two litter-bearers who had once carried the sodden Admiral Pliny to their house. One of them had a little girl with him.

'I never thanked you,' said Turnip-nose, wiping away a tear, 'for saving my daughter last year.'

'Aristo! We love you,' cried a group of teenage girls. 'Don't go!'

Flavia and Nubia exchanged wide-eyed grins of astonishment and Nubia slipped her arm through Aristo's. He kissed the top of her head and all the girls groaned.

Floridius was there – a sacred chicken under each arm – and Cletus the town idiot with a small bunch of wild-flowers for the girls.

'Thank you,' he dribbled, presenting the bouquet upside-down to Flavia. 'Thank you for helping us.'

'Goodbye, Nubia!' cried Mnason the beast-catcher. 'Watch out for snakes!'

They were nearing the docks but the crowd was pressing closer than ever, so Flavia clutched Aristo's other arm for protection. Glancing behind, she saw Jonathan's Jewish relatives kissing him goodbye, their religious differences forgotten at this moment of parting.

'GIVE THEM AIR!' bellowed Praeco, the town herald. 'MAKE WAY, MAKE WAY!'

The crowd parted and there stood the *Delphina*, with passengers and crew standing astonished at the rail: Flavia's father, Diana, Caudex and Alma. Scuto and Nipur put their heads over the rail, both panting happily. Tigris barked a greeting up at them. Bald Punicus and grey-haired Atticus were up in the rigging, trying to get a better view.

To the left of the gangplank stood a small group of half-naked beggar boys. Flavia saw that their leader was the tawny-haired beggar-boy called Threptus. He held a small palm branch. 'Three cheers for Lupus!' he cried, and rattled the branch. 'Do you like the procession we arranged?'

On the other side of the gangplank stood Marcus Artorius Bato, one eyebrow raised above his pale ironic eyes.

'Farewell, Flavia Gemina,' he said and swept out one arm in the orator's classic gesture of display. 'You can see that you and your friends are well-loved and that you will be missed. I, on the other hand, will look forward to a period of calm.' Then he smiled and leaned forward and kissed her cheek. 'Go with Hercules.'

Flavia was too astonished to reply, but now Bato was shaking Aristo's hand and she was going up the gangplank. At the top she turned for a moment to look back at them. But because of her tears, the sea of smiling Ostian faces became one big blur.

The crowds had dispersed by the time the *Cygnet* pulled the *Delphina* far enough out to catch the offshore breeze. It wasn't a strong wind, but Captain Geminus had decided to set sail anyway. Flavia and Nubia stood beside the dolphin stern ornament, with the three dogs panting beside them. Lupus and Aristo were helping on deck, Jonathan had gone down below to rest.

Diana came up to join them on the stern platform. 'Your father told me to wait up here,' she said, 'while he and his men do whatever it is they do.'

'It's the safest place,' said Flavia.

Diana smiled shyly at Flavia. 'That was quite a farewell.'

'I know,' said Flavia. 'We weren't expecting that. But it was wonderful.'

'Are you sad to be leaving Ostia?'

Flavia swallowed hard, too emotional to speak, but Nubia said: 'Little bit, not so much.' She ruffled the fur on top of Nipur's head. 'I am happy to be going back to Ephesus, to the children and to our friends who follow the Way.'

'And your handsome new husband,' said Diana with a smile.

Nubia flushed.

'Don't worry.' Diana put her hand on Nubia's arm. 'I'm over Aristo. I love Marcus very much. He's what I need.'

'And he needs you,' said Nubia. She looked at Flavia.

'Yes,' said Flavia. 'Pater needs a wife. But what changed

your mind about men? You once said you'd rather die than marry.'

Diana stared down at the deck. 'When you went missing, I blamed myself. After all, I was the one who encouraged you to seek adventure.'

Flavia glanced ruefully at Nubia. 'I didn't need much encouragement,' she said.

'Then, when I saw your father in the forum last week, he looked so sad and vulnerable. My heart melted for him.'

When she said this, Flavia felt her own heart melt for Diana.

'And somehow,' said Diana, looking at Flavia's father, 'I just knew. I knew he was the one.'

'You'll be good for him,' said Flavia. 'I'm glad you're married.'

'Thank you, Flavia,' said Diana. 'Thank you for accepting me into your family.' She gave Flavia a quick hug and gazed back towards Ostia and the lighthouse beyond. 'And you, Flavia?' asked Diana. 'Will you miss Ostia?'

'Yes. I love Ostia. And I'll miss it so much.' Even as Flavia said it, she felt fresh tears well up and she began to cry. Nubia and Diana put their arms around her and this made her cry even more.

Flavia cried for all the things she loved that she would never see again: the red-brick granaries, with their warm smell of bread; the black-and-white mosaics, the plume of smoke from the lighthouse at Portus, the soft blue Ostian sky, her beloved umbrella pines and the spicy scent of the grasses in the necropolis. A sudden memory made her smile and she blinked through her tears at Diana. 'Remember the time you were teaching us to be virgin huntresses? And you gave us each a bow and arrows?'

'Yes,' Diana's eyes were also swimming.

'Did you know I accidentally shot a man instead of a deer?'

'Juno!' exclaimed Diana. 'I hope you didn't kill him.'

'I only shot him a little. In the calf.'

They all giggled and then Nubia pointed. 'Behold,' she said. 'Those men are waving at us.'

'Where?' said Flavia, following Nubia's finger. The *Delphina* was moving slowly southeast along the coast.

'There. Those men in the little boat behind us.'

'Oh no!' said Flavia. 'Maybe Domitian changed his mind and sent men to arrest us.'

'I don't think the emperor would send unarmed men in a fishing boat,' said Diana. 'Besides, one of them has a dog.'

'A dog?' said Flavia. She wiped her eyes and shaded them against the late afternoon sun. The water was dazzling and it was hard to make out the silhouette of the man waving at them. 'Great Juno's peacock,' whispered Flavia. 'I think it's Floppy.'

And she fainted.

SCROLL XXXIII

'Flavia? Flavia are you all right?' A deep voice with a patrician accent.

Flavia opened her eyes. 'Floppy?'

'I wish you wouldn't call me that.' He was kneeling over her, looking tired but impossibly handsome. He stood and pulled her to her feet. 'I think you fainted.'

'Yes,' she said. 'I fainted.'

'You've faced bears in the arena and murderers and slave-dealers and imperial torturers and you never fainted then, but I made you faint?'

'Yes. You make me faint.'

He laughed. 'Flavia, I'm coming with you. And in a few years, when you're ready, we'll be married.'

'What about your responsibilities?'

'I don't really want to be a priest. It's not as glamorous as it sounds. Just a glorified civil servant.'

'What about being a lawyer?'

'I can practise law in Ephesus.'

'What about your servants?'

'Lyncaeus is the only one I like. I've brought him with me.'

He tipped his head towards the bow and she saw Lyncaeus standing with her father and Diana and Nubia and Aristo and the dogs. Alma and Caudex were there, too, while Lupus and Atticus were watching them from the rigging. And bald Punicus stood at the helm. When they saw her looking, they all turned their heads quickly away and pretended to busy themselves with other matters. Flaccus laughed and smiled down at her. He was standing very close, holding her lightly by the shoulders.

Flavia looked up into his beautiful dark eyes. 'What about your sister?' she said. 'Don't you have to look after her?'

'She'll be married soon and besides, we don't really get on. She's happy because I altered my will to leave her the townhouse.'

'Your will?'

'It was the only way. I'll have to pretend to die.'

'But what about your poem. What about the *Argonautica*?'

'I left it with Pliny. He understands how important it is to me. If anyone can get it published for me posthumously, he can.'

'But it's not finished.'

He shrugged. 'I couldn't think how to end it.'

'But you know the ending.'

'No,' he said. 'I don't.' His face was very close to hers. So close that she could smell the faint sweet scent of mastic on his breath.

'Floppy?' she said.

He rolled his eyes and grinned. 'Yes?'

'You know the ivory love-tablet you gave me? I dropped it in the bath. And all the writing washed off and I never saw what you wrote on it. Will you tell me?'

He smiled and pulled her into his arms and whispered in her ear. His declaration of love was almost as wonderful as the feel of his warm breath in her ear. She shivered with delight. 'Oh, Floppy!'

'Only you,' he said, 'are allowed to call me Floppy.'

Then he kissed her, and her heart beat so fast that she thought she might swoon again.

Three years later, in the Roman port of Ephesus, Pulchra was thumbing shimmery blue stibium on Flavia's eyelids. 'It's too bad Flaccus died in that shipwreck,' she sighed. 'He was the most eligible bachelor in the empire. I'll never forget hearing the news that he had called off his betrothal to Prudentilla. It was the talk of Rome, and of Neapolis, too. And then his tragic death. But I can see I'm upsetting you.'

'Not at all,' said Flavia. 'Jason is just as wonderful as Flaccus. More so, in fact. He cares more about Justice and Truth than about Fame or Renown. He's a brilliant lawyer who defends widows and orphans, as well as important men. He's already gaining a reputation here in Ephesus.'

'And he's handsome?' Pulchra was applying kohl around Flavia's eyes, to make them look more exotic.

'Very.' Flavia sighed dreamily.

Pulchra huffed. 'Well, I can see why you gave up being a detectrix after Titus died. You were wrong about almost everything.'

'That's what we thought, too,' said Flavia mildly. 'Until last week.'

'What happened last week?'

'We got a letter from Mordecai,' said Flavia, 'sent from Babylon. He told us he had met another rabbi there, a man who had been Titus's doctor. It was Pinchas ben Aruva, of course, and he told Mordecai about the autopsy and how Titus had died. In his letter to us, Mordecai confessed that he had been

waiting for Titus in the latrines that day with a venom-dipped stylus.'

Pulchra stopped applying the kohl for a moment. 'Jonathan's father was there that day? Jonathan wasn't imagining it?'

'Yes. And listen to this: because he had seen a boy who looked very much like Jonathan, at the last moment he couldn't do it. He dropped the stylus and ran. He got on the first ship out of Ostia and for two years he lived as a hermit in the deserts of Judaea. Last spring he went to Babylon. That was when he discovered he really had seen Jonathan that day.'

'And Jonathan had really seen him.'

'Yes.'

'Then there was venom on the stylus?'

'Yes.'

'Why didn't you die? You pricked your finger, didn't you?'

'Only a little, and I got the right treatment: heat not cold.'

'Great Juno's peacock!' breathed Pulchra. 'That means if Jonathan hadn't gone to Rome, his father would have stabbed Titus with that stylus and there would be imperial blood on his hands.'

'Yes. But Jonathan did go. And his being there stopped Mordecai doing something terrible.'

'Maybe Jonathan's vision was from the gods after all!' Pulchra resumed applying the kohl: 'Where is Jonathan?'

'He's practising medicine now here in Ephesus, but he sometimes takes time out to look for Popo. A few months ago we had news of a little boy fitting Popo's description living with a fair-haired mother in Hispania,' said Flavia. 'Jonathan went there to investigate. But he's going to be here for the wedding. He promised. He doesn't even know about his father's letter,' she added.

'Why didn't you and Nubia and Lupus go with Jonathan to Hispania?'

'We're still trying to restore the last of the kidnapped children to their families. But every time we match a child to their parents, someone brings us a new waif or stray. Besides, I told you: I don't solve mysteries anymore.'

Pulchra sighed. 'If you say so.'

A few moments later she put down the kohl stick and rose to her feet. Nubia and Leda had just finished weaving the pearl embroidered ribbons into Flavia's hair.

'Stand up,' commanded Pulchra. 'Turn around. Excellent. Diana, bring the veil?'

Flavia's stepmother brought the veil and draped it over her head and Nubia put the wreath of white and yellow flowers on top.

Pulchra adjusted the garland slightly and fixed it with some silver hairpins and then stood back to admire her work. Nubia, Diana and Leda came to stand beside her. They all stood staring at Flavia.

'Well?' said Flavia. 'How do I look?'

'Beautiful,' breathed Nubia.

'Amazing,' said Diana.

'Fantastic,' said Leda.

Pulchra sighed. 'Flavia, I must confess, even I am a little jealous of you.' She carried the make-up tray over to a side table. 'Where will you and your new husband live?'

'Why here, at the Villa Vinea, with Nubia and Aristo and the children. There are twenty-six rooms here.'

'Doesn't this Jason have a house of his own?'

'No.' Flavia glanced at Nubia, her eyes sparkling.

'So he's going to burst in and sweep you up in his arms and carry you through the streets of Ephesus and then bring you back here?'

'Yes,' laughed Flavia.

'To this room?' Pulchra looked around the spacious room

with its sky blue panels and the frieze of cream-coloured cupids on a black border, and its balcony overlooking Ephesus.

'Yes,' said Flavia. 'This will be our bedroom.'

'We're going to scatter the bed with rose petals,' said Diana, 'so it will be ready when they return.'

Nubia cocked her head. 'Hark!' she said. 'I think I hear them.'

Flavia and the others held their breath, and sure enough, they could hear the joyful pulsing sound of flutes, tambourines and drums from outside. They all ran to the balcony.

It was dusk and the first stars were winking in the deep blue sky above Ephesus. Bats flitted in the warm air and from the hill behind came the steady creak of cicadas in the olive groves and vineyards. Flavia was dizzy from the heady scent of jasmine and saffron crocus in her garland, and her rose-scented veil.

She knew which street they were coming up because she could see the flickering glow of torchlight preceding them. Other shutters were opening and some of their rich neighbours had come out on their balconies, too.

The music was getting louder – its exotic pulsing rhythm made her tap her feet – and at last the procession appeared around a corner. Lupus was thumping the beat on a goatskin drum. Two male flautists followed and two youths on tambourines. Flavia recognised them as musicians from the pantomime troupe that Lupus was apprenticed to. They were dressed in jewel-coloured silk tunics, and their spiky garlands made them look like satyrs. Some of the older boys from the orphanage were there, too, ready to throw nuts and sing bawdy songs.

Behind the musicians at the head of the procession Flavia saw her father walking beside Pulchra's husband, Julius Menecrates, who had accompanied her to Ephesus. The dogs jostled about their feet, all four wearing garlands and panting happily.

Lyncaeus, Caudex, Ursus, and some men from the guild of tentmakers held pine-pitch torches; the scent made her think of night adventures. Sisyphus was there, too, wearing the biggest garland of all; he was one of the few friends from Italia she had invited. Walking beside him was a tall youth in a hooded cloak, with a satchel over one shoulder: Jonathan. He must have come straight from the harbour. She could tell from the slump of his shoulders that he had not found the missing twin.

'Jonathan!' she called, remembering too late that the bride was supposed to be trembling in her mother's arms, not leaning over the balcony. Jonathan looked up and saw her. He gave her a tired smile and a wave. Sisyphus and some of the others in the procession waved up at her, too, and she waved back.

Then Flavia caught sight of her groom. He wore a garland over his glossy dark hair and he was talking to Aristo and laughing. He was near-sighted and hadn't seen her yet.

'Great Juno's peacock!' gasped Pulchra. 'It can't be!'

'It is,' said Flavia, her heart pounding. 'That's him. That's Jason.'

Pulchra turned and stared at Flavia, open-mouthed. 'But that means he gave up everything for you,' she spluttered. 'Wealth, name, reputation. I don't believe it. I just do not believe it.' She shook her head in wonder.

The procession was now almost directly below the balcony. Flavia saw Aristo say something in the bridegroom's ear and point. Her beautiful husband-to-be followed Aristo's pointing arm and at last he saw her. He smiled up at her, his teeth very white and his dark eyes sparkling in the torchlight, and he mouthed something up at her. The music drowned out his words but Flavia laughed.

'What did he say?' demanded Pulchra. 'I couldn't hear.'

'He told me he loved me,' said Flavia. 'And he called me by his pet name for me.'

'And what is that?'

'Puella docta,' said Flavia without taking her eyes from him. 'His clever girl.' She waved as he disappeared around the corner towards the front door of the villa.

'I cannot believe he's alive,' said Pulchra, as they moved from the balcony back to the bedroom. 'You've deceived everyone in Rome.'

'You won't tell anyone, will you?'

'Of course not,' said Pulchra.

'Not even your father? Especially not your father!'

'No, Flavia. I know how to keep a secret.' Pulchra paused and put her hands on her hips and turned back to Flavia. 'Will you do me a small favour in return?'

'What do you mean?' asked Flavia. She could hear pounding on the front door downstairs, then excited laughter and squeals from some of the little girls guarding it.

'You said you don't solve mysteries anymore. But that was before you found out you were right all along. So now you can solve mysteries! You can solve my mystery.'

'I suppose . . .' Flavia glanced at Nubia, and her friend smiled and nodded. 'I suppose I can!'

Downstairs the sound of music suddenly grew louder: the girls had opened the front door.

'Excellent. It's not a very big mystery.'

'Is it urgent?'

'Not terribly,' said Pulchra.

'I can't go back to Italia, you know. I'm still officially in exile.' Flavia could hear her bridegroom taking the stairs two at a time.

'You'd only have to go to the isle of Samos,' said Pulchra, 'which they say is very beautiful this time of year.'

Flavia nodded. 'Very well,' she said. 'I'll take the case. But

I won't be able to start the investigation for a few days. At the moment I'm a little busy.'

As if on cue, the door burst open and the groom came striding towards her. He was smiling, but the intensity of his gaze frightened Flavia a little so she threw her arms around Nubia and buried her face in her friend's neck. Nubia hugged her back and they clung to each other tightly. Some of the musicians had come into the room and the sound of music filled her head along with the sweet scent of roses and saffron.

She felt his hands grip her waist and she clung, giggling, to her friend, but Nubia was laughing too hard to hold on and now he was swinging her up into his strong arms. His dark hair fell over his eyes and he tossed it back impatiently with a flick of his head, then gazed down at her with laughing eyes.

'Oh, Floppy,' gasped Flavia, 'I love you,'

'Only you,' he said, 'are allowed to call me Floppy.'

THE LAST SCROLL

When the emperor Titus died suddenly on 13 September AD 81, some Romans suspected that he had been assassinated. The most likely suspect was his brother Domitian. But nothing could be proven and Domitian became emperor of Rome. Was Titus's death in fact murder? Or did he die of natural causes? It was a mystery then, and it remains a mystery today. In telling the story, I had to do some detective work myself.

Some of the strangest facts in this story are true, or at least historically attested. We know that Titus was about thirty years old when he led four legions against Jerusalem in AD 70 and gave the order to destroy Jerusalem and the Temple of God. On his way home he made a detour to a town in Asia Minor (Turkey) to see a wise philosopher and prophet called Apollonius. This man told Titus to beware his father Vespasian's enemies while he was alive, and – after Vespasian's death – to beware those closest to him. Apollonius also told Titus that he would die *like Odysseus from the sea*. One of Apollonius's disciples interpreted this as meaning the venom of a stingray or 'trygon'. According to one account, Odysseus's son by Circe – Telephorus – killed his father with the spine of a stingray.

Titus returned to Italia and in late June of AD 79, his

father died and he became emperor. Within a month of Titus becoming emperor, disasters began to occur. In August, Vesuvius erupted. Within six months, Rome suffered a terrible fire and plague. Soon after Titus came to power, he began to have terrible headaches and the only relief came when an anvil was banged or music played. Titus was often depressed and tearful, and gradually stopped performing his duties. Then, just days before he died, Titus botched a sacrifice and there was 'thunder in a clear sky'. In September of AD 81, on his way to his family villa in the Sabine Hills, Titus came down with a fever. He put his head out of the litter and cried that he didn't deserve to die. He was packed in ice to bring down the fever. But he died shortly after, at his Sabine Villa, having reigned just over two years. His last words were: 'I have only one regret.' Nobody knows what he meant, though many have guessed.

According to the Babylonian Talmud (Gittin 56b) an autopsy was performed on Titus. When his head was split open, the doctors found a strange growth in his brain. A Jewish eyewitness, Pinchas ben Aruva, said it was a mosquito the size of a sparrow. The rabbis believed it was sent by God to punish Titus for his crimes against the Jews.

We know from Suetonius that Titus's younger brother Domitian liked to spear flies with a needle sharp stylus, that he was a skilled archer and that he once gave dinner to terrified guests in a black triclinium. The remains of his nymphaeum grotto and Alban Palace are in Castel Gandolfo near Rome, but can only be viewed by special arrangement. The mouth of the Emissario is still visible and – at the time of writing – is open to anyone who can find it.

One of the things I invented for this story is Nero's Eye. Nero really did have a lens-shaped emerald but I invented the name, the Delphic prophecy and the use of the emerald as a sign of favour.

Most of the characters in this book are also made up: Flavia, Nubia, Jonathan, Lupus, Aristo, Sisyphus, Senator Cornix, etc. However, Gaius Suetonius Tranquillus was a real person. He became a famous biographer and his book, *Lives of the Twelve Caesars*, is still a bestseller today. Gaius Valerius Flaccus, whom I call Floppy, was also a real person. Not much is known of him, only that he started an epic poem called the *Argonautica* in about AD 79, but died before it was completed. The rhetor Quintilian mentions his death with regret. We can tell from the nomen Valerius that he was a patrician, but we don't really know how he died or how old he was. We do know that despite his poem being unfinished, it was published posthumously: so his name lives on today.

The emperor Domitian did have a blind torturer called Messallinus, a secretary called Vibius Crispus and a fat gourmand friend named Montanus. The astrologer Ascletario was a real person, too, and met a sticky end near the end of Domitian's reign in AD 96. But I will leave that delicious story for a future book.

THE VERY LAST SCROLL
EVER FOR THIS SERIES

This is the final book in a series of seventeen full-length novels and a dozen mini-mysteries all about the same characters. If this is your first Roman Mystery, you might want to go back and start at the beginning with *The Thieves of Ostia*. Flavia first meets Jonathan, Nubia and Lupus in that book and together they solve the mystery of who is killing the watchdogs of Ostia. I suggest starting there and reading them in order. You can see the order in which the books occur at the beginning of this book.

Although *The Man from Pomegranate Street* is officially the end of the stories about Flavia, Jonathan, Nubia and Lupus, they inhabit a world I love and hope to write more about. So keep an eye out: they might get a mention – or even appear – in some of my future books.

ARISTO'S SCROLL

Aeneas (uh-*nee*-uss)
Trojan son of the goddess Venus who escaped from conquered Troy to have many adventures and finally settled near the future site of Rome

Aeneid (uh-*nee*-id)
Virgil's epic poem about Aeneas (see above) whose descendents ruled Rome

Alba Longa (*al*-buh *lon*-guh)
ancient colony founded by Aeneas's son Ascanius at Lake Albano near Rome

Alban (*all*-ban)
referring to the hills about ten miles southeast of Rome

Alexandria (al-ex-*and*-ree-ah)
port of Egypt and one of the greatest cities of the ancient world

aloes (*al*-oze)
succulent plant known for its skin-healing properties in ancient times

altar (*all*-tur)
a flat-topped block, usually of stone, for making an offering to a god or goddess; often inscribed, they could be big (for temples) or small (for personal vows)

amici (uh-*mee*-kee)

    Latin for 'friends', can also mean 'advisors' or 'imperial councilors'

amphitheatre (*am*-fee-theatre)

    an oval-shaped stadium for watching gladiator shows, beast fights and executions; the Flavian amphitheatre in Rome (now called the 'Colosseum') is the most famous

amphora (*am*-for-uh)

    large clay storage jar for holding wine, oil or grain

Amulius (a-*mule*-ee-uss)

    great-uncle of Romulus and Remus; according to ancient legend, he tried to depose their grandfather Numitor and get power for himself

apodyterium (ap-oh-di-*tare*-ee-um)

    the changing-room in a bath-house, usually with wall-niches for clothing

Apollo (uh-*pol*-oh)

    Greek and Roman god of the sun, music and plague

Apollonius (ap-uh-*lone*-ee-uss) of Tyana

    (c AD 2–98) well-known philosopher, mystic and contemporary of Jesus, he lived in Tyana in southeast Turkey and was sought out by many people for his views

Appian Way (see Via Appia)

Aquae Cutiliae

    modern Cittaducale, a mineral spring 9 miles east of Rieti, the Flavians had a residence there; it is famous for being right in the centre of Italy

Aramaic (ar-uh-*may*-ik)

    closely related to Hebrew, it was the common language of first century Jews

Argonautica (arr-go-*not*-ick-uh)

    account of Jason's search on his ship *Argo* for the golden

fleece; the most famous was by Apollonius Rhodius but there is an unfinished version by Valerius Flaccus

Argos (*ar*-goce)

faithful dog of Odysseus in Greek mythology

Aruva (uh-*roo*-vuh)

Pinchas ben Aruva is the rabbi who recounted the story of Titus's autopsy according to the Talmud (Gittin 56b)

as (ass)

a copper coin worth a quarter of a sestertius in the first century AD

Ascanius (ass-*kane*-ee-uss)

son of Aeneas; he founded Alba Longa after his father's death; he was sometimes known as Iulus or Julus

Ascletario (ask-luh-*tar*-ee-oh)

Domitian's astrologer is mentioned by Suetonius in his *Lives of the Caesars*

Asia (*ayzh*-uh)

In Roman times Asia meant what is now modern Turkey, rather than the Far East, as it does today; the province of Asia included Rhodes and other islands

atrium (*eh*-tree-um)

the reception room in larger Roman homes, often with skylight and pool

augur (*ah*-gur)

prophet who interpreted divine meaning behind the flights of birds and other natural signs

Augustus (ah-*guss*-tuss)

a title conferred on Roman emperors, it meant illustrious and hinted at an unbroken line of succession from the first emperor: Octavian Augustus

Aventine (*av*-en-tine)

one of the hills of Rome between the river Tiber and

the Palatine Hill; it is named after the great grandfather of Romulus and Remus

Aventinus (av-en-*teen*-uss)

descendent of Aeneas and great great-grandfather of Romulus and Remus

ben (ben)

Hebrew for 'son of'; Pinchas ben Aruva means Pinchas son of Aruva, Jonathan ben Mordecai means Jonathan son of Mordecai, etc

Berenice (bare-uh-*neece*)

beautiful Jewish Queen who was Titus's lover in the AD 70s

Bovillae (bo-*vill*-eye)

town near Lake Albanus at the fourteenth milestone on Appian Way

brazier (*bray*-zher)

coal-filled metal bowl on legs used to heat a room (like an ancient radiator)

Britannia (bri-*tan*-yuh)

Roman name for Britain

Britannicus (bri-*tan*-ick-uss)

son and heir of the Emperor Claudius, and friend of Titus, he was reputedly poisoned by Nero and died aged 14

Caesar (*see*-zur)

title adopted by the emperors of Rome starting with the first emperor Augustus; after Julius Caesar adopted him in his will, his name became Gaius Julius Caesar

caftan (*kaf*-tan)

long-sleeved loose robe, worn by men and women in hot countries

caldarium (kall-*dar*-ee-um)

hot room of the public baths with a hot plunge

Capena Gate (see Porta Capena)

carruca (ka-*ru*-ka)

a four-wheeled travelling coach, often covered

Castor (*kass*-tur)

one of the famous twins of Greek mythology, Pollux being the other

Catullus (ka-*tull*-us)

Roman poet who lived about 140 years before this story takes place; famous for his passionate, witty and often rude poetry

cavea (*kah*-vay-uh)

the curved seating area of a Roman theatre

ceramic (sir-*am*-ik)

clay which has been fired in a kiln, very hard and smooth.

Cerberus (*sir*-burr-uss)

three-headed mythological hellhound who guards the gates of the Underworld

Chrestus (*kres*-tuss)

Fairly common Greek slave name in the first century and also a possible mispronunciation of 'Christos' (Christ), the Greek word for anointed (Messiah)

chrysolite (*kriss*-oh-lite)

Greek for 'golden stone' but actually a transparent grass-green semi-precious stone

cicada (sik-*ah*-duh)

an insect like a grasshopper that chirrs during the day

Cicero (*siss*-ur-oh)

Marcus Tullius Cicero (106–43 BC) was a famous philosopher, orator and lawyer who lived during the time of Julius Caesar

Circus Maximus (*sir*-kuss *max*-i-muss)

famous course for chariot races, between the Palatine and Aventine Hills in Rome

Claudius (*klaw*-dee-uss)

fourth emperor of Rome who ruled from AD 41 to AD 54; he commissioned the building of a new harbour at Portus near Ostia and befriended young Titus

Clivus Scauri (*klee*-vuss *skow*-ree)

a steep road on the Caelian Hill near the Colosseum, still visible today

Clodius Pulcher (*klode*-ee-uss *pull*-kare)

rich politician of the first century BC; he had an opulent villa on Lake Albano

Collina Gate (see Porta Collina)

colonnade (call-a-*nade*)

a covered walkway lined with columns

Colossus of Rhodes (kuh-*loss*-iss)

gigantic statue of Helios on the island of Rhodes; it lay on the ground, having been toppled by an earthquake 66 years after it was finished

Corinth (*kor*-inth)

Greek port town with a large Jewish population

corona (kuh-*ro*-nuh)

Latin for 'crown' or 'garland'

cryptoporticus (krypt-oh-*port*-ik-uss)

Greek for 'secret corridor'; an underground passage-way, usually vaulted

cupid (kyoo-pid)

Cupid (the Roman equivalent of Eros) was the son of Venus; chubby versions of him called 'cupids' became popular in imperial times and were often shown as naked winged babies with bow and arrows of love

Curia (*kyoor*-ee-uh)

AKA Curia Julia, the senate-house built by Julius Caesar in the Forum Romanum

cursus honorum (*kur*-siss on-*or*-um)

Latin for 'course of honours'; the steps a patrician took to reach a high position in public office, ideally that of consul

Cyclops (*sigh*-klops)

mythical giant with a single eye in the centre of his forehead

dactylic hexameter (dak-*til*-ik heck-*sam*-it-er)

the meter of epic poems such as *The Iliad, The Odyssey* and *The Aeneid*

Delphic oracle (*del*-fik *or*-uh-kul)

the god Apollo was believed to speak through a priestess called the Pythia at his sanctuary at Delphi in Greece

detectrix (dee-*tek*-triks)

female form of 'detector', someone who uncovers things: detective

Diana (Artemis in Greek)

virgin goddess of the hunt and of the moon: she despises men and loves her independent life of adventure, hunting with her maiden friends and her hounds

Dionysius (die-oh-*niss*-ee-uss) of Halicarnassus

(c. 60–7 BC) Greek historian and orator who wrote an account of Rome's origins

Domitia (doh-*mish*-uh)

(c. AD 53–130) Domitia Longina was the wife of Domitian, she is about thirty-eight in this story

Domitian (duh-*mish*-un)

the Emperor Titus's younger brother, is thirty-one years old when this story takes place

eheu! (*eh*-ho)

Latin exclamation meaning 'alas!'

Emissario (em-iss-*ar*-ee-oh)

emissarium is Latin for 'outlet'; the four-century BC Emissario on Lake Albano can still be seen today

ephedron (*eff*-ed-ron)

a plant mentioned by Pliny the Elder still used today in the treatment of asthma

Ephesus (*eff*-ess-iss)

perhaps the most important town in the Roman province of Asia; site of one of the Seven Sights of the ancient world and also of early churches

epsilon (*ep*-sill-on)

fifth letter of the Greek alphabet, equivalent to our letter 'E'

Eretum (eh-*ray*-toom)

perhaps modern Fara Sabina; the exact location of this Sabine town on the Via Salaria is not know, but some ancient writers place it about 15 miles outside Rome

ergo (*er*-go)

Latin adverb meaning 'therefore'

Etruscan (ee-*truss*-kan)

race of people who inhabited the regions to the northwest of Rome long before the so-called 'Latins' arrived; their domination was ended by the Roman sack of Veii

euge! (oh-gay)

Latin exclamation meaning 'hurray!'

eureka! (yoo-*reek*-uh)

Greek for 'I've found it!' (pronounced 'heureka!' in ancient Greek)

Eurydice (yoo-*rid*-diss-ee)

wife of the poet Orpheus; she died of a snakebite on

their wedding day and he tried unsuccessfully to bring her back from the Underworld

ex machina (eks *mak*-in-uh)

Latin for 'from a crane'; usually referring to the part of a play where an actor dressed as a god or goddess is lowered onto the stage to put everything right

Flaccus (*flak*-uss)

for Gaius Valerius Flaccus, see The Last Scroll

Flavia (*flay*-vee-a)

a name, meaning 'fair-haired'; Flavius is another form of this name

forica (*for*-ik-uh)

Latin for latrine or public toilet

forum (*for*-um)

the civic centre of Roman towns, usually an open space surrounded by shady colonnades and official buildings

Fortuna (for-*toon*-uh)

Roman goddess of good luck and success

Forum Romanum (*for*-um ro-*mah*-num)

Rome's most famous forum, the political hub of the empire

freedman (*freed*-man)

a slave who has been granted freedom, his ex-master becomes his patron

frigidarium (frig-id-*ar*-ee-um)

the room of the public baths with the cold plunge

fuller (*full*-ur)

ancient launderer; they used urine, mud and sulphur to whiten wool and linen

gladius (glad-ee-uss)

Latin for 'sword', especially the short thrusting sword of the legionary

Hades (*hay*-deez)

the underground Land of the Dead, in Greek mythology

Halicarnassus (hal-ee-car-*nass*-uss)

(modern Bodrum) ancient city in Turkey; site of one of the Seven Wonders

haruspex (*ha*-roos-pecks)

priest who interpreted omens by inspecting the entrails of sacrificed animals

Hebrew (*hee*-brew)

holy language of the Old Testament, spoken by (religious) Jews in the first century

Helios (*heel*-ee-oss)

Greek for 'sun'; the divine son of Apollo, he drove the chariot of the sun

Hercules (*her*-kyoo-leez)

very popular Roman demi-god, he was worshipped by sailors in particular

Hispania (hiss-*pan*-ya)

name given by the Romans to the Iberian peninsula: modern Spain and Portugal

hospitium (hoss-*pit*-ee-um)

Latin for hotel or guesthouse; often very luxurious with baths and dining rooms

Hydra (*hide*-ruh)

mythological snake with many heads, when you cut one off, two new ones grew in its place

Ides (eyedz)

thirteenth day of most months in the Roman calendar (including September); in March, May, July, and October the Ides occur on the fifteenth day of the month.

imperium (im-peer-ee-um)

Latin for 'power', 'command', 'authority' particularly military; imperium was officially granted to new emperors by the Senate

Italia (it-*al*-ya)

Latin word for Italy, the famous boot-shaped peninsula

Janus (*jane*-uss)

two-faced Roman god of gateways, beginnings and ends

Jerusalem (j'-*roo*-sah-lem)

capital of the Roman province of Judaea, it was destroyed by Titus in AD 70, eleven years before this story takes place

Jonah (*jo*-nuh)

Hebrew for 'dove'

Josephus (jo-*see*-fuss)

Jewish commander who surrendered to Vespasian, became Titus's freedman and wrote *The Jewish War*, an account of the Jewish revolt in seven volumes

Judaea (joo-*dee*-uh)

ancient province of the Roman Empire; modern Israel

Julia (*jool*-yuh)

Titus's only child Julia Flavia was seventeen and married to Titus Flavius Sabinus when this story takes place

Julius Menecrates (*jool*-yuss m'-*nek*-ra-teez)

we know from a poet called Statius that a man named Julius Menecrates married the eldest daughter of Pollius Felix and that she had at least three sons by him

Juno (*jew*-no)

queen of the Roman gods and wife of the god Jupiter

Jupiter (*jew*-pit-er)

king of the Roman gods; together with his wife Juno and daughter Minerva he forms the Capitoline triad, the three main deities of Rome

Kalends (*kal*-ends)

The Kalends mark the first day of the month in the Roman calendar

kohl (kole)

dark powder used to darken eyelids or outline eyes

kylix (*kie*-licks)

elegant, flat-bowled Greek drinking cup, especially for drinking parties

Lacus Albanus (*lah*-kuss all-*bah*-nuss)

modern Lake Albano; a volcanic crater lake in the Alban Hills southeast of Rome

Laetus (*lie*-toos)

Latin for 'happy': the cognomen of Tranquillus' father Gaius Suetonius Laetus

lararium (lar-*ar*-ee-um)

household shrine, often a chest with a miniature temple on top, sometimes a niche

Latinus (luh-*tee*-nuss)

legendary king of Latium, he promised his daughter to Turnus, then later to Aeneas

Latium (*lat*-ee-um)

area to the south of the Tiber, from the coast to the Alban Hills; it was the part of Italy first settled by Aeneas and its language became Latin

Laurentum (lore-*ent*-um)

village on the coast of Italy in Latium, a few miles south of Ostia

Lavinia (luh-*vin*-ee-uh)

daughter of Latinus, the king of Latium at the time of Aeneas's arrival in Italy

litter (*lit*-tur)

Latin 'lectica'; a couch on poles carried by two to eight

slaves, the most comfortable way to travel in Roman times

Livy (*liv*-ee)

AKA Titus Livius (c 59 BC – AD 17) was a historian who wrote about the origins of Rome in his book *Ab Urbe Condita* (From the Founding of Rome)

Lucrine Lake (*loo*-kreen)

Neopolitan lake which was famous for its oysters in Roman times

Ludi Romani (*loo*-dee ro-*mah*-nee)

Roman harvest festival held in September and celebrated with chariot races

Lusca (*luss*-kuh)

Latin for 'one-eyed'

Massilia (m'-*sill*-ee-uh)

modern Marseilles, a port on the French Riviera

mastic (*mass*-tik)

ancient Roman chewing gum; a resin from a shrub native to the Greek island of Chios; the taste is like sweetish spicy carrot; origin of the word 'masticate'

mater (*ma*-tare)

Latin for 'mother'

mausoleum (maw-zo-*lee*-um)

tomb which housed more than one body or urn with ashes; we get the word from the Mausoleum of Halicarnassus, one of the 'Seven Sights' of the ancient world

Menecrates (see Julius Menecrates)

mensa secunda (*men*-suh sek-*oon*-duh)

Latin for 'second table', meaning the dessert course of a dinner

Messallinus (mess-uh-*leen*-uss)

Lucius Valerius Catullus Messallinus, Domitian's blind

advisor, was called 'mortiferus' (death-dealing) by the poet Juvenal

Minerva (m'-*nerv*-uh)

Roman equivalent of Athena, goddess of wisdom, war and weaving

Montanus (mon-*tan*-uss)

Titus Junius Montanus, Domitian's fat advisor, is mentioned in Juvenal's fourth satire (4.130–143)

Neapolis (nay-*ap*-oh-liss)

modern Naples, a city near Vesuvius on a bay of the same name

nefas (*nef*-ass)

Latin word for sin, wickedness or moral wrongdoing

Neptune (*nep*-tyoon)

god of the sea and also of horses; his Greek equivalent is Poseidon

Nero (*near*-oh)

(AD 37–68) notorious emperor who was reported to have strummed his lyre while Rome burned in the great fire of AD 64; he ruled from AD 54–68

Numa Pompilius (*noo*-muh pom-*pill*-ee-uss)

second king of Rome, after Romulus; according to legend, he was a Sabine, born on the day of Rome's founding (753 BC) and was a wise, peace-loving ruler

Numitor (*noo*-mit-or)

king of Alba Longa, he was deposed for a time by his brother Amulius until his grandsons Romulus and Remus restored the kingdom to him

nymphaeum (nim-*fay*-um)

Latin for 'fountain'; ruins of the so-called Nymphaeum Bergantino at Lake Albano grotto can be seen today by special arrangement

Odysseus (uh-*diss*-yooss)

Greek hero whose return from Troy took ten years; according to Eugammon of Cyene, he was unwittingly killed by his son from Circe with stingray venom

ornatrix (or-*nah*-triks)

Latin for hairdresser, usually a female slave

Orpheus (*or*-fee-uss)

musician and poet of Greek mythology who could tame animals with his music, he tried and failed to bring his wife Euridyce back from the Underworld

Ostia (*oss*-tee-uh)

port about sixteen miles southwest of Rome; it is Flavia Gemina's home town

Ovid (*aw*-vid)

famous Roman poet who lived about seventy years before this story

paedagogus (pie-da-*gog*-uss)

male slave or freedman who took boys to and from school; a kind of bodyguard

Palatine (*pal*-uh-tine)

one of the seven hills of Rome; the greenest and most pleasant; the site of successive imperial palaces (the word 'palace' comes from 'Palatine')

palla (*pal*-uh)

a woman's cloak, could also be wrapped round the waist or worn over the head

pantomime (*pan*-toe-mime)

Roman theatrical performance in which a man (or occasional woman) illustrated a sung story through dance; the dancer could also be called a 'pantomime'

papyrus (puh-*pie*-russ)

the cheapest writing material, made of pounded Egyptian reeds

Paradeisos (par-ah-*day*-soss)

Greek word based on a Hebrew word based on the Persian word for royal park or walled garden; Jesus said to one of the men on the cross 'today you will be with me in paradeisos' Luke 23:43

Paris (*pair*-iss)

name of a mythological hero but also of a real pantomime dancer who lived in the first century AD

pater (*pa*-tare)

Latin for 'father'

pater patriae (*pa*-tare pa-*tree*-eye)

Latin for 'Father of the Fatherland' a title conferred upon emperors

Paternus (puh-*tare*-nuss)

Lake in the Sabine Hills below the Villa of Titus

patina (**puh-***tee*-nuh)

Latin for 'dish' or 'pan': a kind of flan with eggs, either savoury or sweet

Pear Street

ancient street on the Quirinal Hill in Rome, perhaps near the modern Via delle Quattro Fontane; the poet Martial lived there for a time

peperino (pep-air-*ee*-no)

grey or dark brown volcanic rock known as lapis albanus and often used by the ancient Romans to build walls and fountains

peristyle (*perry*-style)

a columned walkway around an inner garden or courtyard

Persephone (purr-*sef*-fun-ee)

daughter of Demeter who was kidnapped by the god Pluto and had to reign with him as queen of the underworld for six months out of every year

Pinchas (*pin*-khuss)

Pinchas ben Aruva is the rabbi who recounted the story of Titus's autopsy according to the Talmud (Gitt 56b)

plaustrum (*plow*-strum)

cart or wagon, usually two-wheeled and drawn by oxen

Pliny (*plin*-ee)

'Admiral Pliny' refers to the man we know as 'Pliny the Elder', author of the Natural History who died in the eruption of Vesuvius; 'Pliny' alone refers to 'Pliny the Younger' his nephew, aged nineteen at the time

Pluto (*ploo*-toe)

god of the underworld, he is the Roman equivalent of Hades

Podagrosus (po-duh-*gro*-suss)

name of a mule on a mosaic from the cartdrivers' baths in Ostia: it means 'gouty'

Pollux (*pa*-lucks)

one of the famous twins of Greek mythology, Castor being the other

Pomegranate Street

ancient street on the Quirinal Hill in Rome, perhaps near the modern Via delle Quattro Fontane; the emperor Domitian lived there in his youth

pontifex maximus (*pon*-tee-fecks *mack*-sim-uss)

Latin for 'highest priest'; this was usually the emperor

porta (*por*-tuh)

Latin for 'gate' or 'door'

Porta Capena (*por*-tuh kuh-*pane*-uh)

gate in the Servian (fourth century BC) wall of Rome leading out onto the Via Appia; three aqueducts passed overhead and it was known as the 'dripping gate'

Porta Collina (*por*-tuh co-*leen*-uh)

gate in the Servian (fourth century BC) wall of Rome leading to the Via Salaria

Portus (*por*-tuss)

harbour a few miles north of Ostia, built by Claudius to handle the increasing volume of shipping coming in and out of Rome's port

posca (*poss*-kuh)

a refreshing drink made by adding a splash of vinegar to water, very popular among legionaries; the vinegar makes even bad water potable

Praetorian Guard (pry-*tor*-ee-un gard)

special cohorts of Roman soldiers employed to guard the emperor

Princeps (*prin*-keps)

Latin for 'first' or 'first citizen'; a title often used by the emperor

principate (*prin*-sip-ate)

the power to rule, from Latin *princeps*: 'first, chief'

puella docta (poo-*ell*-uh *dok*-tuh)

Latin for 'educated or clever girl' first coined by the poet Propertius

puellae (poo-*el*-lie)

Latin for 'girls'

pueri (*poo*-air-ee)

Latin for 'boys'

Pythia (*pith*-ee-uh)

the prophetic priestess of Apollo at Delphi in Greece

quadrans (*kwad*-ranz)

tiny bronze coin worth one sixteenth of a sestertius or quarter of an as (hence quadrans); in the first century it was the lowest value Roman coin in production

quadriga (*kwad*-rig-uh)

chariot pulled by four horses, the central two yoked, the outer two on traces

Quintilian (kwin-*til*-yun)

Marcus Fabius Quintilianus, c. AD 35–100; a famous orator and teacher

Quirinal (kweer-in-*all*)

one of the seven hills of Rome, northeast of the forum, mainly private houses and gardens in the first century AD, with a few temples as well

Rabirius (ruh-*beer*-ee-uss)

Rabirius was the architect who built Domitian's Alban Villa on Lake Albano and later rebuilt the imperial palace on the Palatine Hill in Rome

Reate (ray-*ah*-tay)

modern Rieti, a town forty miles northeast of Rome in the Sabine hills

rostra (*ross*-tra)

the famous speakers' platform in the Roman forum; it got its name from the prows (rostra) of conquered ships attached to it

Rutupiae (roo-*too*-pee-eye)

modern Richborough in Kent, England: famed in Roman times for oysters

Sabina (suh-*been*-uh)

the lush hilly region to the northeast of Rome, famous for its olive oil

Sabine (*say*-bine)

having to do with Sabina, the hilly region northeast of Rome

Sabinus (suh-*been*-uss)

Titus Flavius Sabinus – Vespasian's nephew and Titus's son-in-law – was a very real contender to succeed Titus in AD 81; Domitian had him put to death a few years later for allowing himself to be saluted as 'imperator'

Salaria (see Via Salaria)

Salvete! (*sal*-vay-tay)
Latin for 'hello!' to more than one person

Samos (*say*-moce)
Greek island off the coast of Turkey; known as an ancient health resort

satyr (*sat*-ur)
mythical creature of the woods, in Roman times depicted as man with goat's ears, tail, legs and horns

scaena (*sky*-nuh)
AKA scaena frons; the tall backdrop behind the stage (proscaenium) of a Roman or Greek theatre

scroll (skrole)
a papyrus or parchment 'book', unrolled from side to side as it was read

Scylla (*skill*-uh)
mythological monster with six terrible female heads, always found close to the whirlpool Charybdis; encountered by the argonauts on their way home

senate (*sen*-at)
the group of upper class men who helped rule Rome; by the time of this book their number was six hundred and their power was small in comparison to the emperor's

Seneca (*sen*-eh-kuh)
a.k.a Seneca the Younger, a philosopher who wrote about how to die a good death

sesterces (sess-*tur*-seez)
more than one sestertius, a brass coin

shalom (shah-*lom*)

the Hebrew word for 'peace'; can also mean 'hello' or 'goodbye'

Sibylline books (*sib*-ill-line)

AKA libri fatales: Greek verse predictions concerning the future of Rome; they are called Sibylline after the Sibyl, the prophetess who supposedly compiled them

signet ring (*sig*-net ring)

ring with an image carved in it to be pressed into wax and used as a personal seal

Silvius (sill-vee-uss)

Latin for 'of the woods'; surname of many of Aeneas's descendents down to Romulus and Remus

Sisyphus (*siss*-if-uss)

mythological figure tormented in Hades by having to roll a stone to the top of a hill; it always rolled down again so he had to do this for ever

spongia (*spunj*-ya)

sea-sponge – usually on a stick – for wiping the bottom in the latrines

sponsa (*spon*-suh)

Latin for 'fiancée' or 'betrothed'

stibium (*stib*-ee-um)

powder used by women in Roman times to colour their eyelids

stola (*stole*-uh)

a long tunic worn mostly by Roman matrons (married women)

stylus (*stile*-us)

a metal, wood or ivory tool for writing on wax tablets

Succot (sook-*ot*)

another name for the Feast of Tabernacles, one of the

great festivals of the Jewish year; for eight days Jews eat and sleep in shelters ('succot')

Suetonius (soo-eh-*tone*-ee-uss)
famous Roman biographer who wrote the Lives of the Caesars, an account of the first emperors from Julius Caesar to Domitian, about 13 at the time of this story

Surrentum (sir-*wren*-tum)
modern Sorrento, south of Vesuvius: site of the Villa of Pollius Felix

susinum (*soo*-sin-um)
fabulously expensive perfume made of lilies, saffron, roses, myrrh and cinnamon

synthesis (*sinth*-ess-iss)
garment worn by men at dinner parties, probably a long unbelted tunic with a short mantle of matching colour

tablinum (tab-*lee*-num)
the study of a Roman house, where scrolls and writing material were kept

talpa (*tall*-puh)
Latin for 'mole'; the Romans believed moles were deaf as well as blind

Tartarus (*tar*-tar-uss)
mythical Land of the Dead ruled by Pluto, who is sometimes known as Tartarus

tessera (*tess*-er-uh)
tiny chip of stone, pottery or glass; it takes hundreds or even thousands to make up the picture in a mosaic

Theseus (*thee*-syoos)
Athenian hero who had to enter the labyrinth on Crete and overcome the minotaur

Tiber (*tie*-burr)
famous river that flows through the Sabine hills and

Rome and then empties into the Tyrrhenian Sea at Ostia; Rome is at the first fording place

Titus (*tie*-tuss)

Titus Flavius Vespasianus died on 13 September AD 81, after ruling as emperor for just over two years; he was forty-one years old

toga (*toe*-ga)

a blanket-like outer garment, worn by freeborn men and boys

Tranquillus (tran-*kwill*-uss)

Latin for 'calm', today Tranquillus is known to us as Suetonius

Transtiberim (tranz-tie-*bur*-rim)

modern Trastevere, the area 'across the Tiber' in Rome; in ancient times this was where most Jews lived

tribunicia potestas (trib-*yoo*-nik-ee-uh po-*test*-ass)

Roman emperors could not legally be tribunes but were granted the power of a tribune by means of this title; (among other things, a tribune could propose motions and convene the Senate)

triclinium (**trick-*lin*-ee-um**)

ancient Roman dining room, usually with three couches to recline on

Trojan (*trow*-jun)

inhabitant of Troy, the city besieged by Greeks about a thousand years before this story

Troy (troi)

city in Asia Minor (modern Turkey) which went to war with Greece

trygon (try-gon)

Greek for 'stingray', a sea-creature with a venomous spike in its tail: Pliny the Elder describes it in his *Natural History* (32.13)

tunic (*tew*-nic)

a piece of clothing like a big T-shirt; children often wore a long-sleeved one

Turnus (*turn*-uss)

legendary prince who fought Aeneas for the hand of Princess Lavinia and rule of Latium

Tyana (tee-*an*-uh)

modern Bor in Cappadocia (southeast Turkey) about 400 miles east of Ephesus

Tyrrhenian (tur-*ren*-ee-un)

sea to the west of Italy, named after the Etruscans

Veii (*vay*-ee)

an important Etruscan city northwest of Rome, its inhabitants warred with Rome for 400 years until it finally fell after the draining of Lake Albano c. 396 BC

Vespa (*vess*-puh)

Latin for 'wasp'; the first name of Lupus's ship, the *Delphina*

Vespasian (vess-*pay*-zhun)

father of Titus and Domitian and emperor from AD 69 to AD 79

Vesuvius (vuh-*soo*-vee-yus)

the volcano near Naples which erupted in August AD 79

Via Appia (*vee*-uh *ap*-pee-uh)

Latin for Appian Way, a very famous ancient road that runs from the southeast of Rome all the way to Italy's heel, via Capua

Via Corona (*vee*-uh kuh-*ro*-nuh)

Latin for 'garland road'; possibly the name of the ancient road that encircled Lacus Albanus

Via Salaria (*vee*-uh suh-*lar*-ee-uh)

ancient 'Salt Road' that lead northeast from Rome to the Sabine Hills

vigiles (*vij*-ill-aze)

the policemen/firemen of ancient Rome; the word means 'watchmen'

Virgil (*vur*-jill)

AKA Publius Vergilius Maro, a famous Latin poet who died in 19 BC, about a hundred years before this story takes place

wax tablet

a wax covered rectangle of wood used for making notes

yattush (yat-*toosh*)

Hebrew for 'gnat' or 'mosquito'; mentioned in the Babylonian Talmud (Gittin 56b) as the divine instrument of Titus's death